MIDNIGHT SHADOWS

A WILDEFIRE NOVEL

BY ELLA GRACE

Published by Ella Grace
Cover Art by Patricia Schmitt/Pickyme
Copyright 2015 by Christy Reece
ISBN: 978-0-9916584-5-9

PROLOGUE

Tallahassee, Florida
Four Years Ago

"Come on you lowlife, scum sucking son of a slimy slug. Do something so I can go home."

Placing her cellphone at an inconspicuous but strategic angle, Private Investigator Sabrina Wilde waited for something to happen. Would this guy ever do anything interesting? For the past six days, she had been following Harold Benoit around town, watching, waiting, and snapping more photos than she'd ever wanted of a possible cheating husband. And what did she have to show for it? Just a bunch of pictures of Harold having dinner with various women. That might prove he liked to eat at nice places and his diet was a cardiologist's nightmare, but it certainly didn't provide evidence that he was an unfaithful husband.

The women he'd dined with were as eclectic as they were surprising. Two had been attractive but as mistresses went, just didn't look the type. One had been, as her Aunt Gibby might've said, as homely as a rutabaga, bless her heart. And one woman had been old enough to be the man's grandmother.

So just what was Harold Benoit up to?

Other than his unusual dinner companions, the man's life was boringly routine. He went to work at nine and left his office at six sharp. Twice she had followed him home, where, according to Sabrina's client, Delores Benoit, he'd dined and slept with his wife. It was the other nights that Delores wanted to know about.

For several weeks Harold had been coming home late, claiming he was overloaded with work. Delores didn't believe him. She was certain he was cheating on her and had hired Sabrina to find out with whom and provide photographic proof. So far all Sabrina had been able to prove was that he enjoyed an eclectic variety of dinner companions.

Having learned the hard way, Sabrina considered herself an excellent cheat detector. So should she continue following this guy around when she was almost certain he wasn't having an affair? Her innate curiosity said yes. Even if Benoit wasn't a cheating slug there was definitely something going on with him and she wanted to know more.

"Have you had a chance to look at the menu?"

Pulling her gaze away from her subject, Sabrina gave a distracted smile to the server and ordered the first thing that came to mind. "I'll have the grilled salmon."

"Um…ma'am, we don't have grilled salmon. How about tuna or swordfish?"

Neither choice sounded good to her. And she suddenly realized she was ravenous. Having scarfed down a meager breakfast of cold cereal and missing lunch, her stomach was insisting on something more substantial.

Taking the menu she hadn't even glanced at, she hurriedly perused her choices. The spaghetti and meatballs jumped out at her. Not as healthy as grilled fish but she couldn't resist.

She placed her order, took a sip of her iced tea, and then returned her attention back to the man three tables away from her. What she saw made her sit up straight in her chair and take definite notice. Benoit's dining companion had finally joined him. This one didn't just surprise her...she was stunned.

Either Benoit's taste was even more eclectic than she had imagined or something else was definitely going on. One thing she had to admit, taking photos of this one would be no hardship at all.

The dinner companion was not just a man. He was gorgeously masculine, handsome without a hint of prettiness. Dressed in a navy pinstripe suit that had to have been tailored to fit his tall, muscular frame, the man exuded not only an air of confidence and sophistication but danger, too. She got the idea that beneath the elegant suit was a man who could handle himself in any kind of situation. And had done so many times.

His thick brown hair was slightly tousled as if he'd run his fingers through it a time or two. Or perhaps a wife or lover might have. His skin was lightly tanned. Not unusual in Florida but he didn't look the type to spend a lot of time on the beach and definitely not in a tanning salon.

Since he was seated across the table from Benoit, she should be able to get a good clear view of him. Angling the phone an inch to the left, Sabrina clicked on her camera, taking multiple shots. Many more than was necessary, but so what. It was good to have a variety to choose from.

She was too far away to tell his eye color but she thought perhaps dark brown, maybe a couple shades darker than his hair. A slash of thick brows above his eyes made them look even darker. Those brows arched in reaction to something Benoit was saying to him. His cheekbones were prominent, slightly etched, as if he was of Slavic descent. The dark stubble on his face made her think of sexy pirates or maybe marauding highwaymen.

A shiver of excitement zipped up her spine, as surprising as it was uncharacteristic. Sabrina Wilde did not get turned on so easily. Falling into lust, especially over a stranger, was not her thing.

So distracted by her reaction, she literally jumped when a steaming plate of spaghetti and meatballs appeared in front of her.

Thanking her server with a slight smile and nod, Sabrina absentmindedly twirled spaghetti onto her fork and brought it to her mouth. She took a bite, realizing too late that she had more on the fork than she could fit in her mouth. She chewed what she could, uncomfortably aware that several strands of spaghetti hung from her mouth like tentacles. Which, of course, is exactly when the man she'd been practically drooling over looked straight at her.

Hastily dropping her gaze to her plate, Sabrina concentrated on the mass of food in her mouth, willing herself not to choke. Finally swallowing the last of it, she surreptitiously lifted her eyes again. Though he was no longer looking her way, a small, enigmatic smile played around his sensual mouth as if he was fighting an all out grin.

Great going, Sabrina. Not only did you let your surveillance target catch you spying on him, you humiliated yourself in front of the most fascinating man you've ever seen.

Deciding she had more than enough photos, she dug into her meal with the fullest intention of enjoying herself. So what if she had embarrassed herself. She would never see this man again after tonight.

Proud that she hadn't weakened and checked out the man for several more bites, she rewarded herself for her remarkable self-control by looking at him again. He was alone. Benoit had apparently left and though she should probably have followed him she couldn't work up any regret. Tomorrow, she would call her client and tell her that though her husband did indeed seem to have something clandestine going on, in Sabrina's opinion, he wasn't cheating.

The captivating stranger stayed seated at the table, seeming in no hurry to leave. He sipped on a glass of wine as he played around with his iPhone. Sabrina told herself to look away. If she didn't, he would catch her staring at him again. But for the life of her, she couldn't drag her gaze from him.

And then he did something so surprising, so extraordinary... so infuriating. He lifted his phone, pointed it directly at her and clicked several photos.

What the hell?

Ian Mackenzie couldn't resist taking the shots. The instant he'd come into the restaurant, he had noticed the blonde in the corner. Not only was she stunning with her short cropped white-blonde hair, creamy magnolia skin, and light green eyes, she was focused entirely on him.

Hard for a man to ignore a beautiful woman who seemed as fascinated by him as he was by her. Also hard to ignore the fact that she had taken multiple photographs of him and his dinner companion.

This gig had just gotten infinitely more intriguing. When Blue Sea Industries had contacted him for this job, he'd been tempted to turn it down. Not because corporate espionage wasn't interesting but because he already had three other cases that were equally as interesting and time consuming. When they'd offered a twenty thousand dollar bonus if he completed his task within the month, he hadn't been able to say no. With that money, along with his other cases, he should be able to hire a second full time employee.

And now this added bonus. A fascinatingly beautiful woman who was apparently quite interested in Harold Benoit, too. He discounted the idea that she was here to see Ian specifically. The woman had been here when he arrived. Plus Ian hadn't known until an hour before his appointment time where he would be meeting Benoit for dinner.

No, she was definitely here for Benoit. Question was, why? And more importantly, just who was she?

Taking one last sip of his Merlot, Ian grabbed his phone and stood. Withdrawing his wallet, he threw down another twenty for the waiter. Benoit had paid for the meal, but Ian had noted the man had been decidedly stingy on the tip. Made him dislike the slimy weasel even more.

His eyes on his target, Ian moved toward the woman at a leisurely pace. When he saw her eyes widen in alarm, he couldn't help but grin. He reached her just as her hand closed over her cellphone, the one she'd used to take numerous photographs of him.

Covering her hand on the phone with his, he said mildly, "I'm afraid I'm going to have to confiscate your photos."

"What? I don't know what you're talking about."

Settling into the chair across from her, he kept his hand on hers, enjoying the soft, silky skin beneath his fingers.

"Listen buster, you need to get your paw off my hand before you lose it."

"My paw? Gee, I didn't realize my hand was so ugly."

Her smooth brow wrinkled with a frown. "Paws aren't ugly and neither is your hand."

"I have scars."

She glanced down at his hand still holding hers. The scars weren't that noticeable anymore, having faded over the last few years, but he'd had a few people mention them. Explaining how they came about wasn't his favorite topic of conversation. War and his experience in the military were taboo subjects even his family honored. So why had he even mentioned the scars?

Most women who noticed them either asked what happened or politely ignored them. This woman continued to surprise him. Instead of asking questions or pretending she didn't see them, she used her other hand to trace a scar that started on his ring finger. His suit jacket prevented her from seeing that this one extended up his arm to just above his elbow. He wished he were wearing short sleeves so she could follow it all the way up.

"Shrapnel?"

"Yes. How'd you know?"

"I have friends who've served."

When she stopped tracing the scar and removed her hand, he felt the loss of her touch like a blow. Glad that he still held her other one, he squeezed it gently. "So...care to tell me why you were snapping photographs of me?"

"I'm an artist?"

"Are you asking me?"

A delightful pink tinged her cheeks. "No...no. Of course not. I am an artist." Her voice grew with confidence. "Whenever I see an interesting face, I take snapshots so I can recreate it later."

"I'm honored you find my face interesting. So...water color, charcoal, or oils?"

"Um...charcoal."

"Fascinating." He withdrew a notepad and pen from the inside pocket of his jacket and pushed them across the table. "Draw my face. If you convince me you're an artist, I'll let you keep the photos."

"That's ridiculous. I'm not going to draw a picture of you. My work is private…deeply personal. Now please let go of my hand and I'll be on my way."

"Do it and I'll delete the photos I took of you with spaghetti hanging from your mouth."

Her cheeks went pinker. "You didn't get any shots of that."

"Did too."

Glaring at him, she snapped, "I'm right-handed. You'll have to let go of me first."

Unable to resist and willing to take a slug to the face if she saw fit, Ian lifted her hand to his mouth for a light kiss and then released it. Before she could react to that impropriety, he grabbed her phone. "I'll just hang on to this for the time being."

Eyes sparkling with a bright green fury, she snatched up the paper and pen and started drawing. He had no idea if she was actually sketching him or just doodling circles and figure eights. He couldn't take his eyes off her face.

The soft pink coloring her velvety cheeks made him think of a creamy white rose he'd seen in his mom's yard. He remembered that it bloomed solid white but after a few days, took on a rosy, blush-colored hue. The flower, however, paled in comparison to this enchanting creature's beauty.

She wore a sleeveless, light green blouse almost the exact shade of her eyes. Her arms were a light golden color and though slender, were well toned as if physical fitness was a priority for her. She looked both strong and delicately feminine.

"Here." She shoved the drawing toward him.

Dragging his gaze away, he looked down at the notebook and choked on a strangled laugh. She had indeed drawn him and not very flattering. "I never realized how large my nose was."

"Nosy people rarely do."

He slid her phone across the table, placing it where it'd been before. "Care to tell me the truth about the photos?"

She eyed him speculatively. He withstood the scrutiny, knowing she was trying to determine if he could be trusted. "If I tell you, will you answer my questions?"

"I'll do my best."

"Benoit's wife hired me to prove he was cheating on her."

"You're a private investigator?"

"Yes."

"And what have you decided about dear old Harold?"

She lifted her slender shoulders in a delightfully feminine manner. "He eats too much red meat, is a lousy tipper, and picks his teeth when he thinks no one is looking."

"True and quite gross, but not exactly evidence of infidelity."

"He's also doing something underhanded...sneaky."

"Really? Like what?"

"You tell me."

Ian leaned back against his chair. With anyone else he might have told a lie or at the very least skirted around the truth. This woman made him want to share information. Get her take and opinion. He was an excellent judge of character and knew to his soul that she could be trusted.

"Harold Benoit works for Blue Sea Industries, which among other things, develops women's cosmetics."

"Yes, I know that much about him."

"Harold has been working on a project for cell rejuvenation. Cutting-edge research. If FDA approval comes through, it could have a major impact on the aging process and make a boatload of money for the company. And—"

"And Deep Blue thinks Benoit is trying to sell this formula to the highest bidder."

"In a nutshell, yes."

"And he is, isn't he?"

"Yes, he is."

"So he is a scum-sucking, lowlife creepazoid. Just not a cheating one."

"From my research of him and observations, no, he isn't…a cheater, that is. The other description is most definitely true."

"And you were hired by his employer to catch him?"

"Yes. Tonight was my final meeting with him. I was undercover, pretending to work for a competitor. I made him a lucrative offer. He eagerly accepted."

"So what happens now?"

Ian glanced at his watch. "I'd say that even as we speak Harold is making his one allowed phone call to his attorney. I texted his employer just after he left the table."

"So you're a PI, too?"

"I am."

"Care to tell me your name?"

"I will if you will."

She held out her hand to shake his. "Sabrina Wilde, Wilde Investigations."

Taking her hand back into his, Ian knew an odd moment of serenity, as if he was not only touching the soft, smooth skin of a beautiful woman but also someone who would become very important to him.

"Ian Mackenzie."

"I've heard of you."

Reluctantly releasing her hand, he cocked his head, surprised. "Really?"

"Yes."

"And?"

She flashed him an unabashedly cheeky grin. "I've heard you always get your man."

Unable to resist, his own grin just as cheeky, he said, "And my woman, too."

CHAPTER ONE

Miami, Florida

Armando Cruz stepped out of his limo into the back alley of his club and took in a deep breath. Ah yes, the smell of success. Oh, some people might think of it as stink. The stench of debauchery or filth. But Armando knew better. This was life, humanity. *This* had made him wealthy beyond his dreams. *This* was his destiny.

Who knew that a few days ago he could have felt this good or optimistic? After Lauren had left him, he'd been distraught. Yeah, he could admit that to himself now. She had broken his heart, almost broken his spirit. After all he'd done for her, given her. She had betrayed him in the worst way possible. He had been set on vengeance. Finding her and making her pay his only priority. But then he'd been made to see reason and now had a new lease on life.

Only three people knew how this had happened—Armando, the shrink who'd helped him, and Robert, his most trusted friend and advisor. If news got out he had seen a head doctor, Armando knew he'd be ruined for sure. Admitting weakness in this business was tantamount to asking to be killed or taken over. But his one true friend had suggested the shrink. And Armando knew Robert would never tell a soul.

Though wary of sharing his inner most thoughts with anyone, especially a stranger, he had agreed to a visit. After all, Robert had never steered him wrong yet. And once again his friend had been right. That visit had changed his life—made him see things in a whole new light. He now knew why he acted the way he did, did the things he did.

His newly discovered self-awareness hadn't stopped him from performing his job. If anything, understanding his motivation had only increased his productivity. As the doc had assured him, understanding one's inner demons would keep Armando grounded. Didn't mean he stopped being a tough guy. Oh hell no. In fact, just yesterday he'd taken over the territory of one of his oldest rivals, ordering the elimination of the man's entire family. Only a strong, courageous leader would have the balls to do something so bold.

Yeah, he was definitely back on his game.

Even though the shrink believed he needed more than one visit to be completely cured, Armando disagreed. He had overcome a difficult time in his life and he was moving on. It was over… done with.

This morning he'd called off his team of investigators, told them to come back home. He had better things to do than go after some nobody who didn't appreciate him. There were plenty more women in this world. Lauren Kendall meant nothing to him anymore.

"Boss, everything okay?"

Abruptly aware that he'd been standing in one place, staring at the back door of his club, Armando gave a stiff, arrogant nod. So what? He had nothing to be embarrassed about. This was his place…his kingdom. If he told this dumb-ass to stand here until next week with his underwear down around his ankles and his ass hanging in the wind, then that's what the guy had better do. Armando was the ruler of his world.

"I'm fine."

The words were nothing less than a growl. Nevertheless, Armando straightened his shoulders and walked through the door that was being held open for him. The dark hallway led to his offices. Few knew that the lower floors existed. The nightclub was a notorious place of sleaze and human vermin where lowlifes and gangbangers came to get drunk, get laid, and make deals.

Armando liked places like this. It reminded him where he'd come from and how far he'd risen. He could leave here and go home to his mansion, fly anywhere in the world in his private jet, make people do anything he wanted. But the sleaze that came here day after day would never be more. In every way possible, Armando was far superior from that sludge.

A part of a wall slid open, revealing the interior of an elevator. As Armando descended, he stood proudly before the mirror on the elevator door and took stock of his appearance. Just over six feet tall, smooth, slightly olive skin, glossy, thick black hair, chocolate brown eyes, and a slender physique. His dark brown suit had been tailored to perfection, enhancing but not overwhelming his good looks. He was tough looking but elegant, too—the image of a successful businessman. As he'd learned early in his career—image was everything.

A minute later he was in another world. This one of wealth and privilege. The fragrance of rich leather and thousand dollar cigars permeated the air. Decadence surrounded him. While he basked in elegance, the fools above him slogged around in the trenches of filth. But without them, he wouldn't be here. He loved the irony.

"Everything's ready for you, sir."

Armando didn't bother to acknowledge the asinine words. Of course it was ready for him. There would be hell to pay if it wasn't.

He seated himself at his table and immediately dug into his Porterhouse steak. Prepared by the chef of the most exclusive restaurant in Miami, the meal was exquisite. The Cabernet, a perfect accompaniment, had been flown in from France just last week. At five thousand dollars a bottle, few people could afford it.

Armando paid no attention to the people surrounding him. They were there to do his bidding. And just like the furniture or decor, they could easily be replaced.

Hunger appeased, he took one last swallow of his wine and stood. The remains of his meal would be removed, the table cleared. He gave a nod to one of his men who clicked on his stereo. The soothing sounds of light jazz filled the room. That was also a signal to bring in tonight's guests for drinks and some fun. One hunger had been appeased, another remained.

The door opened and two people entered, a man and woman. He knew the man well. Ryan Walker had been working for Armando for years. Caught between two worlds, Walker had proved his loyalty and cunning numerous times.

Walker had brought the woman round before, but Armando had been too immersed in his grief over losing Lauren to really notice her. And damn what a sight he'd missed. Medium height, silky black hair that just touched her shoulders, and a body that wouldn't quit. Good sized knockers that would overfill his hands, slender hips, but not too skinny, and long legs that could wrap all the way around a man's waist for a good, hard ride.

Her smooth white skin reminded him of cream and silk. Armando's mouth watered. He couldn't wait to see if she tasted as good as she looked. And oh yeah…her mouth. Even if she were as ugly as a donkey's ass, that mouth would've sealed the deal. A woman's mouth was made for only two things and neither of them involved talking. He looked forward to putting that luscious mouth to good use.

"Welcome!"

Walker shook his hand, while the woman stood back, looking slightly awkward and shy. Yes indeed, he was going to have a good time tonight.

Giving his other men a nod of dismissal, Armando waited until they'd closed the door behind them, leaving him alone with Walker and the woman before saying, "Who's your friend, Ryan?"

"Mr. Cruz, I'd like to introduce you to Lilah Green."

"Come over here, sugar, and let's get a good look at you."

Her slender neck moved as she swallowed nervously. Green eyes darted over to Walker, as if asking permission.

"No use looking at him. I'm the one who calls the shots here." Armando's voice went hard—she needed to learn obedience, quick. "Now come over here before you're made to."

She stumbled slightly but moved forward. He looked at her feet and figured walking in four inch heels might not be easy, but they sure made her legs look good. He patted the empty space on the sofa. "Come on. I don't bite. Well, not too hard, anyway."

He and Walker shared a knowing grin.

The woman settled beside him and he drew in her delicate fragrance. That subtle perfume teased his senses, making him both hard and irritated. Lauren had used perfume sparingly, too. Most of the women he had been with seemed to bathe in it. He'd told Lauren that was one of the things that convinced him she was a lady. The fact that this woman did the same brought back memories of betrayal and he didn't want that.

Armando looked up at Walker. "Go into the bathroom and get the perfume that bitch from last week left behind."

While he waited for Walker to do his bidding, Armando concentrated on getting to know the sweet, young thing beside him a little better. "Tell me about yourself, honey. Where are you from? What do you do?"

"I'm from Nebraska. I moved down here a couple of years ago."

Armando liked her voice. It held a softness and refinement that was often missing in the women he met. "And what do you do for a living, darling?"

"I'm a hostess at Maxi's."

"Somebody as classy as you working in a joint like that? We'll find you something better, won't we, Ryan?"

Walker handed over the oversized bottle of perfume he'd fetched. "Yes sir. That's real kind of you, sir. Isn't it Lilah?"

"Umm...yes, thanks. I'm not real fond of it. It's just a place to work till something better comes along."

Armando leaned over and whispered in her ear, "You please me tonight and I'll make sure something better comes along."

Her delectable body stiffened and she shot Walker a look that could've melted iron. Any other time Armando might have been amused by her reaction, but tonight it didn't sit well with him. The bitch needed to learn her place.

His hand wrapped around the back of her neck and he pushed her up until she stood beside him. "Cuffs, Walker."

She jerked away from him and sent another look to Walker. "What? Ryan, no, this isn't what I—"

"Um...Mr. Cruz." Walker said. "I don't—"

"Silence! Both of you," Armando snapped. Had Walker been about to refuse him this treat? The very idea had Armando seething. First he would show the girl her place, then he would deal with his disobedient employee.

Still holding the woman by the scruff of her neck, he took the cuffs Walker handed him. "Put your hands behind your back like a good girl and I won't hurt you. Resist and pay the consequences."

Armando felt the tremors in her delectable body as she complied. Was there anything sweeter than a beautiful woman terrified and bound for his pleasure? He snapped the cuffs on, making sure they weren't too tight. Marring her lovely skin, at least at the beginning of their relationship, wasn't in his plans. There would be plenty of time for that later on when they got to know each other better.

Armando pushed the girl down to her knees. "Close your eyes. I don't want to blind you."

He was pleased that she did as he asked. Holding the big bottle of perfume, he walked around the kneeling woman, gave her several good sprays on her neck, cleavage and bound wrists. Once he stripped her, he'd find a few more places but this should do for now.

"Look at me."

She opened her eyes and looked up. For just an instant, he saw something behind her fear. Anger yes—he had expected that, but he also saw steeliness and courage. Maybe there was more to this one than he'd thought.

He unzipped his pants and took himself in his hand, already rock hard. Time to find out if that mouth lived up to its potential. "Let's make use of that beautiful mouth in the best way possible."

Her eyes went wide and she shook her head, jerking away from him. "No way in hell, you lowlife, scum sucking maggot."

Fury engulfed him. No one spoke to him like that and lived. She would pay for those words with her life, but for now, she would pay with her mouth. Pushing her head down, Armando bent her to him. "You damn well better do as you're told or you'll—"

She butted at him with the top of her head. Armando jumped back, barely getting out of the way in time.

"Why you little—"

Shouts outside the door caught his attention. And then a pop...pop...pop.

Gunfire? What the hell?

The door burst open. Four men stood there. All holding guns...all wearing merciless, cold expressions. Armando caught a glimpse of bodies lying in the hallway behind them. His men, dead or unconscious.

The instant he recognized the man in the lead, uncertainty rushed through him. Holden Marsh had a reputation that made even Armando flinch.

He tried to keep his tone genial, unthreatening. "What's going on here? What have you done to my men?"

"Long time no see, Cruz."

At the hard ice in Marsh's voice, terror entered Armando's heart. But this made no sense. The man Marsh worked for was Armando's most trusted friend and advisor. Surely this wasn't something Robert had sanctioned.

"What do you want?"

"Just a little conversation. Looks like you were about to get your rocks off, but I'm afraid that's going have to wait." Amusement curled his mouth. "Besides, it appears she would've had to work awfully hard for it."

Armando looked down at his now limp dick. Every good feeling he'd had tonight had been obliterated. Quickly tucking his shrunken member back into his pants, he zipped up. His humiliation was complete when he saw a glint of amusement in the girl's expression.

"What is the meaning of this? What is it you want? You come in, mow down my men. What gives you the right?"

"The boss man wanted a little information from you. If you have the time, that is."

"Of course." Armando tried for a jovial, friendly look. His men could be replaced. "I always have time for the man who brought me into the business." He gave Walker a look. "You and your girl can go. I'll be in touch."

"No one leaves." Marsh nodded at the girl. "Stand up."

With surprising ease and grace, the girl stood.

"Uncuff her."

His hands shaking slightly, Armando took the girl's wrists and unlocked her. She breathed out a heavy, relieved sigh as she stepped away from him.

Armando gave her a glare. "Don't think this is over, bitch."

"Tsk. Tsk. Armando," Marsh said. "That's no way to speak to a lady."

The cuffs that had been around the girl's wrists only a moment ago suddenly encircled Armando's. "Wait. What are you doing?"

"Seems someone's been talking, Cruz. Boss just wants to get to the bottom of it."

"Talking? Who?"

"You ever hear of Dr. Terrence Cummings?"

"Of course I have. Your boss is the one who recommended him to me. What do you want to know about him?"

"Seriously?" Marsh's voice held a mocking condescension. "Do you really think the boss doesn't know what you've told him?"

"It doesn't matter what I told him...the man's a doctor. He can't reveal anything. And I've always been loyal. He's got no reason to distrust me."

"Until you met that sweet morsel named Lauren."

"What's she got to do with this? She's gone."

"Yes, but what did she abscond with?" His mouth quirked up in an amused sneer. "Besides your balls, that is."

Armando forced himself to ignore the insult. Time enough to make the bastard pay for it later.

"I don't know what you're talking about."

"We'll just see about that." Marsh motioned at two of the men. "The pool table looks like a good place."

"Good place for what?" Armando asked shakily.

Before he could protest or fight back, two men literally picked him up by his elbows and carried him to the pool table on the other side of the room.

"Put me down! What's this about? You can't just—"

"Garrett, be so kind as to gag him until we get him ready."

The indignity got worse as a cloth was shoved into his gasping mouth and then covered by duct tape. Armando struggled, jerking at the hands that grabbed at him. Before he knew it, his clothes had been cut from his body and he found himself lying naked, spread eagle on the surface of the pool table. They'd uncuffed his hands and then used tape to bind his ankles and wrists to the four corners of the table.

Even though his heart was thundering in his chest, Armando tried to tell himself he wasn't in that much danger. He had never once thought of betraying the man who'd dug him out of the sewer and given him a chance. Once they realized how loyal he'd been, they'd let him go. So what if he had to suffer a little embarrassment in front of Walker and the woman. It would be no worse than that.

"Okay, now that you're all comfy, let's hear what you've got to say."

The moment the gag was removed, Armando started talking. "I've done nothing to betray him. I promise."

"Really?" Marsh said.

Agony exploded in his kneecap. Armando squealed and screamed. Opening his tear-glazed eyes he saw one of the men had a hammer. They'd busted his knee!

"Why are you doing this?" Armando sobbed. "I've done nothing wrong."

"Tell me who else you've been blabbing to."

"No one. I swear."

"Come now, Armando. In one freaking visit, you told that shrink every little secret you've had since you were in grade school. He can't be the only one you've shared secrets with."

Armando shook his head, feeling an unaccountable betrayal. Cummings was a respected psychiatrist. Doctor and patient confidentiality should have protected Armando. And Robert? How could he have done this to him?

"I can see you're shocked, Armando. Let me assure you that Dr. Cummings felt quite torn for telling your secrets. However, his oath didn't extend to the man who ordered his brother-in-law killed."

"What are you talking about?"

"Remember Rodney Hawkins?"

"No, never heard the name."

"That's probably because you've killed so many, but believe me, Dr. Cummings remembers. When the boss approached him with the offer of serving as your doctor as payback, he jumped at the chance. Boss knows that everyone has a price. He proved it. So let's get back to the business at hand. Who else have you told your secrets to?"

"No one. I swear!"

"Not even Lauren?"

"Of course not. She knows nothing."

"Why don't we ask her ourselves? Where is she?"

"I don't know. I can't find her. I told Dr. Cummings I couldn't. I—"

Agony exploded again, this time in his other knee. Armando bit down on his lip, tasting blood. Behind the blur of excruciating pain, he heard the woman scream, "Stop!"

Armando gave little thought to the oddity that the woman was the only one who was trying to end this atrocity.

"Please…please," Armando pleaded. "I promise. I don't know where she is. Dr. Cummings is the one who persuaded me to stop looking for her."

"You're right. He told us that. We just wanted to make sure you were telling the truth. Boss said he wants to know about her though. Where her family is. Where she's from. Said the short time they spent together they didn't do much talking."

He now deeply regretted giving Lauren to the brutal bastard he had called friend. He'd thought it was a nice gesture. Robert had turned fifty. What better birthday present than to give him what Armando cherished the most, his lovely Lauren? When she had returned to him, she'd been bruised, a little battered, but other than one silent accusing look, she had never complained. The next week, after she healed, she'd come back to his bed like she had never left it. He'd thought things were okay, but two months later, she'd been gone.

"I never told Lauren any of my business."

"I thought we'd established that. What I asked was, where is she from? Where's her family from? You need some more pain to help you concentrate better?"

"No...No. She, uh...she's from up north. Maine or New Hampshire. One of those cold states."

"Not exactly pinpointing it for us, but it's a start."

The reality hit him then. His knees were ruined, and as hard as that was to accept, he already knew they weren't through with him.

As if he could read Armando's mind, Marsh said, "I think he needs a little something to take his mind off his knees."

Agony erupted in his ankle. And then pain exploded in his other ankle.

Armando screamed and sobbed. His body jerked and twitched in rebellion, his muscles cramped with strain. The meal he'd recently consumed surged up his throat. Turning his head so he wouldn't choke, he vomited. The sheer atrocity of what was being done to him stunned him for several seconds. How could he get out of this? He couldn't think straight. He had done nothing to deserve such torture.

"I swear I don't know anything else," Armando sobbed. "She said she was from up north, that her name was Lauren Kendall. Her family is all gone. I swear that's all I know."

Marsh's face appeared above him. "I believe you."

Though agony pounded in his knees and ankles, Armando closed his eyes in relief. Finally, at last, it was over. Now—

Something cold and hard pressed against his right temple. Armando opened his eyes. Ryan Walker had a Glock against Armando's head.

"You traitorous bastard!" A last gasping scream of "Noooooo—"

And then there was nothing.

CHAPTER TWO

She was in big trouble.

Sabrina stared at the pool table where the bloody, lifeless body of one of the most notorious drug lords in the country lay. Dying rarely came easy, but for Armando Cruz it had come with an unequaled brutality. The man had been a disgusting, vile specimen of humanity. She could still feel his filthy hands on her, smell his foul breath. The revolting image of his penis wasn't something she could unsee.

Despite her revulsion and disgust of the man, watching his torture and murder had been a singularly unpleasant experience. The sheer barbarism of the act was sickening, but she hadn't expected it to be followed up with a bullet to his head. Who were these people? What had Cruz done to them to deserve such a brutal end?

Silly. Here she was worrying about a lowlife criminal dying when very soon she might be joining him. Every instinct she possessed was telling her to run, but Sabrina stood frozen in place. The gun now digging into her spine was troublesome, the man holding the gun even more so. She had trusted him.

Undercover cop Ryan Walker had been her entry into Cruz's domain. The drug lord's former mistress, Lauren Kendall, had come to Wildefire Security, the agency she and her sisters owned, for protection. Which they had provided. But when they'd taken the case, they had known that providing protection wouldn't be enough. Cruz would always be a threat to Lauren until he was stopped.

Sabrina had gone undercover to get information on Cruz. Her intent had been to help put him behind bars and remove the threat against Lauren. What had just happened here had not been anywhere on her radar.

One thing for certain—Cruz was no longer a threat to Lauren. Problem was, how was Sabrina going to get out of this? Ryan Walker was a dirty cop. A killer. No way in hell did he plan to let her live.

"Sorry you had to see that," Walker said.

Just before going into their meeting with Cruz, Walker had told her to be prepared for anything. Having him double-cross her hadn't been on her list of things to be prepared for.

"Why did you kill him?"

Walker came to stand in front of her, his gun only inches from her face. The cold amusement in the man's eyes wasn't encouraging. "It was time for him to go. Cruz didn't know it but he was a minnow in an ocean of sharks. His biggest mistake was believing he was more than that."

"What are your plans for her?"

The guy asking the question sat on the sofa. He'd been the one to question Cruz, to give orders for each blow of the hammer into the man's bones. But now he looked so relaxed he was practically reclining. It was apparent that this was nothing new for him. The bored expression on his face said he'd been there, done that, and didn't really care if he had to do it again.

"I'm going to take her some place, screw her brains out, and then dispose of her."

Sabrina's shiver of revulsion brought a cruel smile to Walker's mouth. "Don't worry. I'll make sure you go with a smile on your face."

A lot of things—sarcastic and insulting—came to her mind to say. She might be impetuous and rash, but she wasn't stupid. Pissing off a man holding a gun on her wasn't a good idea.

"Boss says hold up," the guy on the couch said. "He wants to talk to her."

The mysterious boss man everyone kept referring to who had apparently ordered Cruz's death. As of yet, no one had been generous enough to offer his name. Cruz had trusted the man. Had said he'd brought Cruz into the business.

Whoever this boss man was, he had a remarkable influence. The gun that had been pointed at her lowered in an instant.

Sabrina eased away from Walker, inch by inch, and eyed the door—her only way out. She was going to have to make a run for it and needed a clear path.

"What does he want with her?" Walker asked.

"Does it matter?"

"She could identify me. I could lose my job at the department."

"You seem to think you're important." The man on the sofa grinned up at him. "You got Cruz's ego issues?"

"I've given dozens of tips, provided tons of information over the years. Hell, I just killed Cruz for him. I'm an invaluable member of his organization."

"You're a snitch and a weasel. And a bad cop."

"I'm an asset." Walker's voice shook, no longer arrogant.

The man on the sofa lifted his gun and without the slightest flinch, fired, shooting Walker twice in the chest.

Sabrina jumped out of the way of the falling dead man as her brain scrambled to keep up with everything that was happening.

In less than an hour, not just the rules but the whole damn game had changed. Without a doubt, she had stumbled into something she'd never had to deal with before.

What now?

As if shooting a cop was just another day on the job, the man on the sofa continued his relaxed pose as he turned his attention to Sabrina. "So the question is, what should happen to you?"

With no weapon and under the guise of being not so bright arm candy, Sabrina had little choice but to maintain her cover of a beautiful ditz. "Seriously, mister. I just came along cause Ryan promised to take me to Club 500 after we left here."

"You don't seem too upset to see your lover dead."

"We weren't lovers. He was just a guy I dated a few times."

"You have very bad taste in men, my dear."

With one notable exception, that was one statement Sabrina Wilde could wholeheartedly agree with.

"I don't know anything about what's going on here. I don't *want* to know."

"Perhaps not, but you just witnessed two murders. That's not something one easily forgets."

"I have a real bad memory."

He gave her a lazy grin. "I like you."

She had no idea if that was a good thing or not.

"You're a tad too perfect looking for me, though. Makes a man want to mess you up."

No, that didn't sound good at all.

Unfolding his long body from the sofa, he stood and gave a lackadaisical one- shouldered shrug. "Unfortunately I don't always get what I want."

Sabrina tensed, readying herself to take flight. She had little chance of surviving, but she refused to stand here like a statue and let him just shoot her at point blank range.

Even if she could avoid being shot, the three other men in the room wouldn't let her get away. Still, she would not go down without a fight.

Instead of pointing the gun at her, the man used it to gesture as he gave out instructions to the other men. "Julio and Dennis, take care of Cruz's body. Put him in the water. Leave Walker here, though. We'll let the cops wonder if Cruz did all this."

He winked at Sabrina. "Gotta keep'em guessing."

He glanced at another man. "Garrett, you're with me. We're going to take a ride with Ms." He frowned. "What's your name, honey?"

"Lilah Green." She didn't have to fake the tremor in her voice. The fear was real.

"Let's take Ms. Green with us."

Sabrina tried to tell herself this was much better. She could handle two men better than she could handle four. Never having been an optimist even on her best day, she ignored the snarky, "Yeah right" comeback that whispered in her mind.

The men, apparently Julio and Dennis, set to work on Cruz's bloody corpse. Taking a tarp from behind the bar, they lifted the body from the pool table and started rolling him. Either Cruz killed so many people that he kept plastic tarps around to clean up the mess or they'd been prepared for this.

The other man, Garrett, jerked Sabrina's arms behind her back and zip-tied her wrists.

She winced at the tightness and tried one more pitiful look at the man issuing orders. "Look, mister, really. I won't tell anyone." She blinked rapidly, working up some tears. "I promise."

"Look at it this way, sugar. If you survive, you'll have an adventurous story to tell your grandkids. Besides, the boss might like you so much, he might decide to keep you for himself."

Oh joy.

Ian sat in a parked car half a block from Armando Cruz's club. Sabrina was in there. He had no idea what she'd gotten herself into or what was going on behind those walls. He only knew that no way in hell was he going to leave her on her own.

She'd be pissed that he had followed her to Miami. Didn't matter. He'd been watching her back too long to stop now. They were no longer PI partners, but so what? Looking out for her had nothing to do with business and everything to do with his sanity.

He glanced at his passenger, his companion of two years—a gift from Sabrina. "What about it, Jack? Should we just sit here like two slobbering idiots panting after the same girl or should we go in and see what we can see?"

Tongue lolling to the side, drool pooled on the leather car seat as sad, droopy eyes gazed at Ian lovingly, trusting him to know what to do.

"Yeah, that's what I thought."

Ian scratched the hound behind one of his long floppy ears and then slumped back into his seat with a disgusted snort. Was he an idiot for just sitting here waiting for something to happen? He knew Sabrina Wilde. Ninety-nine percent of the time, she could get out of any kind of trouble. He'd seen her dodge bullets, knives, and once she'd outrun a pack of wild dogs. No, she wasn't superwoman, but she was intelligent, crafty, incredibly gifted, and fearless. It was that one percent that drove him crazy...kept him awake at night. That one percent would get her killed someday. Ian planned to make sure that was at least a hundred years from now.

She would be furious if she knew he'd added a little safeguard to her wardrobe. It wasn't something he had done a lot. When they'd first started working together, she'd been reckless but had tempered that with commonsense and sound reasoning. The last few months, commonsense had all but disappeared. Something had ignited the wildness in her again.

Of course what that something was, remained a mystery to everyone but Sabrina herself. Hell, sometimes he wondered if she even knew why she took the chances she did.

They had known each other for four years, had started working together within months of meeting. Ian figured he knew her as well as anyone. Meaning sometimes he didn't know her at all.

When she had told him she was going back to her hometown of Midnight, Alabama, to open up a security agency with her sisters Savannah and Samantha, he hadn't liked it but had understood. Family came first. And being one of identical triplets, the sisters had an amazing closeness. Only made sense for her to want to work with them.

So he had put on a stoic face and wished her well. Since he was only a few hours from Midnight, he told himself he'd see her almost as often, he'd just have to drive a little farther.

He had been in love with her almost from that first meeting. Spunky, sarcastic, loyal, brave, beautiful, and absolutely the most maddening woman he'd ever had the good fortune to meet.

When she had told him about Wildefire Security's first case, he had been intrigued but also a little concerned. Messing around with the likes of Armando Cruz wasn't a good career move. Especially since the case involved protecting a woman who happened to be Cruz's ex-mistress.

Still, he had been certain that Sabrina would discuss plans with her sisters before she did anything too dangerous. He'd been wrong. When she had called and told him she had a way inside Cruz's domain, he'd been furious and worried as hell.

He had expressed his concerns in a manner he had deemed appropriate at the time. Meaning he'd demanded she back away from the job before she got herself killed. That hadn't gone over well. Sabrina had never responded well to ultimatums.

And then he'd done something even dumber. He'd extended an invitation to visit his family in Sarasota again. The moment the words were out of his mouth, he'd wanted to take them back. That first and only visit had been a disaster. He had known another one would be out of the question but had promised his mother. Ian figured he was an asshole about a lot of things, but when it came to his mom, he didn't break promises. Sabrina's response had been predictable. She'd run like the proverbial scalded cat.

Sabrina had a commitment phobia. He'd learned that early. It had taken a year and a whole lot of late night surveillance jobs to get her to tell him why. In the dark of night, waiting for a criminal to show his face or an unfaithful spouse to leave a lover's bed, time could drag. In those hours, you found yourself sharing a helluva lot more than you ever planned.

He had opened up with her about his time in Iraq and Afghanistan. Of having one of his best friends die in his arms. Of the brutal days of fighting and the grueling boredom of waiting for something to happen, and the sheer terror when it did.

He'd even told her about his shitty childhood, something only his family knew about. How he'd watched his mother destroy herself with drugs. About his abusive alcoholic father whose favorite pastime, second only to drinking, was beating the hell out of Ian. And he'd shared with her all the emotions and joys that came with his incredible good fortune when Molly and Barry Mackenzie came into his life and he had been adopted.

In return, Sabrina had told him about her parents' deaths when she was ten. Of the devastation and the grief. Of her love for her sisters and aunt—the only family she had left.

She had explained her inability to commit to a serious relationship, blaming it on her former fiancé, Tyler Finley. The man had lied to her, cheated on her, and had taken advantage of her for his own gain. She admitted that he had almost destroyed her.

Ian wished with all his heart that the bastard were still alive so he could teach him a lesson he'd never forget.

Without a doubt, Sabrina fascinated Ian on every level. Vulnerable and tough, affectionate and prickly, funny as hell, loyal to a fault, and much too serious. A dichotomy of characteristics living within the same person. And he loved every single one of them.

The tiny dot on his cellphone went into motion, indicating she was on the move. For the past hour there'd been no discernable movement, but now the signal showed rapid progress. Was she through for the night? He wished he'd been able to hide a microphone on her but hadn't wanted to take the risk. If she was scanned, finding a bug on her could've blown up in his face.

A white stretch limo eased out from behind the club. A black SUV followed close behind. Ian waited. One of the vehicles held Sabrina. Which one? The SUV stopped at a light and the limo veered left. The blip on his screen kept moving, telling him she was in the limo.

Ian pulled from his parking spot and headed in the direction the limo had taken. Something was definitely off. Two hours ago, she had arrived in a silver Jag. So why was she leaving in a different vehicle?

CHAPTER THREE

Sabrina stayed quiet, not wanting to draw attention to herself. After a fifteen-minute limo drive with almost no conversation, she'd been pushed into the back of another nightclub, this one even seedier looking than the last. Other than the shove the guy named Garrett had given her into a chair, she'd been ignored.

Fine by her.

She had learned two things on the way over. The lazy man with the gun was named Marsh. Garrett had slipped and called him that and had received a furious glare in return. She'd also learned he wasn't as lazy as he liked to appear. When she had refused to step into the limo, Marsh had picked her up and thrown her over his shoulder as if she weighed nothing. The loose sweatshirt he wore hid an impressive amount of solid muscle.

She could almost hear Ian's 'I told you so.' He would be furious with her. Even more than he already was. And he had been right. She had walked into this situation with almost no research on the man she had gone undercover with. Just because Ryan Walker had a way inside and she'd only had a limited amount of time to make the decision was no excuse. Enthusiasm had bypassed caution. Yes she could be impulsive, but she rarely gave her trust to someone before knowing them well. One would think she would have learned her lesson.

So here she sat in the corner like a recalcitrant child being punished with a time out. This had been one of her mom's favorite ways to punish her when she was a kid. And being the kind of kid that never wanted to sit still, it had been effective. Her mom had known her so well.

Sabrina gave herself a mental ass-kick. Dealing with guilt and grief at any time was never a top one hundred priority item. Doing so while she needed all her wits about her would be downright stupid.

She drew in a silent, inner breath and looked for a way out. She refused to believe there wasn't one.

The room was apparently used for both an office and storage. Stacked boxes covered one side of the room, the other side held a desk, desktop computer, and a comfortable looking chair.

There were only three ways out, two doors—one she knew led to the back alley, where they'd entered. The other door was across the room. Garrett stood at that door with a look on his face that told her she'd have to mow him down to get out that way. Between the desk and the boxes was a window. Not an ideal exit strategy but if she had to, she'd throw herself through the glass. Better to have a few cuts than a bullet in her head.

The man named Marsh sat at the desk reading something on the computer screen. He'd given occasional grunts as well as one soft chuckle, so whatever he was reading must have been entertaining.

They were waiting for the boss to show up. As curious as she was to find out who that might be, Sabrina knew it would behoove her to get out before he, and whatever goons traveling with him, arrived. One against two armed men weren't the best odds. One against three or more would be downright sucky.

The sound of a jaw-cracking yawn caught her attention. Marsh had apparently finished his Internet reading. He stood and stretched his big body. Catching her eye, he gave her a grin. "How you holding up, sugar?"

"I'd really like to go home." Understatement of the century.

Surprising her, his grin went away and a flash of compassion entered his expression. "Wish I could let you go."

"You can. I promise. Cross my heart. I won't tell anybody about what happened."

"What do you do for a living?"

"I'm a hostess at a restaurant downtown."

"Oh yeah? Which one?"

"Maxi's Place."

"The one on 22nd street? Sugar, that's a strip joint."

She gave an indignant sniff and held her head high. "We serve pretzels and peanuts, too."

Marsh gave a loud guffaw and even Garrett snickered. That was okay with her. Maybe if they liked her, thought she was just an airhead with stilettos and a nice butt, they'd consider her harmless and let her go.

"You ever done any stripping?"

The question came from Garrett. The amusement on his face had turned into a leer. That wasn't exactly the way she wanted him to like her.

"No, I don't do stuff like that."

"Maybe you might like to try." His expression got slimier. "You could audition for us here."

"That's enough."

Marsh's growling reprimand made her feel a little better. At least he didn't appear to want to do anything to her. His next words destroyed any relief. "Boss doesn't want her messed up until he gets here."

Okay, she really needed to get out of here before that happened. "Do you think I could go to the bathroom? It's been a while and well…"

"Sure thing, darlin'." Marsh shot Garrett a hard look. "Take her to the one in the hallway. She has the slightest smudge on her when she gets back, you'll answer to me."

Garrett's responding glare might've intimidated a lesser man but it only made Marsh give the man an amused smirk.

"Get up," Garrett said.

She stood and went with him, but seconds before they reached the door, a loud clanging outside caught everyone's attention.

"Wait," Marsh said. "Check that out first."

"I'm not your damn lackey," Garrett snarled. "You go check it out."

Giving the man a look that could've melted steel, Marsh barked, "Do it!"

Mumbling curses under his breath, Garrett took Sabrina's elbow and pulled her back to the chair. Then with one last glower at Marsh, he stomped out the door.

"Guess I'd better not turn my back on him for a while." The amusement in Marsh's voice said he wasn't worried.

Hoping to glean more information, Sabrina said, "Who are you waiting on? Why can't you let me go?"

"I told you, we're waiting for the boss to arrive. And I can't let you go because he's become intrigued with you."

"How does he even know about me?"

"There were cameras all over that room."

"You mean he—"

"Yeah, he saw and orchestrated the whole thing." He gave her a warning look and added, "And enjoyed every moment of it."

Sabrina couldn't hide her shudder. "What did Mr. Cruz do that made you guys torture him like that?"

"Maybe he kept asking questions that were none of his business."

She got his drift and self-preservation told her to shut up while he was still in a mildly good mood. Questioning him further was only going to rile him. But if she didn't ask, she'd never get more answers. "Did Mr. Cruz work for your boss, too?"

Instead of another warning, Marsh surprised her by answering, "No. They're in the same business. Competing businessmen you might say."

"Is that why he was killed? To get rid of the competition?"

"Nah. Boss wasn't scared of the competition. He's too big for that. Cruz blabbed. In this line of work, you spill your guts, your guts get spilled."

"What does your boss do?"

Marsh stood, a cold, blank expression replacing the casual one. "Your questions seem a little too pertinent for a cocktail waitress in a strip joint. Something you been keeping from me?"

She could do haughty as well as anyone. "Just because I don't have a college degree or work in a high powered position doesn't mean I don't have a brain. I have a right to know who you people are and why I'm being held."

There. Put that in your arrogant pipe and smoke it, you condescending bastard.

Uh oh. The look got meaner. He started toward her and then stopped when he heard another noise outside. Pulling the gun from his holster, he gave her one last warning before striding out the door, "You move a muscle, you die where you sit. Understand, little girl?"

Okay, this guy was really pissing her off. But since he had a gun and she didn't even have the use of her hands, all she could do was glare.

No way in hell was she going to wait and see what he'd do when he came back. She jumped from the chair and ran to the other door. Turning her back on it, she used one of her hands to twist the knob. Dammit, her hands were bound so tightly that the ties were cutting into her wrists. Knowing she'd have more than this small amount pain if she didn't get out of here, she ignored the agony and kept trying. Sweat trickled down her back as she strained with all her might to twist the knob enough to open the door.

Almost there...almost...

A deep voice from across the room drawled, "Need a hand with the door, little lady?"

If he hadn't been equal parts furious and worried sick about her, Ian would've laughed as Sabrina jumped a foot off the floor.

"What are you doing here?"

"Apparently doing what I do best, pulling your pretty ass out of danger."

"How did you even know where I was?"

"You want to get out of here or would you rather sit down and have a chat?"

"Fine." She turned her back on him. "Can you get me out of these? They're tearing into my skin."

Using the knife he'd stolen from one of the men he'd knocked out, Ian cut the ties around Sabrina's wrists. When he saw the deep gouges in her skin, he wanted to turn around and beat the crap out of both men again. As gently as possible, he removed the plastic that had stuck to her. "You're bleeding. Let's call the police and then get you to a doctor."

"Where are Marsh and Garrett?"

"Those the two guys that were holding you?"

"Yes."

"Left them unconscious and tied up in the alley."

"Then we need to get out of here."

"Why?"

"I'll explain as soon as it's safe. But we need to leave now."

He had trusted her with his life more times than he could count. He wasn't about to question her judgment about this. "Let's go. I'm parked around the corner."

As they entered the alleyway, he saw her give a satisfied nod at the two pairs of legs sticking out from behind the dumpster. Less than a minute later, they were in his car, speeding away from the nightclub.

Neither spoke. While Ian concentrated on getting as far from the club as possible, Sabrina took medical gauze from the first-aid kit he'd stored in the console and wrapped her bloodied wrists. That would do for now. When he got to the rental house, he'd treat them properly.

They were on the interstate, headed north before Ian asked, "Want to tell me what the hell happened? Who were those guys and why didn't we call the cops?"

Before she could answer, Jack, who'd been relegated to the backseat, began whining. Sabrina patted her lap. "Come on up here with me, big guy."

With a happy yelp, he jumped onto the console and then into her lap. Wrapping her arms around the dog, she gave him a hug and a kiss on his head, then said to Ian, "Because I don't know who we can trust. All I know is there's someone more evil than Armando Cruz out there and if he finds me, I'm dead."

CHAPTER FOUR

They were barely inside the front door when she started stripping. "Where's the bathroom?"

He had brought her back to the beach house he'd rented when she'd taken on this undercover stint. That she hadn't questioned him about the place told him exactly how shaken she was.

Though every protective cell in his body urged him to hold her and find out what the hell had happened, Ian knew not to touch her. She would want to find control on her own. He wanted answers, but first he needed to make her feel safe.

He pointed toward the direction of the master bedroom, the bathroom beyond it, and watched silently as she dashed toward the rooms. Since she smelled as though someone had upended a gallon of cheap perfume on her, he figured she wanted to remove the stench but it was more than that. Whatever had happened had shaken her to her core.

While she showered, he fed Jack and took him for a quick walk. When they came back inside, the hound waddled to his bed and collapsed onto the cushion with a happy, noisy sigh.

Ian stood in the middle of the living room and listened. Not only was he surprised that Sabrina hadn't come out of the bedroom, he couldn't believe that the shower was still running.

Needing to check, just to make sure she was okay, he strode through the bedroom and then into the bathroom. She'd finally shut off the water and was just stepping out of the shower.

Her clothes lay scattered around the bathroom as if she'd haphazardly flung each piece the instant she'd taken it off. The black wig she'd been wearing hung halfway out of the small garbage can beside the sink. The extra bra padding lay on the floor beside the can as if she'd thrown it and missed her target.

Lilah Green had entered the room but now no longer existed. In her place stood a pale, slender woman with short, white-blonde hair, light green eyes, and a veiled vulnerability that Ian had never been able to resist.

He handed her a large fluffy towel. While she dried off, he went to the medicine cabinet, pulled out gauze, antibiotic ointment and tape. "Come over here."

"I can do that."

The look he gave her cut off any further protests. There was a place and a time for her independence to show itself, this wasn't one of them. Ian would see to her injuries.

She stood before him, held her arms out and watched in silence as he gently smoothed the ointment on her ravaged skin, then wound gauze around the wounds.

"I wished I'd killed them for this alone," Ian whispered.

"You didn't…?"

She left the question in the air. They both knew what he was capable of.

"No, they're probably already awake. Hopefully with massive headaches and multiple bruises."

He concentrated on his task for several seconds, willing the rage to settle down. When he spoke again, it was in a mild, unthreatening tone. "You ready to talk?"

"Can you give me just a few more minutes?"

She still hadn't regained that steeliness she wore like a protective coating. Pushing aside his own needs for the time being, Ian silently put away the medical supplies and left her alone.

Even though the temperature outside was well over eighty, Ian went to the fireplace and busied himself building a fire. Not only would she need the heat to help her deal with her shock, he needed something to occupy himself. Sabrina's fierce independence was often difficult to accept, especially when he knew she was hurting.

Half an hour later she finally appeared in the living room. Her outfit made him smile. He rarely traveled without packing something for her. When she was lounging around at his house, one of his old college T-shirts and a pair of his socks was her usual attire. He'd thrown this one in because it seemed to be her favorite.

Ian handed her a double shot of bourbon, figuring that would get her blood warmed up faster than anything. Her face was still as white as Florida sand and held a pinched, worried expression.

She took a long, healthy swallow. "Thanks. You always know exactly what I need."

No, not always. But he had studied this woman unlike anything or anyone else in his life.

"There's something else you need. Come over here by the fire."

Her look one of absolute trust, Sabrina came to him and took the hand he held out to her.

Kneeling, he pulled her down with her back to him. "Relax." He then began to knead the knots at the top of her shoulders.

She whispered, "Thank you" and then went silent.

Even though a massage would be easier without clothes, Ian couldn't ask that of her. More than anything, she needed to feel safe. He had been her safety net before and would never want to damage that trust.

Her body went limp as if finally giving out and Ian was able to smooth out the knotted muscles in her shoulders and neck. "Lie down, I'll get your back and glutes."

Instead of complying, she surprised him by twisting around and pulling him to her for a kiss. Even though he wanted to respond with all the heat burning inside him, he let her take the lead. Her mouth, soft and sweet, tasting like his mint-flavored toothpaste and Sabrina, was delicious, addictive. When her tongue swept against his lips, he opened up and allowed her tongue to sweep inside. His tongue responded, tangling with hers but never thrusting.

Before things got too heated, he pulled away scant inches and whispered, "We need to talk about what happened. We can't let those men—"

"We will, I promise. But I need this now. Please?"

She never needed to say please to him. She knew beyond a shadow of a doubt that Ian would give her anything she asked.

Sabrina pulled the T-shirt over her head, needing Ian more than she ever had before. Only he could make her feel clean, renewed. Only he could erase the darkness inside her. Make her forget what she'd seen today.

As Ian's eyes swept over her, delicious arousal spread through her, both exciting and familiar. His look spoke of appreciation, affection, tenderness. All the things she had come to rely on in this man. The memories of Armando Cruz and his filthy hands and lust filled eyes were at last fading away.

Wanting to feel his naked chest against hers, Sabrina unbuttoned his shirt. As she did this, Ian thankfully unzipped his pants, toed off his shoes and stripped the rest of his body. By the time she'd finished with his shirt and had pulled it off his shoulders, the rest of him was bare. Sabrina pressed against his warm, hard body, savored the feeling. Ian represented everything that was good and decent in a man.

"Tell me what you want."

"You, Ian. Only…always you. Make love to me."

Lying back on the soft rug, she watched his face as he bent over her, kissing her with tenderness and exquisite care. They'd made love numerous times…their joining usually passionate, fiery, sweaty. But Ian, somehow, always seemed to know just what she needed. At this moment, passion was set aside and his gentleness took over, giving her exactly what she required.

Ian Mackenzie was as rare as a mountain cactus in the ocean. She relished that she'd found someone who understood her so well.

Starting at her forehead, his mouth trailed kisses down her face and her neck. He stopped briefly at her breasts and gave one, then the other, a soft, tender caress before continuing down her body. Gently parting her thighs, he nibbled over every inch of her mound. Sabrina had a distant, cloudy thought that the wax treatment she endured every other week was well worth the discomfort. The extreme pleasure of his lips, tongue, and teeth on her bare flesh drove her wild, shooting fire through her veins. His tongue penetrated her sheath and she groaned her approval. Arching upward, she gave herself over to the incredible sensations zinging through her body and settling deep within her center. When his mouth covered her clit and sucked gently, she zoomed up and then over into an explosive climax.

Shuddering with her release, Sabrina felt renewed from the inside out. Ian lingered over her, drawing out her pleasure as long as possible. When the last throbbing contraction subsided, he started with her again.

"Ian…please," Sabrina groaned. "I need…"

"Shh, baby. I know."

And showing her that he indeed did know, he lifted her until she lay on top of him. Straddling him, she looked into his beautiful face and saw everything she ever needed or wanted to see. Dark brown eyes gleamed with heat and desire but most of all love. His lightly tanned skin was flushed and his mouth held a deliciously sexy slant. That mouth…oh that mouth that gave infinite pleasure. Wavy, dark brown hair, tousled even more from her fingers, was adorably messy and sexy.

"Take what you need, love."

Sabrina did exactly what he asked of her. Rising up on her knees, she held him in her hands and brought him to her. Sinking down slowly, she took one hard delicious inch of him at a time.

Ian ground his teeth until his jaw ached from the pressure. The minute Sabrina grabbed hold of him, he had stopped breathing. Now, as she brought him inside her heat, his heartbeat ceased along with his breathing. If a man could die this way, then he swore it was going to happen this very moment. Every ounce of his control was being used up. He wanted nothing more than to thrust deep and pound away until he exploded. That kind of roughness wasn't what she wanted or needed. So he would give her exactly what she asked for and if he died, then he'd die inside the woman he loved. What more could a man ask?

Once she was fully seated and had taken him as far as she could, she sat down abruptly and he strangled on a groan. Holy hell, this was it. He was a goner. Then she rose up, graceful, slow, and began a beautiful, sexy, up and down ride. The sweet torture of her tight heat and grasping of her inner muscles was the best thing he'd ever felt in his life. The release he'd been holding off rose up swiftly.

She must've felt it because she whispered softly, "No…not yet" and rose up onto her knees.

Now only the tip of the head was inside her and Ian figured this was it...death would now occur. When she dropped back onto him fully, he couldn't prevent the curse that sprang from his mouth. Instead of being insulted, she gave a sultry, beautiful laugh.

Words ground from his clenched teeth. "You're a demon wrapped up in a beautiful package, Sabrina Wilde."

"Your demon, Ian Mackenzie," she whispered.

"Yes, mine. All mine."

Now that she had him seated fully inside her again, he had hopes that she would finish them both off but no, she still wasn't finished with her torture. She glided up and down and just when he thought his head would blow off, she'd stop until they both had their control back.

Dammit, he wanted to give her what she needed, but he wasn't going to last much longer. He felt her inner muscles milking at him and he knew a strong climax was about to hit her. Wanting that to happen for them at the same time, Ian surged up abruptly and taking his fingers where they were joined together, he pinched the top of her clitoris and then let go.

The scream she released was uninhibited and loud enough to wake the neighbors, if he had any. With a harsh groan, Ian followed her into satiated oblivion.

Long minutes later, she was snuggled up in his arms. Their breathing had lessened from rasping to only slightly elevated. Ian held her close in one arm, while he kissed the back of her head, her neck, wherever he could reach.

At last, she spoke. "Cruz is dead."

Ian jerked at the news. "What happened?"

She began with the bare facts, quickly glossing over the details of her almost sexual assault.

"Wait...back up." Ian pushed her onto her back. Propped up on his elbow, he glared down at her. "You're telling me Cruz handcuffed you and was going to make you go down on him? And that bastard cop was going to let him get away with that?"

"That bastard cop is dead, too."

"Shit, Sabrina, what the hell did you stumble into?"

As succinctly as she could, she told him everything she remembered and concluded with what the man named Marsh had told her. "Whoever the boss is, he's a lot scarier than Cruz ever was."

"We need to fix this. Call the Miami police."

"And tell what to whom? We don't even know which ones of them we can trust."

"We have to do something. Whoever this guy is, he'll come after you."

"No he won't."

"How are you going to prevent it?"

Thankful she'd been smart enough to use one of her covers, she explained, "Walker really believed my name was Lilah Green. No one, including the Miami police department, knows who I am."

"How could you go undercover without them knowing more about you?"

"Because my cover is good and my credentials impeccable. Remember I told you that when I became a private investigator, I wanted to make sure nothing I did ever touched my family in Midnight?"

She waited for his nod before she continued, "I created several covers for myself. Only used them once or twice. Had never used my Lilah cover, so with just a little online manipulation, I updated everything and it passed without a hint of doubt or speculation."

"You think Walker knew what would be expected of you? Think that's why he agreed to use you instead of another cop?"

"Yeah, I do. I think he knew exactly what Cruz would want to do. If another cop had gone undercover with him…was sexually assaulted and/or killed, there would've been too many questions. I was just an insignificant nobody. I made sure they knew that Lilah Green was alone in the world. I was disposable."

He was silent for so long she wondered if an explosion would be coming soon. She knew she'd almost gotten herself killed. If not for Ian, she might be at the bottom of the ocean along with Cruz. Which suddenly brought to mind a very important question. "How did you know where to find me?"

"GPS tracker in your shoe."

"What?"

"The heel in your left shoe. I used it to follow you."

She supposed she should be angry with him. He had violated her trust. But how very stupid to be angry when he had saved her life. She was a lot of things, but she wasn't stupid. Ian had saved her once again.

"So what are you going to do?"

"I'm going to tell our client, Lauren Kendall, that Cruz is dead and that she's safe."

"Sounds like she's had a rough time of it. Maybe she can get her life back now."

"I hope so."

"And then what are you going to do?"

"I'm going to go back to Midnight and make sure my family is safe."

"That's it? You're not going to report that Walker was a dirty cop or who killed him?"

"What would I tell them? That a crooked cop killed Cruz and then a man named Marsh killed that crooked cop? That I don't know who gave the order for their deaths or why? They'll find the bodies without me telling them, but there's nothing I can tell them that would help in their investigation." She shook her head. "I need to get back home and make sure my family is okay. They're my priority."

"What are you going to tell your sisters? Savannah and Samantha will want to know what happened."

"I'll tell them as little as possible. Cruz is dead...that's the main thing. His death ends our investigation...our part. The less they know, the safer everyone will be."

She cupped his face in her hands. "Promise me, Ian, that you won't tell anyone."

He didn't want to make that promise, but she was right about one thing. They had no real information. "I promise."

She gave him a brilliant smile of thanks and settled back into his arms.

Ian held her tight again and thought about the upcoming investigation. There were some seriously evil people involved here and if they ever found out about Sabrina, they would kill her. Ian would do everything in his power to make sure that never happened and that meant finding out who these people were and putting a stop to them.

CHAPTER FIVE

Five Months Later
Midnight, Alabama

With graceful, color-filled abandon, dawn broke over the lush, serene landscape of Midnight. Shades of yellow, orange, and light crimson brushed the sky with a delicate artist's stroke, sending a blush of warm golden light over treetops.

Farmers were just beginning their chores of milking cows, plowing fields, feeding livestock. The shirt factory was in the midst of changing shifts. Faye's Diner and other early opening restaurants were baking their first batch of biscuits. And if one listened carefully, the shrill whistle of the steam plant ten miles away could be heard. Midnight was waking to a brand new day.

Sabrina loved mornings in her little town, before the bustle and busyness could begin. It seemed peaceful, almost story-bookish—as if nothing bad could ever happen here. The Wildes knew that wasn't true better than anyone.

Evil had come to Midnight more than once. Sabrina was determined she would not be the cause of it happening again.

As usual, her duties began on Wildefire Lane, at the Wilde mansion where she was raised and now lived again. Making sure her home and loved ones were safe was her first priority. Once she had ensured that all was well, she expanded her search, covering the entire town. Though Midnight wasn't large, going down each street with a thorough and careful eye took some time.

It was earlier than usual to be making her morning rounds, but to accomplish everything she needed to do today, an early start was a necessity.

Some might find her caution laughable, others would call it paranoia. What others thought of her ceased to matter a long time ago. She lived by her own standards, her own rules. At ten years old, she had learned the most difficult lesson of all—actions have consequences. Her life had been shaped by events she never could have anticipated. Those events drove her to protect those she loved at all cost. And because of her reckless behavior five months before, that protection now included the entire town of Midnight. She refused to be responsible for once again causing devastation.

Two hours later, assured that her loved ones and town were safe for one more day, Sabrina raced through the small grocery store with an overloaded cart. For the next few days, company would be calling and she wanted to be prepared.

Her thoughts going in a dozen different directions, focus off what was in front of her, she rounded a corner. The crash was inevitable. Stacked cans of pork and beans collapsed like a demolished high rise and rolled speedily in every direction as if making a long awaited escape.

Cursing beneath her breath, Sabrina dropped to her knees and began the arduous task of restacking cans.

"Sabrina, I just heard about Savannah's baby being born."

She stopped stacking for a moment to give attention to one of Midnight's sweetest citizens, Heidi Pruitt. "Hey, Miss Heidi. Yes, Camille Sage was born on Tuesday night, weighed in at six pounds, three ounces, and twenty-one inches long. Both mama and baby are doing great. In fact, they're coming home today."

"Well, now, that's just wonderful. Please extend my congratulations to both Savannah and Zach. I've got a little something I made for the baby. I'll bring it over tonight, if that's all right."

"I'm sure they'd love to see you. I'm cooking up a storm so be sure to come hungry."

"Aren't you the sweetest thing? I'll just do that. I've got a strawberry rhubarb pie I made just this morning. I'll bring it over, too."

As soon as Miss Heidi strolled away, Sabrina resumed restacking the cans she'd spilled. Scrunching her nose at the less than artistic pile she'd created but satisfied that they at least wouldn't tumble over again, she stood and resumed her shopping.

"Hey, Sabrina. Tell Zach and Savannah congratulations on the new addition."

Sabrina jerked to a stop before the she hit the elderly man standing in front of her. "Thank you, Mr. Milford. I'll be sure to do that. They're coming home today."

"I'll tell the missus. I know she'll want to come visit for a spell." Noticing the overflowing grocery cart, Mr. Milford grinned. "Looks like you're getting ready to feed an army."

Not an army, but possibly half the town. Once word got out that Savvy and Camille Sage were home, the visits would begin. Sabrina wanted to be prepared. It was the least she could do.

"I'm making Faye's gumbo."

His eyes lit up. "Well, now, that sounds awful good." He patted his thick belly like a man who knew what he was talking about. "That Faye can sure make a fine gumbo."

"Then be sure to come by the house. We'll have plenty."

"Thank you kindly. We might just do that."

Sabrina pushed her overflowing buggy to a checkout counter and began unloading it with swift efficiency.

In between working several cases in Atlanta, her sister Sammie was in the midst of wedding preparations. Quinn Braddock, Sammie's fiancé, was busy setting up his private practice in Midnight. On top of being a new dad, Zach had his hands full as chief of police. Sabrina figured cooking for the massive amount of company that would come calling was her responsibility. Fortunately she loved to cook.

Besides, if she didn't do it, Aunt Gibby would try. Not only did the elderly woman not need to be working that hard, no one in their right mind would accept anything to eat if they knew Gibby made it. So far Gibby was the only person in Midnight who didn't know she was the worst cook in Alabama. No way did Sabrina intend her aunt to ever learn the truth.

Thankfully Gibby was with Zach and Savvy at the hospital, getting ready to bring the baby home.

The Pick-Quick, the town's newest grocery store, was well stocked. It was on the bypass and a few miles out of her way, but she'd drive ten times that distance to prevent having to go to the other grocery store in town. Even if she didn't have a morsel of food in the house to cook, Henson's Grocery wasn't a place she'd ever shop at again. The owner, Ralph Henson, was an evil, vile man who should be in jail.

A slightly nasal, elderly female voice called out, "Bri, I heard that Savvy and Zach left the hospital about ten minutes ago."

Sabrina held onto her laughter with difficulty. The tiny, wizened woman standing in front of her stood barely over five feet tall and was so thin she didn't look like she should be able to push an empty cart, let alone a full one. Her denture-filled mouth gleamed with a bright, infectious grin. Inez Peebles was

Midnight's most notorious gossip. It didn't surprise Sabrina in the least that Inez had informants in Mobile, too.

"That's right, Miss Inez. They're coming home today." She nodded at the multiple sacks the grocery bagger was quickly filling. "I'm headed home to cook up a few meals."

"You tell Savvy I wanted to come see her in the hospital, but I've had the sniffles all week and didn't want her or the baby to catch anything."

"I'll be sure to do that. I hope you're feeling better."

"Still stopped up a bit…other than that, feeling almost good as new." She huffed out a breath and Sabrina forced herself not to jump back at the strong scent of garlic. The woman was convinced that garlic had kept her alive and healthy for all these years. "Not that my ungrateful son cares a whit."

"I'm real sorry to hear that, Miss Inez. I know you were a good mama."

Grateful that her groceries were sacked and she could soon leave, Sabrina turned back and made her payment. Inez Peebles would talk as long as anyone was willing to listen. Most times she was entertaining, as she knew more about the residents of Midnight than anyone. However, once she got started on her no account, good-for-nothing, ungrateful son, it was best to hightail it away from her as quickly as possible.

As Sabrina walked out the door, she glanced back at the elderly woman. "Be sure to come by when you're feeling up to snuff, Miss Inez. I know Savvy can't wait to show off Camille Sage to you."

Her wrinkled face wreathed in a bright smile. "You can count on it."

Pushing her massive cart to her SUV, Sabrina took a second to savor the peace. Something she hadn't allowed herself to feel in what felt like forever. The last few months had been rife with worry. After being so afraid that she had made a massive mistake and evil people would descend on her little town, she had barely left the city limits. She had used the excuse that she didn't want to be away from Savvy if she was needed. And after what Sammie went through, she had trouble letting her sister out of her sight.

Besides, their fledging security agency was finally taking off and she needed to be here to work cases.

Her family had allowed her the excuses. She was thankful the questions had stopped about Armando Cruz and what had happened to him. Still convinced the less they knew the better, she hadn't shared with them anything other than her initial statement that the man was dead.

Ian was the only one who knew everything. Well, not everything. She had yet to share what she'd been doing in her spare time. That was one benefit of not sleeping much—the extra time to work on her secret project. She would need to involve Ian soon, though—just not yet.

Turning onto Wildefire Lane, Sabrina laughed at the banner hanging from the rafters above the mansion's front porch. No doubt Sammie and Quinn's doing. '*Welcome home Camille Sage*' was a beautiful sight.

She drove to the back of the house to unload the groceries. Sammie and Quinn stepped outside as soon as she stopped her car.

She hopped out and grinned her delight. "Love the sign."

"According to both Savvy and Zach, she's going to be the most brilliant baby in the universe. We thought we'd give her a reading exam."

Though her words sounded lighthearted, the worry in Sammie's eyes said something else.

"What's wrong?"

Instead of answering, she took Sabrina's hand and pulled her away from her car.

Quinn flashed them both a solemn, compassionate glance. "I'll unload for you."

Her heart thudding with dread, Sabrina tugged at her hand. "What's wrong? Is it the baby? Savvy? Did something happen?"

Her sister shook her head. "They're all fine. Already on their way home."

"Then what's wrong?"

Continuing to pull on Sabrina's hand, Sammie stopped at the stone patio and nodded toward one of the wrought iron chairs. "Sit down."

Her heart twisted. "Ian? Did something happen to—"

"For heaven's sake, Bri, everyone is healthy and fine. Stop worrying."

"Then why the hell are you scaring me like this?"

"Quinn and I took an early morning run, just after dawn."

"And?"

"And we saw you."

"Saw me where?"

"Don't play dumb. We saw you making your rounds."

"I have no idea what you're talking about. You guys aren't the only ones who got an early start this morning."

"Stop it, Bri. Ever since you came back from Miami that last time...when you told us Cruz was dead, you've been watching the town as if you're expecting trouble anytime."

"That's ridiculous, Sammie. So I took a drive around town early this morning. That doesn't mean anything."

"How about the fact that you take an early drive around town every morning and a late night drive every night? How about the fact that you haven't stepped outside of Midnight in months?

How about the fact that you've got shadows so deep under your eyes, I could pack my wedding trousseau in them."

"You know no one has a wedding trousseau anymore, don't you?"

"Don't change the subject."

Sabrina released an exasperated breath. She was actually surprised one of her sisters hadn't called her on this before now. She couldn't deny the facts. It was true she drove through Midnight at least twice a day. Most days more than twice. She was the one who'd threatened her town with her reckless behavior. Damned if anyone would suffer for her stupidity. She'd already been the cause of the deepest kind of grief a family could endure. She could not bear to have that happen again.

"Look, I've told you all I can. So what if I want to make sure everyone stays safe."

"I don't fault you for that. You know I don't. But you've told us zilch about what happened. Don't you think we deserve to know so we can be on alert, too?"

She had gone over and over this in her mind. And she and Ian had argued about it more than once. But she knew, with one hundred percent certainty, that if her sisters knew what had happened, they would dig deep to find the man responsible for kidnapping her. She could not let that happen. Not telling them was the only way to make sure they stayed out of it and stayed safe.

"It's been months. Odds are, nothing's going to happen. No one can trace me here to Midnight."

"And yet you roam through the town several times a day, everyday." That stubborn light that Sammie got sometimes gleamed brighter. "Not buying it, Bri."

"It's the truth."

"Who is this 'no one' that can't trace you back here?"

"I don't know and that's the truth, Sammie."

"Dammit, Bri—"

Quinn's deep voice rumbled behind them, "Sorry to interrupt a good argument but thought you guys would want to know that Zach and Savvy just drove up."

Anxious to welcome her niece home and more than happy to end their discussion, Sabrina jumped to her feet and started for the front of the house. Just before she rounded the corner, Sammie called out, "This discussion is not over, Bri."

Sabrina raced to the front of the house, her arms opened wide for the little bundle of joy in Savvy's arms. This was a day of celebration. Nothing, not even Sammie's digging, was going to spoil it. Worry would have to wait for another day.

CHAPTER SIX

Tallahassee, Florida

Ian closed his laptop with a snap and went to the board on his wall. The Internet had opened doors allowing a floodgate of information to be discovered and he used it voraciously. However, he'd been taught the PI business by an old school investigator and when it came down to connecting dots and seeing the big picture, there was nothing like going back to the basics.

On one side of the board, he had all he knew about Armando Cruz. On the other side was this mysterious, as yet unnamed man who had ordered the deaths of at least two people, Cruz and Ryan Walker. Based on Sabrina's account, there were probably a helluva lot more deaths for which the man was responsible.

Beneath the mystery man was the name Marsh. And beneath Cruz's name was Lauren Kendall.

These were the four main players. Finding their connection and how their paths crossed should lead him to this mystery man.

Armando Cruz was the key though. Sabrina said that Cruz referred to the mystery man as being the one that brought him into the business. So, even though Cruz was dead, the man was being infinitely helpful.

Born in San Salvador, Mexico, Armando Cruz moved to the States with his mother when he was a baby. His mother had been a teenager. She died too young but not before she hooked up with the wrong man. A couple of years after her death, Cruz's abusive, alcoholic stepfather was killed. Ian had some speculation on how that went down.

Left alone in the world, Armando went into the welfare system. He escaped after a year, successfully avoiding being found. He stayed off radar until he was nineteen and then suddenly began to make a name for himself. Joined a gang, rose in its ranks. Had more than a few brushes with the law. Locked up for a few months, here and there, but after each release, went back to his old gang, his old ways and only seemed to become meaner, greedier.

Ian had easily followed Cruz's path up until the man was twenty-five when he somehow fell off the face of the earth. Didn't take a genius to see that someone had taught him how to cover his tracks. The mysterious 'boss'? Cruz's mentor?

The eerie similarities between Ian and Cruz's upbringing were both startling and eye opening. Ian had been born into the same kind of life as Cruz. A drugged out mother who had OD'd on Meth when he was six. A father who drank himself into oblivion almost every night and who frequently took out all his frustrations with his fists on his wife and son. By the time Ian was nine, he was well on his way to becoming a perfect replica of both parents. And then came Molly Mackenzie, who never met a child she couldn't love and wouldn't try to save. And her husband Barry, who'd battled through every legal loophole and asshole to make sure Ian became a Mackenzie instead of another statistic. His adoptive parents were the greatest people on earth. Without them, Ian knew he'd either be dead or in prison.

Barry and Molly Mackenzie had saved him and countless other children who'd been headed down a destructive path. The realization of just how lucky he'd gotten came on his first night in the Mackenzie house. His new family, consisting of four brothers, four sisters, three dogs, two cats, and a hamster had welcomed him as if he'd been there from the beginning. He had experienced his first night of comfort, love and acceptance. His first experience of true peace. He'd been so damned lucky.

Cruz hadn't had a Barry and Molly in his life, but that didn't excuse the sick acts he'd committed. Even though Ian could only find a handful of mentions after Cruz found a way to hide his activities, it was apparent the man had been an evil bastard and had gotten what he deserved. But who was the mysterious mentor responsible for Cruz's death?

Ian felt like he was chasing a ghost and not doing it very effectively. Sabrina had no idea of his investigation or search. These men had kidnapped and hurt her. God only knew what else they would have done if he hadn't rescued her. They needed to be found and stopped.

Needing encouragement and support, he punched a speed dial number on his phone, and went to one of the people he could always count on. He smiled at the cheerful greeting of his mother. "Hey, darlin'. What's up?"

"Nothing. Just wanted to hear your sweet voice."

Molly Mackenzie had been around that block too many times to count. When it came to her kids, she knew them inside and out.

"And how's Sabrina doing?"

"She's good. Her sister Savannah had a baby a couple of days ago. I'm heading to Midnight in a few hours to meet the newest Wilde girl."

"That's wonderful. You be sure to give them my best."

"I'll do that."

"When are you bringing Sabrina down for another visit?"

Ian winced. The answer of 'probably never' would be the truth, but not one he would give. His family could be overwhelming on a regular day, but when he'd brought a girl home for the first time in forever, it had been a red-letter event for the Mackenzie clan. As his dad had said, they'd put on the dog for her. In other words, it had been a major celebration.

To be fair, he had tried to warn Sabrina. With that many Mackenzies running around, it was bound to be boisterous. And the Mackenzies loved to celebrate. With Molly and Barry's ten, plus numerous grandchildren, along with a healthy smattering of aunts, uncles, and cousins, there always seemed to be a reason to have a party.

He had taken Sabrina down on what he'd thought would be a relatively low-key weekend. No birthdays, anniversaries, job promotions, or graduations. When it came to celebrations, his family didn't know the word low-key. Ian was bringing a girl home for a visit. That had been cause for a party.

Sabrina had been charming and friendly. Had seemed to blend in well. No one would have ever known anything was wrong. On the trip home, things had fallen apart. And he had been losing ground ever since.

"She's been busy with their new agency. I'm not sure when she'll be free for another visit."

"I hope our little impromptu party didn't scare her off. I know all the Mackenzies at one time can be a little overwhelming."

Hell of an understatement, but that hadn't been the reason for Sabrina's panic. It'd had more to do with the dozen or so people that had asked that all too sensitive question of: *"When are you and Ian going to tie the knot?"*

By the time they'd gotten in his Jeep to head home, his own head had been spinning. And Sabrina? She hadn't talked the entire trip home—five freaking hours of silence.

Since explaining the problem to his mother would only bring about more questions, Ian went with the blandest, most truthful comment he could come up with. One that was sure to please her and change the subject. "She told me that your risotto was the best she'd ever had and wants your recipe."

His mother, no fool, laughed. "I know what you're doing Ian Mackenzie. However, I'll let you get away with it. I'll email you my recipe so you can give it to Sabrina."

"Thanks, Mom." They both knew his words were for more than the recipe.

"So how is the Mackenzie gang?"

As expected, his mother began a litany, starting with Ian's oldest sibling, and brought him up-to-date. Accustomed to his mother's chatty updates, Ian took the notes he'd jotted down about Cruz and moved them to the board.

He continued to work as he heard that his brother Colin had received a new promotion at his bank position, his sister Sinead was up for partnership in her law firm, and his sister-in-law, Melanie, was considering returning to college for her masters. Good news always traveled fast in the Mackenzie household. Ian was glad to hear it all but came to an abrupt halt at his mother's last bit of news.

"What do you mean Alana passed her drivers test?"

"Made a perfect score."

"She's too young to get her driver's license."

"She's sixteen."

"Exactly. Too young."

"Same age as you when you got yours. How is she younger than you were?"

"She just is."

Yeah, it was a lame comeback but dammit, his baby sister out on the road by herself? With maniacs driving all around her? When had she grown up? He still remembered the day she'd come into the family. Though he'd been a Mackenzie for a while, he was still in awe of just how lucky he'd gotten with his ready made, too loud and loving family. His mom had walked in the door with a tiny, fragile little girl in her arms. Skin pale as milk and big blue eyes showing the exact same fear he'd often felt. He'd become her big brother that day and had done his best to shield and protect her. But now that she was growing up, how was he going to do that?

Another horrifying thought hit him. "Just tell me she's not dating yet."

"No one steady, but she's been on a few double dates." Knowing her son well, she added, "Your dad has interrogated both boys already so there's no need to come down here for the same thing."

The hard lump in his stomach eased. Of course his dad would take care of that. A former US Marine, Barry Mackenzie could be as intimidating as The Hulk. Only his family and close friends knew he was a gentle teddy bear inside.

"Good to know, but if it looks like she's getting serious with someone, let me know."

"I will, but she's got a good sensible head on her shoulders."

Ian couldn't argue with that. His sister was smart as a whip. "True but there are a lot of assholes out there disguised as decent people."

"Language, Ian."

Ian winced. "Sorry, Mom."

"She'll be careful. We'll make sure of it."

That was good enough for him. The Mackenzies took care of each other. Always had. No matter what background or experiences each of them had endured, when he and his brothers and sisters had been adopted, they'd become family. The Mackenzies were enormous not only in numbers but love and loyalty.

They went on to talk about other things for a few minutes before ending the call with his promise to come for a visit soon, along with the assurance that he would ask Sabrina to accompany him. Not that he believed she would accept the invitation.

Ian looked out the window of his backyard, thought about and rejected the idea of mowing the grass before he headed to Midnight for the weekend.

Was he an idiot for holding out hope that Sabrina would change her mind? He knew she'd been hurt by the asshole she'd been engaged to, but dammit, he wasn't the same kind of guy that idiot had been.

Tyler Finley. Sabrina had met the man during spring break while she was still in college. She and Finley had become engaged, but a couple of weeks before they were to tie the knot, the guy had been killed in a car crash. That had been painful enough for Sabrina but when Finley's wife and child showed up to claim the body, it had almost destroyed her. That was when she had learned it had all been a scam. Bilk Sabrina of out her inheritance, leave and go back to his real family.

Finley's widow had actually tried to blackmail Sabrina to keep it a secret. Of course the woman hadn't received a cent. Sabrina hadn't cared about her reputation. What had infuriated her was being taken for a ride.

When Sabrina had told Ian about Finley, he had known immediately why, not that she'd tried to soften the truth. She had wanted him to understand that she would never be interested in a permanent relationship.

Ian understood her reasoning but still felt there was more to the story than just a creep of a fiancé. Her traumatic childhood—losing her parents in the way she had, had shaped her into a wary, vulnerable person. He wanted to heal all of her hurts, the ones he knew about and the ones he had yet to uncover. Unfortunately he was beginning to believe she was never going to allow that to happen.

His gaze shifted back to the charts on the wall. He had dug as deep as he could. Now it was time to bring in someone else to help fill in the blanks. Someone with firsthand knowledge.

Knowing Sabrina Wilde, she wasn't going to like it one damn bit.

CHAPTER SEVEN

Midnight

Sabrina pulled the piping hot skillet of cornbread from the oven, flipped it onto a plate, and set it aside to cool. She was running ahead of schedule. The gumbo was simmering, creating a heavenly fragrance, and the cheese grits and shrimp was done and in the warming oven, waiting to be devoured. Three pies and two cakes were sitting prettily on the kitchen table just asking to be sliced.

Aunt Gibby was watching over the baby while Savannah took a nap. Zach had gone to take care of some things at the police station and Quinn and Sammie had gone to do some work on Quinn's new office. All was quiet in the Wilde house, but that wouldn't last.

Her stomach grumbled, a reminder that breakfast had been hours ago. Even though she'd taste-tested everything, she needed something a little more substantial if she was going to get any work done before company started calling. She had uncovered a new thread last night that she wanted to follow up on.

She took a couple of slices of bread and slathered it with peanut butter. Grabbing a banana from the fruit bowl, she sliced it, and placed it on top of the peanut butter. She was just about to take her first bite when she heard the shouts.

"I got a right to see her!"

What the hell? Sabrina ran to the window and peered out. Spotting the ancient truck, one she recognized immediately, she grabbed her gun from her purse she'd left hanging on a kitchen chair and took off. In seconds, she was on the front porch and pointing her weapon at the red-faced furious looking man standing on the steps.

"Get off our property," Sabrina snarled.

"You get that gun out of my face, missy. I gotta right to see that baby."

Savannah stood at the edge of the porch, blocking Ralph Henson's entry, her rage filled eyes making it clear that the old geezer would have to come through her first.

Sabrina stood beside her sister. "Take one step closer, Henson, and I'll straighten that part in your scraggly hair."

Without taking her eyes off the man in front of them, Savannah said, "Thank you, Bri. I just came down for a little fresh air and this idiot shows up."

"No problem, Savvy. Why don't you go call Zach while Henson and I have a few words."

"Okay, but if you have to shoot him, hit him in a non-vital area. Zach would be disappointed that he didn't get to do that himself." She threw Henson a glare over her shoulder as she walked away.

Her hand steady as a rock, Sabrina gave him some advice. "I suggest you get out of here before Zach shows up. Trespassing on private property is a crime."

"There's no court in this land that'd keep me from seeing my own—"

"Don't you say it," Sabrina warned. "Don't you dare say it. Get out of here before I show you how good I am with this gun."

The sound of a vehicle coming toward the house caught Sabrina's ear. Holding her gun steady on the arrogant asshole that was Ralph Henson, she caught sight of Ian's steel gray Wrangler. Reinforcements.

Ian jumped out of his Jeep and headed toward the front porch, his weapon already in his hand. The sight of Sabrina holding her gun on a man was a surprise, but Ian trusted her enough to know that whatever the reason, it was a good one.

"Might want to leave now," Sabrina said. "Ian's an even better shot than I am."

"Why thank you, darling." Ian directed a dark look at the older man standing so defiantly before them. He was a stranger to Ian, but that didn't matter. Anyone who threatened Sabrina or any of the Wildes was his enemy, too. "I suggest you take the lady's advice and leave."

"Dammit, I got rights, too."

"Rights? Why you lowlife, sleazy, scum sucking—"

A siren blared, cutting into Sabrina's litany of insults. Zach's police car zoomed down the drive and skidded to a stop. The police chief jumped out and sprinted to the porch. "What the hell are you doing here, Henson?"

"I've come to see my granddaughter."

"She's not your granddaughter, old man. Now, you've got five seconds to get the hell off my property or I'll be hauling your ass to jail."

"A man's got a right to see his kin."

The stone expression on Zach's face should have deterred the most persistent of men. "You have no claim on my daughter."

Showing that Henson wasn't the smartest of men, he stood his ground and growled, "She's mine, too."

Zach took a long stride and stood toe to toe with Henson. His voice was low and lethal, leaving no doubt of his intent. "Get the hell out of here before you're carried away in a body bag."

"Zach…don't," Savannah said.

Zach's eyes remained on Henson. "Go back in the house, Savannah. I'll be in as soon as this asshole is gone."

"I'm not going anywhere, Zach Tanner," Savannah said. "We agreed to face every adversity together. Remember?"

Tearing his gaze away from the old man, Zach shared a look with his wife that said more than words ever could—love, anger, pain, sorrow, and acceptance. He then turned back to Henson and spoke softly again, "Leave. Now."

Apparently the man saw something in the police chief's expression that told him this was his last chance before things got ugly. His thin lips twisted bitterly, he backed away with a curt nod. "Fine. But don't think this is over."

No one spoke as Henson strode swiftly to his truck and then peeled out of the drive like a teenager.

Ian kept his eyes on the truck until it disappeared from sight. When he turned, Zach was holding Savannah in his arms. Hearing the whispers of apology and declarations of love, Ian looked at Sabrina, jerked his head toward the front door. "Come on. Let's give them some privacy."

"But I—" Sabrina released a harsh breath. Ian was right. This wasn't the time for her to go after Henson or reassure her sister. This was between Savvy and Zach. But she looked forward to having a one on one conversation with Henson in the not too distant future.

In the kitchen, she dumped her now stale sandwich in the garbage disposal and said, "How about some shrimp and grits?"

"Only if you'll eat with me."

Since her stomach was now tied in knots, swallowing anything was probably not a good idea. However, knowing Ian would hound her about not eating, she pulled two bowls from the cabinet, giving him three times more than her own small serving.

Thankfully he didn't remark on her less than generous portion. They sat across the kitchen table from each other. Ian took a large bite and shook his head. "You know you could open a restaurant, serve only this and make a million."

She took a tiny bite to see how it went down. Pleased that it was easier than she'd expected, she took another. Ian was right. It was delicious.

"Couldn't do that. It's Faye's recipe. That would be stealing."

"Ha. You only say that because you're afraid of her."

She couldn't deny that. If there was anyone in this world who intimidated her, it was Faye Grissom. Tough looking as any drill sergeant and about as humorless as a funeral director. There were dozens of rumors and speculative stories about Faye and no one but Faye knew if they were true or not. No one had the courage to ask her.

"So what's Henson's deal?" Ian asked.

Sabrina grimaced. There went her appetite. "You could probably piece together most of it. It's not something Zach or Savvy like to talk about."

"I'd say that's understandable. Henson is Zach's biological father?"

"Yeah. And that's about it. Zach didn't know for years and considering what happened, would love to never have known the truth."

"What happened?"

As succinctly as possible, Sabrina described the horrific night that Zach had learned the truth of his parentage and the ten years of heartbreak both he and Savvy had endured.

"Hell, I'm surprised your brother-in-law let him leave without the slightest bruise."

"Zach's the police chief. He can't take the law into his own hands."

"You don't agree with his decision?"

Hiding her opinions from Ian had never worked. The man could read her like a book. "We both know that sometimes it's not that simple."

"I'd say that should be Zach and Savannah's choice. Not yours."

She stood and carried their bowls to the sink to rinse them. Responding would only get them involved in an argument. And she didn't plan on breaking the law. No law against telling a man some home truths. It was past time for Henson to hear them.

She turned back to him, eager to move on to happier subjects. "Ready to see the baby?"

"You bet. Then I need to talk with you about a case."

Always eager to discuss an investigation, Sabrina held out her hand. "Let's go meet the newest Wilde heartbreaker and then I'm all yours."

A fleeting sadness whispered across Ian's face. "If only that were true."

With a head full of downy white hair, a tiny bow for a mouth, and pink, chubby cheeks, Camille Sage Tanner was the poster child for perfection. A heartbreaker for sure.

Having a family that numbered the size of a small town, Ian had seen plenty of newborns and had to admit this one was about the prettiest. The fact that he could already see Sabrina's features made her all the more beautiful.

Holding the soft, tiny infant in his arms, Ian glanced up at the beaming parents. "She's perfect, Savannah. Congratulations to you both."

"Thank you, Ian," Savannah said. "We're blessed."

Though he was sure the scene earlier had upset her, Ian was glad to see the happiness and contentment on both Savannah's and Zach's faces. Henson hadn't taken away their joy.

"She looks just like you and your sisters when you were babies, Savannah Rose."

Ian smiled at Sabrina's aunt, Gibby Wilcox, who stood behind them. Sabrina had told him their aunt had agreed to stay a few days to help out. The gleam in her eyes said she was as proud as she could be to be asked.

"I remember the day Maggie brought you three home from the hospital. Never saw prettier babies in all my life." Her smile widened. "Till now, that is."

"Thank you, Aunt Gibby," Savannah said. "I love knowing that."

A small unhappy cry told Ian it was time to return the bundle to her mother. Saying goodbye, Sabrina and Ian left the nursery and headed to her suite of rooms on the other side of the mansion.

"What case did you want to talk about? Is this a new one or an ongoing one?"

"I've been working it on and off for a few months."

"We've talked about it?"

"Sort of."

"Hmm. Sounds mysterious." She opened the door to her suite.

Before the discussion that would most likely erupt into an argument could begin, Ian pulled her into his arms. "First things first." The instant his mouth touched hers, heat ignited. Just like that—that's how it'd always been with Sabrina.

Her moan of pleasure vibrated against his lips as he drew deeply on her. When she opened her mouth, Ian pulled her closer, devouring her sweetness.

Four years and the new hadn't worn off. The love he had for her had only grown stronger. Her taste, the delicacy of her strong but slender body, the sheer beauty of the woman he held in his arms enchanted him. In fifty years, even seventy-five, he would still feel the same way.

Loosening his arms, he looked down at her. The slightly glazed look in her eyes was gratifying. And it was exactly how he felt, too.

Her laugh was breathless and a little shaky. "Now that's what I call a hello kiss."

"I've had five days to think about it."

"Hmm. Maybe when we finish talking about your case, you can show me what else you've been thinking about."

"With pleasure."

She moved to the sitting area and dropped onto a sofa. "Okay, so what's the case?"

Ian took a breath. Here goes. "Armando Cruz."

CHAPTER EIGHT

"Cruz," Sabrina muttered the name she hadn't allowed herself to say in months. "What about him?"

"I've been trying to find the man responsible for killing him."

"Why?"

"Because he needs to be found and stopped."

"And that's the only reason?"

"You know it's not. I couldn't care less about Cruz. Whoever this guy is, he—"

Ian shoved his fingers through his hair and scowled his irritation. "Why the hell am I even looking for an excuse? What better reason is there than the real one? He had you kidnapped, Sabrina. God only knows what he planned to do to you."

She had no idea why this news surprised her. From the moment she'd met Ian Mackenzie he'd gotten in her way, injected himself into her life and made his presence known in a thousand different ways. He had saved her life more than once. Been her partner, became her lover only months after knowing him. He could make her furious one moment and have her laughing the very next.

Anyone else's interference would have infuriated her. Other people had tried to get as close to her and she had shut them down, forced them out of her life. That had never happened with Ian.

He expected anger, she could see. He was braced for it, ready to argue his case and she knew he wouldn't back down. A man of principles and integrity, Ian Mackenzie would fight for what he believed was right. She could prevaricate—argue this wasn't his business, his case. And how stupid would that be?

Instead, Sabrina stood and held out her hand. "Follow me."

Somewhat puzzled at her lack of anger, Ian didn't question when she pulled him toward her closet. This woman continually surprised and intrigued him.

She opened the door and pushed her clothes aside, mostly jeans and t-shirts, which was her usual attire. Another surprise was the door she revealed behind the clothes.

"What's this?"

"Our old playroom…when we were kids. Mama insisted our bedrooms be connected and Daddy insisted we had to have a private playroom where we could share secrets. He had this room built for us. We stopped using it when we got older, but I found a new purpose for it when I moved back."

Sabrina pushed open the door and they stepped inside. The room was about half the size of her bedroom. Shelves filled with books, dolls, Lego sets, puzzles, and board games covered one side of the wall. Normal playroom stuff. It was the rest of the room that blew Ian away.

In silence, he stood before a wall filled with information on the very people he'd been investigating. Just at a glance, he could see she had found some things he hadn't. But he had information she apparently hadn't yet uncovered.

"Why didn't you tell me?"

"I guess the same reason you didn't tell me."

"No. I didn't tell you because I figured you'd be angry that I was pursuing something you felt I should let go."

Her green eyes skittered guiltily away and Ian felt the gut punch to his soul. "Dammit, when are you going to stop trying to protect the whole damned world?"

"I don't know what you're talking about."

Ian grabbed her shoulders and pulled her around to face him. "Yes, you do. I know you, Sabrina Wilde. You're worried that you might have attracted evil men to your town, but instead of involving people who care about you, can help you, you're trying to do this alone. Why wouldn't you let me help?"

But he already knew the answer to that. Not only was she trying to protect the whole damn town, she was trying to protect him, too.

He shook her slightly. "Why do you protect everyone but yourself?"

"Don't be ridiculous, Ian. This isn't about protecting anyone. I—"

"It damn well is and you know it."

"I didn't get angry when you told me you'd been working this case without me. Seems like the least you could do is extend the same courtesy."

Arguing would do no good. And she had a point. "You're right." He looked at the charts, similar to his own. "So, if I show you mine, will you show me yours?"

"Why, Mr. Mackenzie." She batted her eyes at him in exaggerated flirtation. "Are you propositioning me?"

Pulling her close, he dropped a kiss on her forehead, her nose and then a long, lingering one on her soft lips. "You're damned right."

She grinned. "Good. I'll take you up on that proposition, both literally and figuratively." She nodded at an overstuffed chair a few feet away. "But first, have a seat and let me wow you with my impressive investigative skills."

The anger and defensiveness were gone as if they never existed. He loved that about her. Loved her mercurial moods. Her easy ability to move on, focus on the bigger picture.

Ian sprawled into the chair she'd pointed to, prepared to be wowed. She never disappointed.

"I know we probably have a lot of the same information. I'll go over what I have. You can fill in any blanks."

"Sounds good."

As if she were teaching a class, Sabrina grabbed up a marker and using it as a pointer, shared with him what she had discovered.

As she went into detail, giving him information, much of it he'd already uncovered, he watched her. Green eyes glinting with excitement, beautiful mouth tilted upward. Her slender body practically vibrated with energy. He loved watching her work. Sabrina always approached a case like it was a puzzle to be unraveled, and when she found clues or connections, her delight in the discovery was like a kid at Christmas.

"Cruz was born in Mexico. Came with his mother to the States when he was a toddler. Mama was unmarried but trying her best. Unfortunately she hooked up with the wrong man. He got her hooked on drugs. She OD'd. Stepdad ended up dead in a back alley. Cruz got locked into the system. He followed in his mother's footsteps and hooked up with the wrong people."

"Yeah, except he went a different way."

"Exactly. Instead of taking the drugs, he sold them. Hell of a note to sell the crap that killed the only person who gave a damn about you."

"I doubt he worried about that too much. I traced him through various gangs. He's served some time but nothing significant. He got called in for questioning on several suspicious deaths, but nothing could ever be proven."

"I'd say he avoided being called in for questioning even more than that. Looks like when he was nineteen he might've had his first kill."

Ian shook his head. "I don't think so."

"Really?"

"No. I think his first kill was his stepfather."

Sabrina turned back to her notes, noted timelines, location. She nodded slowly. "I'll bet you're right. Should've seen that. He didn't even get called in for questioning."

"He was a kid and already a good liar."

"I can find almost nothing about him after his nineteenth birthday."

Ian stood and walked over to her board. Taking his iPhone from his pocket, he pulled up the info he'd stored on Cruz. "I've got him in Chicago for a few more years. Up to his mid-twenties." He took the marker from her hand and jotted the notes on the board.

"How'd you find him there?"

"Found a couple of records that mention a kid named 'Mando'. It gave enough information for me to catch on that it was Cruz."

"So he went to Chicago. When did he come back to Miami?"

"Hard to say. He stayed below radar there."

"You think that's where the boss man—Cruz's mentor, lives? In Chicago? That might've been why it was taking so long for him to get to the club where Marsh and Garrett held me. That's a long flight."

"Could be."

"So...Who's going to Chicago?"

"Since you haven't left Midnight in months, I'd say the answer to that is an easy one."

She grimaced. "Sammie called me on that today."

"I'm surprised it took her that long. I understand why, but it's been almost six months. If they knew you were here, they would've come for you long before now."

"I agree. I just want to wait a little while longer. With Savvy just giving birth and Sammie planning her wedding, I don't want to be caught blindsided. Keeping them safe is too important."

"And you still won't tell them what went down?"

She gave an emphatic shake of her head. "There's no way to keep them out of it if I told them. They'd want to help."

"And that's a problem why?"

"I'm the one who caused this, Ian. I can't put them at risk."

"You didn't cause this. You were doing a job. That's the nature of the kind of work we do."

"True, but it shouldn't cause problems for our loved ones."

Ian could argue until he was out of breath and it would do no good. Sabrina had set herself up as protector of those she loved. As much as it infuriated him that this lovely, delicate looking woman thought she should take all of this on by herself, he couldn't help but love her for being so caring.

"Then we'll protect them together."

A brilliant light entered her eyes as she slid her arms around him. "Thank you, Ian. I don't know what I'd do without you."

"We make a good team."

"Yeah." Her smile was both sweet and seductive. "We do."

He dropped back into the chair he'd vacated and then pulled her down into his lap. In an instant his hands were sliding beneath her shirt, meeting soft, silky flesh.

She pressed her face against his neck, breathed him in. "This is another part of working together I miss. Work and then slow, sweet seduction."

"Slow?"

"Fast and hard works for me, too."

Already iron hard with arousal, Ian's pulse leaped at her words. "When we were partners, this was always my favorite part of the day."

Melting into his arms, Sabrina laughed softly. This had been a favorite part of their day for her, too. "Do tell? I want— "

She caught her breath as a rough, callused hand covered her bare breast and then hummed in pleasure when his fingers lightly pinched her nipple. "Yes…that's what I want…just like that."

"Oh yeah," Ian growled, "definitely the best part of my day."

Closing her eyes, Sabrina lay back in his arms and surrendered to the magic of Ian's hands and mouth. For several long moments, the only sounds were gasps and groans, mostly from her. Only with Ian had she ever been able to lose herself in total abandon. In his arms she became a wholly sensual creature, giving herself freely to his desires and her needs. Only Ian could make her fly without wings.

"Look at how beautiful you are."

She opened to eyes to see his admiring gaze roaming over her. She'd barely noticed that her shirt was unbuttoned, her bra was off, and her skirt was bunched up at her waist. She lay sprawled out in his arms like a willing sacrifice awaiting his pleasure.

"You make me feel beautiful."

"Let me make you feel good." His hand, strong yet tender, parted her legs further and then delved beneath her panties.

Sabrina tried to keep her eyes open, she really did. She loved watching him. When he was turned on, his eyes would glimmer hot, like golden brown embers, and his mouth would take on a sensual slant, tilting at the edges.

But despite those intentions, her eyes closed as desire swamped her, drowning everything but her need for fulfillment. His fingers, one…then two, pressed into her. She grasped his wrist, digging her nails into his skin as he took her higher, then higher still. Her hips moved sensually, then frantically. He covered her cry of delight with his mouth, devoured her sounds of ecstasy, swallowed her breath, took her essence inside him. When he lifted his head, the feral look in his eyes told her all she needed to know. He wanted her. Right here. Right now.

Sabrina shifted around to straddle him and with fingers much too shaky and excited for finesse, hurriedly unzipped his jeans. She felt the same urgency…had to have him inside her right this minute.

Her hand had just barely skimmed his hard silky flesh when a noise outside the room penetrated her pleasure filled mind.

The pounding on the door was followed by Sammie's voice. "Bri? Are you here? We've got company arriving."

"Oh no." Sabrina dropped her forehead against his shoulder. "I didn't close the closet door. I don't want her to see the board."

Harsh, breathless laughter rattled through Ian. "Go. I'll be behind you in about five minutes when I'm able to walk again."

"I'm sorry." She planted a quick, hard kiss on his mouth. "I'll make it up to you tonight."

Though his smile was pained, his eyes glittered with promise. "I'll make sure you do."

CHAPTER NINE

Sabrina checked her watch as she headed to the guest-house. Their new client was supposed to arrive at nine this morning but was early. Sammie hadn't arrived yet, but according to April Cantrell, their receptionist, the man had asked to speak with Sabrina only. Maybe she'd worked with him before though she hadn't recognized the name Holden.

Both her sisters were better at dealing with clients than she was—their people skills more honed. Sabrina had a tendency toward bluntness when diplomacy would work better. She could be agreeable…she just had to work harder at it. She would get the facts of the case, and when Sammie arrived, her sister could soothe any ruffled feathers.

If Ian hadn't gone for a long run, he could have come with her. His people skills were excellent. She'd seen him charm, soothe, and ease the most frazzled of nerves. How on earth they got along so well was anyone's guess.

In between feeding the massive amount of company who stopped by to welcome the newest addition to their family, the weekend had been spent sharing and reviewing all the information they'd both gathered on Cruz.

Tomorrow, Ian would head to Chicago where they believed the man who ordered Cruz's death lived. What would happen once they identified him was still a mystery. The man was responsible for at least two deaths that they knew of. Who knew what else the guy had done?

For a brief moment, Sabrina stopped in front of the newly rebuilt guesthouse to admire the structure. Last year the original one had been destroyed by fire. She and her sisters had never hesitated to rebuild, all agreeing that their parents' murderers had taken too much from them already. The guesthouse was part of their legacy and now served as the main offices for the Wildefire Security Agency.

They had rebuilt it identical to the one that had been destroyed. A smaller replica of the Wilde mansion, the house held all the charm of an old Southern mansion but was built with twenty-first century material. The structure could withstand the fiercest of storms. Fire could still destroy it, but the only person who would want that was rotting in prison, serving a life sentence for the murder of her parents.

She walked through the foyer and then stopped at the door to the reception area. April stood in front of their prospective client, holding out a cup of coffee for him. Hearing the woman giggle like a schoolgirl made Sabrina smile. Apparently the man had charmed his way into their receptionist's heart already. That was no easy feat. The mother of four boys, April was nobody's fool.

"Hello," Sabrina said. "Sorry, I didn't get your full name Mr. Holden. I'm—"

April stepped aside and Sabrina caught her breath. Without missing a beat, she pulled her weapon from her side holster, her heart pounding with dread. Even though every molecule in her body was telling her to run and warn Savvy, she held the gun with unwavering calm on the man in front of her. How the hell had he found her?

Her eyes never moved from her target. "April, go to the main house. Lock all the doors."

"What's wrong, Sabrina? Should I tell Savannah or Zach?"

"No. Not yet. I'll call you when it's safe. If Ian comes back, send him over here, please."

Thankfully April didn't argue. The instant Sabrina heard the door shut behind her, she said coolly, "You have five seconds to tell me why the hell you're here before I call and have you arrested."

"Relax, Sabrina. I'm not here to hurt you."

"Oh yeah? I suppose that's why you held me against my will, tied me up. Just a little friendly kidnapping?"

"Actually I paid a big price for letting you get away."

"Gee, forgive me if I don't feel a bit of remorse for that. And you didn't 'let' me do anything."

"That's true. I believe Mr. Mackenzie was your rescuer."

This man knew way too much about her already. She wanted answers. Now.

"Who are you? Why are you here? What do you want?"

"Mind if I sit?"

"Answer my questions."

"Fine. I found you through Mackenzie."

"Try again. The truth this time."

"It wasn't him directly. When he came for you, the cameras caught his image. I found out who he was. From there, it wasn't hard to put two and two together and find you."

"It took five months to get that information?"

"Actually no. I got that information within hours of you leaving. There was just no reason to pursue you."

"And now there is?"

"Look, I really would like to sit down. With this humid weather, my knee is killing me."

"Fine. Sit." Her gun remaining steady in one hand, with the other she withdrew her cellphone from her jeans' pocket and hit Ian's speed-dial number.

"Hey, babe. What's up?"

"Are you headed back to the house?"

"Yeah. Got maybe a mile to go."

"Can you come straight to the office?"

"Sure thing. Something wrong?"

"I'll explain when you get here." She slid her phone back into her pocket, gave a quick nod to the man in front of her. "Start talking."

"You don't want to wait for Mackenzie?"

"No. He'll try to persuade me not to shoot you. I want to make that decision after I hear what you have to say. Now start talking."

"Very well. I'll cut to the chase. My name is Holden Marsh. I'm a DEA agent working undercover to bring down Robert Silva."

"And he is?"

"I'm not surprised you haven't heard of him. He likes to stay off the grid, work behind the scenes. Suffice to say he's one of the most dangerous criminals in the world and our government, along with several others, has been trying to apprehend him for years."

"And what was he to Armando Cruz?"

"His one time friend and mentor."

"A friend who had him killed. Which you sanctioned, by the way."

"Not my decision, but I had no choice but to let it move forward. Cruz was a dead man the minute he spilled his secrets to a shrink."

"So why are you here, now, to see me?"

"I need your help."

Sabrina unsuccessfully swallowed a snort. "And I should help you…why?"

"Because I'm trying to save a woman's life."

"Who?"

"Lauren Kendall. Cruz's former mistress."

The lead block that had developed in her stomach the instant she recognized Marsh settled deep. "I know who she is."

Dawning understanding flickered in his eyes. "Now it makes sense. That's why you were there, wasn't it? You weren't just looking for evidence on Cruz. You know Lauren. She was your client?"

She wasn't ready to share anything with this guy until she got answers. "What's happened to her?"

"Silva has her."

"What makes you think I care?"

"You disappoint me, Wilde. You don't look the type to play games." When she continued to just stare at him, Marsh released a harsh breath. "Look, I know you have questions but I can explain."

The front door opened and Ian called out, "Sabrina?"

"In here."

"What's going on? What—"

Keeping her eyes and gun on Marsh, she heard rather than saw Ian pull his gun from beneath his shirt. The man rarely went anywhere unarmed.

"What the hell's he doing here?"

"Seems Mr. Holden Marsh has come to ask for our help."

"That's a rather simplistic way of putting it," Marsh said, "but yeah, I do need your help."

"We need to get out of here. If this asshole knows you're here, then so does his boss… Let's get your family to a safe place."

"Once again, my so called boss has no idea who you are, much less where you are."

"And we're supposed to believe you, why?" Ian snarled.

"He says he's DEA." Sabrina said. "Undercover."

"That right?" Ian said. "I have some friends in the DEA. Could they verify that?"

"Doubtful." Slight sarcasm entered his tone. "The whole under-cover thing sort of hinders the everyone knowing about it scenario."

"So we're just supposed to take your word for it?"

"No, but if you'll let me explain, I think you'll be more inclined to believe me."

"Fine." Ian said. "Talk."

"I started working for Silva almost two years ago. It's taken me almost that long to gain his trust, get inside his inner circle. When you escaped, I was on shaky ground. I managed to pull it off so it looked like you did it on your own."

"What does this Silva know about Sabrina," Ian asked.

"Nothing…and I'd like to keep it that way. For now, he knows only what Walker told him—what you'd told Walker. That you were Lilah Green, a private investigator who had some kind of information about Cruz. That you wanted more and then you'd share what you had."

"So Walker was on this Silva's payroll, too."

"Silva used him as a gofer and a weasel—two things Walker excelled at."

"Silva knew I would be there that day?"

"Yeah."

"Sabrina wasn't supposed to survive, was she?"

"Hard to say. Silva isn't big on sharing his plans. I was going to have to figure out a way to get you out of there, but Silva nixed my plans. He liked the way you looked."

"Gee, guess I got lucky."

"We both did. I would've blown my cover if I'd tried to spring you inside Cruz's place."

"How did you explain my getting away?"

"Wasn't easy. Fortunately the security cameras only work half the time. Silva knew that so when he asked for footage, I told him the camera was down."

"And your friend Garrett? How did he explain my escape?"

"He didn't. Since I couldn't make him lie, I had to take him out."

"You killed him?"

"Don't worry. As you'll recall, he wasn't a very nice man."

"And you told this Silva I killed Garrett and then escaped on my own?"

"No. I admitted to killing Garrett. Told him the man tried to rape you and I had no choice. That's how you got away. That I was fighting Garrett…you saw your chance and took it. Since Silva didn't want you touched until he got his hands on you, he was basically all right with the killing."

"Basically?" Ian asked.

Marsh shrugged. "I took some punishment for it. Silva likes things to go smoothly. When they don't he has a volatile temper."

He returned his gaze to Sabrina. "Don't mourn too much over Garrett's death. The bastard helped kill an entire family a month before that, including a five-year-old child. Like I said… not a very nice man."

Sabrina swallowed hard. "This Silva ordered the death of an entire family? Just what kind of evil is he?"

"The worst kind. No remorse, no conscience. His word is law and if you betray him, you're marked for death."

"Sounds like you're walking a fine and dangerous line," Ian said.

"Part of the job."

"If you've been working on this Silva for two years, why's it taking so long? When's he going down?"

"As I said, your escape set me back a bit." A darkness entered his expression. "I had to prove my worth all over again."

Sabrina didn't even want to know what he'd been forced to do.

"So why are you here?" Ian asked.

"He says he knows where Lauren is."

"And that's all you want? To tell Sabrina about Lauren?"

"Not exactly."

"Then what exactly?" Ian asked.

"I need Sabrina's help in saving Lauren."

"Why? Where is she?"

"Silva has her again. This time he doesn't have to let her go."

"Silva is hung up on her?" Sabrina asked.

"You might say that. Do you know what happened when he had her before?

Sabrina shook her head. "Just the little I got when Cruz was being tortured. She spent some time with Silva?"

"Yeah. For his fiftieth birthday, Cruz gave him Lauren. Silva had her a week."

"Shit," Ian said softly. "Can't decide who's the biggest bastard."

"Both of them," Marsh said. "Only Silva has more money and power, along with a high dose of sadism."

"You could do nothing to stop it?"

"I didn't know anything about it until the week was almost over. I'd been out of town on a job for Silva. When I returned, I heard several of his men lamenting that this week's entertainment was almost over."

Bile surged up Sabrina's throat. "He shared her with his men?"

"No. Silva doesn't share, but he used her in front of them. He enjoys humiliation almost as much as he does doling out pain."

"When she described what Cruz had done to her, she didn't tell us about that."

"I'm sure what Cruz had done to her was enough to convince you to help. I didn't know that much about the man's day-to-day activities, but if he was shitty enough to give his girlfriend to a sadist for a week, he was slime."

Cruz had treated Lauren horribly. When she'd come to Wildfire Security for protection from Cruz, Lauren had told them hideous stories of abuse. Of the murders and torture she had witnessed. She had endured hell. Sabrina had never fathomed just what the woman had gone through. No wonder she hadn't shared everything.

Had Logan Wright known about it? He and Brody James, Wildfire Security's partners, had been Lauren's bodyguards. But Logan had been more than that. He and Lauren had become close. Had she revealed to him just how horrible her experiences had been? Sabrina thought not. It would take more than a few months of knowing someone before you told something like that. Sabrina knew all too well that there were certain secrets that could never be revealed, no matter how much you trusted someone. Her own nineteen year old secret was one she planned to take to her grave.

"So Silva has Lauren. How long and how bad off is she?"

"He's only had her a few days. And so far, I don't believe she's been hurt. Silva is in Chicago attending his daughter's wedding. Lauren's being held for him… he hasn't seen her yet. If any of his men touch her, they know they'll die. Which means she's safe for now. When he returns…"

Marsh left that hanging, leaving no doubt that Lauren would soon be in dire danger.

"When's he due back?" Sabrina asked.

"In four days. I need to figure out a way to get her out before he returns."

"He wants to kill her?"

"Most likely. Once he's done entertaining himself with her. And her death won't be as painless as Cruz's."

Sabrina could only gawk at Marsh. Cruz's death most certainly hadn't been a painless one.

Correctly interpreting her expression, Marsh nodded grimly. "Believe it or not, Cruz got off easy. Silva had some kind of twisted affection for the man. I've heard about weeks of torture Silva has inflicted."

"Why can't the DEA or another law enforcement agency help her? If she's being held against her will, why can't they save her?"

"We can't afford for my cover to be blown. Whatever I do to get Lauren out will have to be done without harming Silva. We can't risk our case against him falling through."

Ian gave a slow nod of understanding. "They don't know you're here, do they? Your people at the DEA? They don't know you're trying to save her."

"One woman's life compared to the ones we'll save when we finally bring Silva down?" Marsh shook his head. "No, they can't sanction a rescue."

"Then how do you want me to help?" Sabrina asked.

"Silva was royally pissed when you got away. He's not put a lot of man-hours behind finding you simply because you covered your tracks so well. Not even the Miami police knew your real name. However, he'd be more than thrilled to find you."

An ominous chill swept up her spine. "And?"

"He's got feelers out, just in case you can be found. I want to take you to where he's keeping Lauren. Once you're inside, I'll help both of you escape."

CHAPTER TEN

Ian's head was shaking long before Marsh finished his sentence. Put Sabrina at the mercy of this Silva person? No way. No way in hell was he about to let that happen.

"I understand why Silva can't be taken down at this point, but couldn't we do the rescue covertly? Go in and rescue her straight out? Why would I need to be taken to him?"

"Silva has a house where he keeps his…playmates. I've never been invited to it. As much research as I've done on the man, I've yet to uncover the location. Once he learns you've been found, he'll instruct me to take you there."

"But when Lauren and I both disappear from his house, won't he suspect you?"

"No, he won't know I had anything to do with it."

"How's that?"

"As I mentioned, Silva has feelers out for you. One of them will pay off and make a call to one of his men. Silva will order me to make the grab." His face twisted in a distasteful grimace. "I've become the asshole's go-to man when it comes to shit like this."

"How do I know we'll be able to get out? He might just kill me on the spot."

Ian shot her a glare that should've singed her. It would have if she'd been paying him any attention. Instead her focus was on Marsh. Ian could almost see the wheels turning in her head, planning on how she could work this.

"He won't kill you," Marsh assured her. "He'll want to talk. Find out who you are. How you got away. That'll give us some leeway in pulling off the escape."

Okay, he had heard more than enough. "No. Hellfire, no. You're insane if you think Sabrina's going to go undercover like this."

"Ian, stop. We need to—"

His gun still steady on Marsh, Ian sent Sabrina a warning look. "You are not going to get anywhere close to this Silva. We'll figure out another way to save Lauren, but putting yourself in his hands is not even an option."

"She's a Wildefire client. We agreed to protect her."

"And you did the job she hired you to do. Got paid for it. The job was done and she left of her own freewill. She's not your client any longer. Not your responsibility."

"So what am I supposed to do? Ignore that she's been kidnapped. Hope it all works out for her?"

"Hell, no. Like I said, we'll get her out. But putting you in the same kind of danger can't be the solution."

"Do you have a better one?"

"We'll find a better one."

"Would you two like to be alone to discuss this?" Marsh asked.

They answered simultaneously, only Ian's was a "Hell, yes" and Sabrina's an emphatic "No."

"Look, Mackenzie," Marsh said. "I can understand your concern, but Lauren's living on borrowed time. Once Silva gets hold of her, I don't know what all he'll do to her. I can guess and believe me, none of it will be pleasant."

Two sets of accusing eyes stared at Ian. Marsh's he couldn't care less about. Sabrina was his only concern.

"And what happens when he gets hold of Sabrina? You know damn well he'll want to do the same things to her. What's going to prevent him?"

"I'll get both of them out before it can happen."

Ignoring Marsh again, Ian focused on Sabrina. "We don't even know this guy. You watched him kill a man, order the death of another. He kidnapped you, held you hostage. And now you trust him enough to go along with this harebrained scheme? That's insane."

"We'll verify what we can, Ian. But if it checks out, I don't see any other way. We can't let this Silva guy get to Lauren again."

"There's got to be another way."

"That's not your decision, Ian."

No it wasn't, but he'd hoped his opinion meant something to her. Once again he was reminded that his influence with Sabrina only went so far.

"What are you going to tell your sisters?"

"That depends." She looked to Marsh again. "If we're to get Lauren out, we'll need all the help we can get. Agreed?"

"What are you thinking?"

"That we need to include Wildfire Security in the rescue. The entire agency."

"The less people involved, the cleaner and easier it'll be."

Sabrina shook her head, the mutinous look on her face one Ian knew all too well. "Nope. It's a package deal…not up for debate. I bring Wildfire Security in on the rescue or I back away, too."

Marsh was silent for several seconds as he apparently adjusted to that ultimatum. Finally he nodded. "Fine. Since I'm off the grid on this, I'm alone. Maybe we can make it work."

"Savannah will stay here. Zach will stay here, too…make sure she, the baby and Aunt Gibby are safe. Quinn's former military so he could help. That's five…" Her eyes flickering with a myriad emotions, Sabrina turned to Ian. "We could use your help, too."

With a hard knot in the pit of his stomach, Ian gave a silent, grim nod. What the hell choice did he have?

Sabrina was surprised Ian waited until Holden Marsh left before he detonated. But then, Ian Mackenzie had an enormous amount of self-control. The tick in his jaw told her that his incredible control was being sorely tested.

The instant Marsh shut the door with her assurance that she would call him as soon as she'd talked to her family, she had expected an explosion of some import.

It didn't come. Instead he just looked at her, silently.

She smiled at him, not nervous, exactly. "I think I'd rather you yell at me."

"Yell at you for what? Agreeing to do something that would put your life in jeopardy? What's the point? You would do it anyway. Or should I yell because you don't think about the people who love you before you jump into the fire? You just go gung-ho, damn the torpedoes, full speed ahead."

"You've been watching too many John Wayne war movies."

He didn't laugh, didn't even crack a smile.

"Ian…please. I don't have a choice."

"That's bullshit and you know it."

"What should I do then? Just tell this Marsh guy sorry but whatever happens to Lauren is her problem, not mine? That Silva can do anything he damn well wants because I'm not going to put myself out to save her?"

"Putting yourself out? Sabrina, the man is a killer. You're agreeing to willingly put yourself into his home, his territory. What's to keep him from shooting you on sight?"

"According to Marsh, he's not that kind of a killer. Other people do his wet work for him."

"Forget the fact that I trust this Marsh guy as far as I can throw this house. If what he says is even a fraction right, Silva is a rapist and sadist." He shrugged. "But hey, no big deal."

She reached out to touch his arm, hoping contact would diffuse his anger. "Don't be like that. I'll be fine."

Ian backed away from her touch. For the first time ever she felt a rejection from the one man she depended on never to let her down.

It was difficult but she managed to ask, "So you've changed your mind? You're not going to help me?"

"I'll help...don't worry about that. I'm just getting damn tired of watching you punish yourself."

"I have no idea what you're talking about."

He released a humorless laugh. "Yeah well, neither do I, but I've seen it too much not to know it's there. When we first started working together I saw it but thought you'd fought it back. Then last year, right before you decided to work with your sisters, it came back, worse than ever. It's like you have a damn death wish."

She shook her head. That wasn't it...that wasn't why she did the job. Why she put her everything into her work. It was just who she was. She believed in doing the right thing and had enough confidence in herself to get the job done. That was it, nothing more.

"That's not what I do."

"You're lying to yourself, Sabrina. And someday you're going to get your wish. You're going to get killed."

CHAPTER ELEVEN

Chicago
Silva's Estate

Robert Silva puffed on his cigar as he watched live feed of Lauren Kendall waiting for him on his yacht. She'd been there a few days but still had a air of defiance about her. Those slender shoulders were too proud, the gleam in her eyes too haughty. That would change, and soon.

It would be a few more days before he could attend to her… the wait would do her good. Nothing like a little terror-filled anticipation to sweeten a woman up. By the time he arrived, she would have lost much of her arrogance. He'd have fun destroying the little that was left.

A knock on his office door at this time of night was unusual. When he called out "Enter" he was surprised to see his wife Erica.

"Robert? May I speak with you? Please?"

He took one last look at his newest pet and then turned off the monitor. "Yes? What is it?"

Her eyes glued to the floor, she spoke in a soft, respectful tone as she had been taught. "I wanted to ask a favor."

They had been married almost twenty years. In that time, he could count on one hand the favors she had asked of him. He didn't particularly like that she was asking one now. Still, he was curious. "What is it you want?"

"To go with you when you return to Florida."

"Why?"

"Perhaps I could be of assistance to you there."

He almost laughed. The only assistance a woman could give a man wasn't something he wanted from her anymore. He'd done his duty...given her children because it was expected. Anything else he could get elsewhere. He kept her as his wife because that was what he had been taught, just as his father had stayed married to his mother and his grandfather to his grandmother. The women bore the children, oversaw the servants, handled the minutia of everyday life. And he, just as his father and grandfather before him, handled the business. Their roles were clearly defined, the lines never to be blurred.

"What kind of assistance do you think I require?"

"I don't know. I just thought—"

"Do I look like a man who requires assistance?"

"Oh no. Of course not. I just thought—"

"Perhaps you think too much. Perhaps you don't have enough to occupy you now that our oldest daughter has married."

"Not at all, Robert. The children keep me busy."

"How old is Elena?"

She looked at him then, her light blue eyes wide with worry and a satisfactory amount of fear. "She'll be two next month."

Robert stood. Perhaps his duty had not ended. "Take off your clothes."

She knew better than to question his orders. Within seconds she was naked. Even through five pregnancies, her body had held up well. Maybe a little more flab around the stomach area and her hips looked a little wider than when they'd married. He'd give her one more brat, then get her fixed for good—no more childbearing. After that, extensive plastic surgery to take care of the flaws. He was Robert Silva—he demanded and deserved perfection in every aspect of his life.

"On your hands and knees."

"Robert...please."

"Are you denying me?"

"No, of course not. I just wanted—"

"And you think your wants matter to me?"

The woman he could've sworn had rubber for a backbone straightened her spine and said, "I'm your wife."

His voice went soft as a whisper. "Are you challenging my authority?"

As if she realized she'd gone too far, she shook her head quickly and went to her hands and knees as he commanded.

Robert checked his watch, then removed his belt and unzipped his pants. He had an important conference call in twenty minutes. Plenty of time to take care of his husbandly duty and get in some much needed discipline, too. By the time he was finished, he was quite sure that traveling anywhere with him would be the last thing on her mind.

Midnight

The family meeting Sabrina called that night wasn't remotely one she looked forward to but it had to be done. If they were going to be working this case, then her family needed to know everything. How she became acquainted with Holden Marsh had to be revealed and discussed.

Staying as sketchy as she could on the less savory details, Sabrina explained about Cruz's death. About Ryan Walker's betrayal. About Ian's rescue of her.

The room was silent as they absorbed the information she gave. She sat on the edge of her chair watching the expressions of those she loved. She had a feeling that glossing over the less savory details hadn't worked. Savvy and Sammie looked horrified. Zach and Quinn, angry and grim.

And Ian, who stood on the other side of the room, held a granite-like expression of quiet fury.

She and Ian hadn't talked since he'd walked out the door a few hours ago. His parting words had stunned her. She refused to believe there was the slightest sliver of truth to his accusation.

She took a swallow of water to wet down her parched mouth. No one had made the slightest comment yet and despite herself, she was getting nervous. She cleared her throat. "So, anyway, Marsh has asked for our help and I'd like the entire agency to be involved."

Savvy was the first to speak, her voice thick with simmering emotions. "Why didn't you tell us, Bri?"

"Because I knew it would upset you. You didn't need that worry, Savvy. When all this happened, you'd just had that scare with the baby. And Sammie had just gone through her ordeal. I figured you both would try to find this man…this Silva. I couldn't risk that."

"You put your family in jeopardy by not telling us, Sabrina," Zach said.

The cut went deep to her heart. "Telling you guys would've added more worry and that wasn't something anyone needed."

"Keeping everyone in the dark is never a good idea," Quinn said.

Okay, she could see Quinn's point since everything that had happened to him and Sammie had been because he'd been left in the dark. But this had no real correlation to what had happened to him. Sabrina had kept secrets to protect her family. Not hurt them.

She sent pleading looks to her sisters. Of all the people in the world, she needed their support and love. If she lost it, she didn't know what she would do.

"I just wish you had trusted us, Bri," Sammie said.

"It had nothing to do with trust."

Zach shook his head. "Whatever your reason, Sabrina. It was wrong to hold it back. Your sisters deserved better. Your family deserved better."

Sabrina took a shaky breath, opened her mouth, ready to apologize again.

"Okay, that's enough," Ian growled. "Do you even know what kind of pressure she's been under? Maybe it was wrong not to tell you, but everything she did was to protect you, not hurt you."

"That's why you haven't left Midnight," Sammie said "Why you're constantly driving through town. You thought he might come here."

"I didn't believe there was any way they could find me."

"And yet this Holden Marsh did," Zach said. "Do you believe him?"

"I talked to a couple of my contacts at the DEA," Ian said. "He is who he says he is. Whether he's telling the truth about Lauren is another issue."

"Why didn't you tell us, Ian?" Savannah said. "You're as culpable as Bri."

Ian arched a brow. "Culpable? So we're criminals here?"

Sabrina released a frustrated breath. This was getting so messed up and not anything like she intended. "Don't blame Ian...it's not his fault. He wanted me to tell you. This is all on me." She took a shaky breath. "I understand if you don't want to help. I can—"

"Not help?"

Before she could react, both Savvy and Sammie came to sit on either side of her, each wrapping an arm around her.

"Good Lord, Bri, you're our sister," Savvy said. "We love you. Of course we're going to help you."

Sammie squeezed her shoulder. "Just because we're angry doesn't mean we'd let you do this on your own. We're family. We stick together, no matter what."

Appreciating their love and quick forgiveness, she glanced over at Quinn and Zach.

Zach said. "Of course we're with you."

Quinn nodded. "Whatever you need, Sabrina."

Relief almost made her dizzy. Telling her family had been what she had dreaded the most. Now they could move forward. "We need to call Brody and Logan in."

"We'll have trouble keeping Logan from doing this on his own," Sammie said. "He's not been the same since Lauren left. And I know he hasn't stopped looking for her."

Zach waved away their concerns. "You leave Logan to me. Once he understands we're all in this to rescue her, he'll cooperate."

"So what's the plan?" Savvy asked. "I can't do anything physical yet, but I want to help."

"You'll help plenty, Savvy. We'll need all the information you can find on Robert Silva. And if you can find out more on Holden Marsh without sending out flags, see what you can dig up."

"What about the rest of us?" Sammie asked. "How are we going to get this done?"

"Marsh is coming back tomorrow morning. Let's get Logan and Brody here and we'll talk about what we need to do."

Silva's Yacht

As prisons went, this was surely one of the most luxurious imaginable. An elegant two hundred foot yacht with a staff of five whose only responsibilities it seemed was keeping her well fed, entertained, and oh yeah, prisoner.

So what if she lounged around the pool all day or was treated to the most current movies or books in the evening. So what if the food was prepared by some fancy chef with a foreign accent. And so what that though her guards' eyes gleamed with lust and violence, no one had touched her since they'd dumped her here. She knew what was coming when Silva arrived.

The guards were superfluous. She was in the middle of the damn ocean. Just where the hell did they think she would go?

Sometimes, when she wasn't living in fear or running for her life, she wondered what might have been. She'd had a family once—one that had loved her, but she'd always been a rebel at heart. Always thought she knew best. Always wanted more.

Leaving home at eighteen, sure that with her looks and talent, she could be a Hollywood superstar, had been the first of many bad decisions. When the money she'd saved ran out, she had waited tables, certain that she would be discovered. The only discovering that had been done had been on her part. She'd discovered that in Hollywood good looks and talent were a dime a dozen. Too stupidly stubborn to go home, she'd stuck it out and then it had been too late.

The call had come in the middle of the night. Her parents had been killed in a hit and run accident. And she, Lauren Kendall, rebel without a single cause, had learned about loss. Regret. And a whole shitload of guilt that never ceased.

One would think she would have learned her lesson, but instead of straightening out her less than spectacular character, she allowed herself to dig deeper into the mire. She wished she could blame it on someone else but was too honest with herself to even try. Every bad decision she had made in her life was her own damn fault...no one else's.

Hooking up with Armando Cruz had been the pinnacle of those bad decisions. She'd fallen for his silky tongue, his good looks and yes, his money. Let's not forget the money.

She had been his girlfriend, then his mistress. It wasn't until close to the end of their relationship that she realized she was just his whore. She had witnessed atrocities that would haunt her until death. Instead of finding a way to escape, she had stayed, determined to get as much money from him as possible before she left. If she had walked out the door and just disappeared, how much easier would her life have been?

The day Robert Silva had come to call on his old friend Armando had been the beginning of a new, gruesome hell. Her life, already covered with a thousand pounds of shit, got a million times worse. She hadn't known it at the time. Armando had introduced her to Silva and then told her to leave. She had gladly complied. The dead look in Silva's eyes had scared the crap out of her. She hadn't known that she had caught his interest.

Then, in the way a man loans a car or a boat to a friend, Cruz had loaned her to Silva. A loan of property for a short time, to be used and abused as each saw fit. A birthday gift to a friend... but just for a few days.

What had been done to her still woke her up sometimes, screaming with agony and debasement while bile surged up her throat.

She had never told anyone. Even when Silva had returned her to Cruz, even when her supposed lover had asked her why she had bruises, cuts, and marks all over her body, she wouldn't say. If she had told him, allowed herself to speak the words, she would have killed him.

Once she'd gotten away from Cruz, she had felt free for the first time in years. But she had known she wasn't completely free. He would come after her. Not only for the money she'd stolen but also because she'd damaged his ego. An evil man with a bruised ego was a dangerous thing.

When she'd gone to Midnight and hired Wildefire Security to protect her, she had felt almost safe. She'd covered her tracks. No way would Cruz ever trace her all the way to a tiny little town in South Alabama.

How nice it would be if the story ended there. If all of her bad decisions just melted away and, for once in her life, Lauren Kendall had started making wise choices. For a time, that's what it had seemed. She had a safety net of people who could keep her out of Cruz's clutches. Good people who had actually cared about her. And she'd had Logan Wright.

Oh God, why hadn't she stayed?

Logan was the first man to treat her like a lady…like she was someone special. The first man whose touch had made her feel clean. He had known almost everything she had done, most everything that had been done to her, and still he had stuck with her, by her. And how had she repaid him? By doing the very thing she'd been doing most of her life. She'd run like a chicken-shit coward. The instant she'd learned that Cruz was dead and couldn't touch her anymore, she'd hightailed it out of Alabama like a band of demons was on her tail. She had left Logan in the dust.

And what good had it done her? Instead of that freedom she'd thought she wanted, she was right back to being a prisoner again. Only this time it was worse, so much worse than before.

Lauren surged to her feet and paced the small confines of the cabin. Freedom? That wasn't why she'd left Logan. There was no point in lying to herself. She'd left him because what he made her feel had scared the hell out of her. She had known how much he cared for her and realized that with her record, she would never be good enough for him.

Of course none of that mattered now. She was well and truly caught. When Silva showed up, it would be the end for her. Even if he allowed her to live, she already knew she couldn't survive a second dose of him. If he so much as laid a finger on her... She shook her head. She didn't know what she might be capable of doing, but she swore if he touched her, it would be the last thing he did—even if it meant her life.

CHAPTER TWELVE

Midnight

Holden Marsh sat in the elegant but comfortable living room and eyed his fellow.... What could he call them...teammates? He hadn't planned on having any and beneath the aggravation, he felt an odd sort of amusement. He who had worked alone for too many years to count, now had eight people involved.

When he'd come to Sabrina Wilde with his proposition, he hadn't seen it as more than her going in to Silva's 'guest' house. And him, with Sabrina's help, bringing Lauren out. It had been complicated already. Adding this many people was, in his opinion, a sure road to disaster. Unfortunately, Sabrina Wilde wouldn't have it any other way.

Family was an odd concept to Holden. By accident of birth you were born into one and for that reason alone you were supposed to love them? Trust them? He'd had a family once, but love hadn't been part of the equation. At least not the kind that these people apparently had for each other. Even Brody James and Logan Wright seemed to have been included.

Holden had done his research before coming here. The Wilde family had an interesting history. Triplet sisters who'd lost their parents to a supposed murder/suicide. Raised by their grandfather, the sisters, though independently wealthy, had gone on to make something of themselves. Savannah was a former assistant district attorney, Samantha a former homicide detective, and Sabrina a private investigator.

Seemed like odd choices for three Southern belles who really hadn't needed to be employed in order to have every material possession they might want. In Holden's estimation, that said a lot about a person.

Zach Tanner, chief of police of Midnight, had an interesting story, too. As did Dr. Quinn Braddock. The Wilde family sure as hell wasn't without their drama.

Logan Wright and Brody James, friends of Tanner's, had run a successful security company in Mobile. A few months back they'd formed a partnership with Wildefire Security. Holden didn't have much intel on either man...not near enough to form a solid opinion. Their being friends with Tanner was enough for Holden right now. Still, he would keep an eye out for any possible problems.

On the other hand, Ian Mackenzie was seemingly an open book. Holden didn't trust the obvious. Mackenzie had been adopted when he was a kid by Molly and Barry Mackenzie— 'do-gooders' who had adopted and raised a total of ten kids.

What concerned Holden was the lack of drama or trouble surrounding Mackenzie. He appeared to be a straight shooter. He might've had a rough start in life but once adopted became the model son and citizen. A decorated war hero who'd served in both Iraq and Afghanistan. On returning to the States, the man finished up his college degree in criminal justice and worked for a private investigator. When the old man retired, Mackenzie took over the business.

The PI was well respected, had a reputation for uncovering obscure, hard to find information, and was well liked by his peers. Holden wasn't buying it. The guy had to have something dark. Everybody had secrets.

Holden didn't like unsolved mysteries and he didn't trust people with a squeaky clean past. Ian Mackenzie had to be hiding something and even while they all worked together to rescue Lauren Kendall, he was determined to find out what that secret was.

Sabrina stood at the front of the room and addressed the small group of people. "We're all here, so let's get started." She nodded at him. "Mr. Marsh?"

"Just so we're clear," Holden said, "what's said in this room can go no further. I'm not only putting my ass on the line but also every person involved in bringing Silva down."

"You can trust us," Sabrina said. "Everyone in this room is a professional…knows the importance of this job. Now tell us what you can about Silva."

"He's one of the least known but most powerful criminals in the United States. His family, grandfather and father, started their businesses in Columbia. From all accounts they were sadistic bastards who taught young Robert everything he needed to know about being evil.

"Silva came to the US when he was in his early twenties. Guess he wanted to make his own way, but he had plenty of help from them, in both contacts and capital. By the time he was thirty, he had amassed his own wealth—his own reputation of filth."

"And why can't he be stopped?" Savannah asked. "If your people know this much about him, why can't he be tried and convicted?"

"Money, influence. He's got politicians and law enforcement...hell, even the media's in his pocket. They either owe him favors or he pays them off."

Savannah shook her head. "I don't buy that. I worked as a prosecutor. Sure there are some dishonest people in law enforcement, but the majority is there to seek justice, legally. You make it sound like everyone's corrupt."

"Not what I'm saying at all. In fact, I agree with you. But whenever Silva has been brought up on charges, he either finds a way out of them or they go away. He's had plenty of people try to go up against him. But evidence disappears, witnesses mysteriously vanish, die, or change their stories. And slick attorneys find holes for the bastard to weasel through.

"A long term undercover project is our only hope. As I told Sabrina, I've been working as one of his lackeys for close to two years trying to get enough verifiable evidence to bury the bastard. He doesn't trust easily. Even though I've witnessed and been involved with enough filth to fill a garbage bin, I still don't have anything substantial. Not enough that will hold this bastard. We could probably get him locked away for a year or two, but that's not going to do anything but amuse him. I've got to have enough to bury him for good.

"I was close to gaining his complete trust...becoming one of his top goons. He'd never put me in charge of anything major. Then I got the assignment for Armando Cruz." He saw Sabrina's surprise and nodded. "Yeah, that was a first for me. I knew some of the plan, not all of it. Silva had cameras planted in the room, was watching the whole show. I was supposed to wait until you and Walker left before coming in."

Surprise and then gratitude gleamed in Sabrina's eyes. "You saw what Cruz was about to do to me. You came in and stopped him."

"Yes."

"What's he talking about, Bri?" Savannah asked. "What was Cruz going to do to you?"

"I'll tell you later." She nodded her head at Holden. "Thank you."

He acknowledged her gratitude with a nod of his own. "Once I was in, I knew I was going to have to make it look good. Silva was cursing in my ear, telling me how I'd already screwed everything up and would pay. He told me I'd better make sure everything else went off without a hitch."

"The information Cruz gave you about Lauren. It wasn't much."

"That was a ruse. I wasn't there for information. Silva already knew the answer to every question I asked Cruz. I didn't know going in but I was sent there for one reason—to kill Cruz. Silva called all the shots—I just delivered them."

"What about Walker?" Sabrina asked.

"Silva's orders, too. He'd planned on getting rid of Walker soon. He decided to go ahead and get rid of him then."

"Because Silva decided he wanted me," Sabrina said.

"Yes."

"What would he have done with me?"

"What he does with every other woman he takes—rape, torture, slavery, eventually death."

"Then thank you from all of us," Samantha said, then shook her head, confused. "But weren't you holding her for Silva?"

"I needed it to look that way. Silva was still a couple of hours away. I was going to get her out of there." His mouth twisted in a grim smile as he remembered what happened next. "I had a friend on his way over."

"And then I showed up and messed up your plan." Mackenzie said.

"Not really. Garrett was going to have to go either way. Could've done without the headache you gave me, but for the most part, it worked."

"As an officer of the law, gotta say I'm not comfortable with the murder of three people, no matter how bad they might have been. However, as Sabrina's brother-in-law, I'm grateful for any help you gave her." Tanner leaned forward. "Now tell us why a man who seems to have no compunction to arbitrarily kill people is so anxious to save one woman."

He couldn't dispute Tanner's criticism. And his question was a fair one. Shame wasn't necessarily a new concept to Holden. Yeah, he'd done a lot of shitty things, especially in the last couple of years, but most of those didn't bother him all that much. With the kind of job he had, a man had to make some difficult choices. If he got bogged down by every one of them, he wouldn't be a very effective undercover agent. But he did have some regrets, especially one in particular.

"Lauren is a victim. Those assholes weren't."

Seeing that this hadn't satisfied them, Holden continued, "As I told you, I didn't know about Cruz's birthday gift to Silva. Lauren arrived when I was on an assignment. When I got back, she'd already been there six days...was to be returned to Cruz the next day. I got there in time to watch Silva's last performance."

"Performance?" The harsh grimness of Logan Wright's face told Holden he wasn't asking a question. It also told him that Wright had feelings for Lauren beyond a bodyguard.

"Silva likes an audience. I won't go into detail about what he did."

"And you did nothing to stop it?" Wright snarled.

No, and that was his hell to live with. It was also something he swore he would never allow again. As sick and disgusting as

Silva's abuse of Lauren had been, it'd been limited simply because he was going to have to return her to Cruz. Now that Cruz was permanently out of the picture, he would have no such restraint. There was no telling what Silva would do to the woman.

"Where is she? Where's he keeping her?"

"I don't know."

"What do you mean you don't know? How the hell—"

"Logan, let him explain," Sabrina cut in.

"Silva has a house specifically for his women. I don't know where it is. He's never invited me, but he goes there once or twice a month for entertainment."

"Then how are we going to get her if you don't know where she is?" Samantha asked.

Before Holden could answer, Sabrina stood and addressed the room. "Silva wants me. He's been looking for me ever since my escape. Marsh is going to arrange for one of Silva's men to be notified of my whereabouts. Marsh will get the call to pick me up. He'll take me to the house where Lauren is being held. Once I'm in, I'll work with Marsh to help Lauren escape."

A long, taut moment of silence followed Sabrina's statement. Then the air exploded with protests and curses.

Sabrina steeled her spine, bracing herself, prepared to take them on. When she felt a hard, strong body behind her and then a comforting but supportive hand on her shoulder she twisted her head to look up. *Ian.*

"I've got your back, Sabrina. Always have, always will."

His support giving her the strength she needed to handle her family's objections, she flashed him a glowing smile of thanks and turned back to them, now prepared more than ever to take them on.

Her sisters were already angry and disappointed with her and now they were worried, too. Even as she listened to their protests, deflected and reassured, she felt the pain of that. It hurt more than almost anyone could comprehend. The fact that she deserved their censure and disapproval made it a million times worse.

For most of her life she had defied what other people thought and said. If someone disapproved of her, she took it as a point of pride. But when it came to family, most especially Savvy and Sammie, she wanted and needed their approval and love to an almost desperate degree.

She didn't question why she felt this way. Even those who knew her best weren't aware of her extreme vulnerabilities. Hiding the deepest parts of herself was an ingrained habit. On a fateful day, nineteen years ago, she had committed what she considered the most awful transgression possible. Everything that followed had been influenced and led by that one terrible sin.

No one knew about it. She was determined no one ever would. However, because of it, she had done everything she possibly could to ensure she never hurt her family again.

Oh she had astounded them, possibly embarrassed them, but never would she purposely hurt them.

When they finally paused for a breath, she tried for levity, hoping to break through the tense atmosphere. "So what does a woman wear to meet a sleazy drug lord? Any suggestions?"

Neither sister looked impressed with her lame attempt at humor. Okay, so she wasn't a comedian.

"Seriously, you two, what am I supposed to do? Just let Lauren be abused by this creep for the second time?"

"Of course you can't, Bri," Savvy said. "We have to help her any way we can."

"But that doesn't mean we aren't worried about you," Sammie added.

"Telling you not to worry won't do any good. You're going to do that anyway. For what's it worth, this seems like the most solid plan."

"It'd be a lot easier if Silva could be taken at this time. Sneaking in to rescue you and Lauren without anyone knowing about it won't be easy." Savvy cut her eyes over to where Holden Marsh stood talking with the men and then lowered her voice. "You're sure Marsh can be trusted?"

"Not a hundred percent, but why would he agree to get everyone involved? If he'd tracked me down just to take me back to Silva, it'd be a lot easier if you guys knew nothing about this. He could've caught me off guard somewhere and taken me. No one would have ever known."

"Except you're not exactly easy to catch off guard or be taken," Sammie said.

"Maybe not, but I'd be easier than all of you guys together. I think he's telling the truth."

"Then we're going to do everything we can to make sure both you and Lauren come out safe." Savvy grimaced "I just wish I could be there."

"The information you dig up on Silva will be just as important."

"Quinn will be coming along, too" Sammie said. Her grim tone said she wasn't completely happy about that.

"I'm sorry I got us into this."

Savvy gripped Sabrina's wrist, pulled her around. "Stop it, Bri. We're in this together, just like all of our cases. If you hadn't gotten involved in Cruz's business, we wouldn't even know that Lauren had been taken. I hate to think of her in Silva's grasp. She's been through so much already."

"I agree," Sammie said. "And yes we're disappointed you didn't tell us what happened with Cruz, but only because this shouldn't have been your burden to bear alone. I wish you had trusted us."

"Trust had nothing to do with it. I just hated getting you guys involved when you had so much going on."

"Can we at least agree that if anything like this ever happens again, you don't keep it from us? Remember we Wildes stick together, no matter what."

Sabrina smiled her thanks for Sammie's quick forgiveness. "I believe I can keep that promise."

Savvy gave an emphatic nod of approval. "That settles that then. And bottom line, this is the reason we created Wildefire Security…for cases like this. So let's talk about what we need to do to bring both you and Lauren back home safe."

CHAPTER THIRTEEN

"At last she wakes."

Ian's morning voice always sounded so sexy and gruff, like silk over sandpaper. Brown eyes, the color of the Kentucky bourbon her granddad had been so fond of, gleamed down at her. The perpetual five o'clock shadow stubbling his handsome face gave him a rakish look that never failed to increase her heart rate. He was smiling just a little, giving her a teasing glimpse of the dimple in his right cheek.

"Good morning."

"Get much sleep?"

No, she hadn't. Nightmares had chased her all night. Ian knew better than anyone how unusual an easy sleep was for her. Intimacy was difficult for Sabrina for a lot of reasons and one of them had to do with her inability to sleep the night through without nightmares. No one in her family knew about them. She couldn't bear for them to ever find out. Nightmares had been part of her life since she was ten years old. Awake or asleep, they shadowed her but it was in sleep, when she was her most vulnerable, that they tortured her soul.

Ian had questioned her many times about them. How could she tell him when she didn't have the courage to tell her sisters? Thankfully he no longer asked. Besides, it was easy enough to use her parents' deaths as an excuse for the nightmares. He didn't have to know about the other things that haunted her.

She smiled now, wanting to push those dark thoughts away. "Enough. How about you?"

"Not really."

"You're worried about me."

"A perpetual state of being these days."

She didn't want to argue with him. It would do no good...her course was set. Tomorrow she would become a willing prisoner of Robert Silva.

She was grateful Ian had gotten over his anger. Having him mad at her was almost as difficult as having her sisters upset with her. She depended on him for so much. His acceptance of the person she was, including all her weird hang-ups and flaws, was as close to unconditional love as she could imagine.

They'd all been working like demons for the last couple of days to ensure everyone was comfortable with their plan. Being too much of a realist to believe the plan would proceed without glitches or problems, Sabrina didn't bother to reassure Ian that she would be completely safe. He was no dummy and knew the risk she was taking. If somehow this was their last time together, she wanted the memory to be a good one.

With that thought in mind, she cupped his face with her hands and brought his mouth to hers. And just like that...like always, need exploded. There had never been anyone like Ian in her life. Ruthlessly tender. Sexy. Dominant without being overbearing or obnoxious. She had never known that a man could be so tough but oh so gentle, too.

Threading her fingers through his thick hair, their shared breath a thing of beauty, she let him take her to a place she'd never known existed before he'd touched her that first time.

Lifting his mouth from hers, Ian spread small, soft kisses over her face, down her creamy neck. His tongue licked, then swirled around a beautifully taut nipple that beaded and tightened with his attention. Sucking greedily, he listened to her rasping, excited breaths as she became more aroused.

He knew what she was doing. Knew part of it was to comfort, part of it was to distract. She was worried about him, just like she worried about all the people she cared about. And, whether she wanted to acknowledge it or not, she was showing her love for him. Sabrina was many things, but she wasn't a user, and she didn't fake affection. She loved him but in his heart he feared she would never willingly acknowledge it.

Ian took in a breath, inhaling all the delicate scents of the woman he adored. The musk of her arousal blended with the tangerine lotion she'd slathered herself with last night. When they'd first started dating, he'd mentioned that tangerines were his favorite fruit. Somehow she'd found lotion that smelled just like tangerines. One of the many ways she showed her love for him.

"Ian. Come inside me."

"Soon," he murmured. His tongue swirled around a nipple, nibbled a little, and then lightly bit down. She arched her body on a gasp of arousal. Holding his head to her breast, she urged him on.

When he lifted his head, she moaned at the loss of contact. "Shh..." he whispered. "I'll make it good for you. Promise."

"You always make it good. You never disappoint."

He chuckled softly. "High praise indeed. Let's see if we can go from good to spectacular." His mouth covered hers, he plunged his tongue deep, loving her taste, the generous way she gave herself up to his desires, his needs.

Raising his head, he trailed more kisses down her body, following shadows, licking and savoring wherever his mouth led him. From the hollow of her neck, he followed a path down her torso, swirled his tongue around her navel, moved his mouth to the inside of her thigh, licked, nibbled, licked again. Her legs spread wide in invitation as her body arched.

Ian laughed softly. "Eager are we?"

"For you? Always."

"Let's see if we can make you even more so."

Settling between her legs, Ian parted the soft folds of her sex and devoured the sweetness he found there. She came quickly, almost crying in her need to reach the pinnacle.

He settled back onto his knees and watched her. Never had he seen anyone more beautiful, more giving. Sabrina was a lovely woman…no one with eyesight could deny that fact. But Ian saw so much more than her physical beauty. He'd seen firsthand her love for her family, her compassion for anyone hurting, her need to right wrongs. How many animals had she rescued since he'd known her? How many people had she tried to help? When they were working together as partners, almost every week she'd take a case pro bono.

She would deny it, but she had the softest heart of anyone he'd ever known.

"Ian?" For once she sounded a little self-conscious. "Why are you just staring at me?" Her eyes shifted downward to where he was hard, hot, aching. "We're definitely not finished."

Lowering himself onto her, Ian slid easily into the softest, most welcoming warmth he could ever imagine. "Oh no, my darling Sabrina, we're not finished. Not by a long shot."

And with that he proceeded to show her that good could definitely become spectacular.

Sabrina lay beside Ian, her body so sated she didn't want to move. Their lovemaking had always been wonderful. Ian was the most giving lover she could ever imagine. This time had been even better than any other. If she was making memories, then apparently Ian was, too. She refused to believe there was a need to worry that this would be their last time. Everything would work out. She had to trust her instincts.

"I guess we need to get up and have one last meeting with everyone. Marsh said he wanted to leave at dawn tomorrow. We still have a couple of things to iron out."

He didn't respond, didn't move.

"Ian?"

A harsh breath exploded from him as if he'd been holding it back, and then he surprised her by saying, "If I asked you not to do this...for me. What would you say?"

"We've already had this discussion."

"It doesn't mean we can't have it again. It's not too late. We can find another way to get to Lauren. Putting yourself on Silva's radar could come back and bite you in the ass."

"I'm already on his radar. He's been looking for me. It might be only a matter of time before he finds me. Let's rescue Lauren so Marsh can concentrate on bringing down the bastard for good. That's the only way we'll ever be sure I'm safe from him."

"That is if Marsh is on the up and up. You're taking an awful lot on faith with him."

"I don't see that I have a choice. And you checked with your sources at the DEA. He's definitely undercover."

"Yeah, but that doesn't mean he's not gone bad. Look at what happened with Ryan Walker. Besides, even if Marsh is on the up and up, it doesn't mean he'll take care of you if something happens. What if Silva finds out what's going on before we can get to you? How do we know Marsh won't throw you under the bus to save himself?"

"I can take care of myself."

"Dammit."

Startling her, he shot up from the bed and his feet thudded to the floor. With angry, jerking movements, he slid into his jeans and then glared down at her. "The thing is, whether you want to admit it or not, you put yourself in dangerous situations more times than necessary. You said you don't have a death wish. I don't believe you. But one thing for certain, the day will come when you can't fight your way out of trouble. Your number will be called and I won't be around to pick up the pieces. Think on that."

Stunned at his outburst, Sabrina watched him stride across the room. He opened the door, cast her one last furious glare and then was gone.

CHAPTER FOURTEEN

"You ready?" Marsh asked.

"As ready as I can be, I guess."

The grim toughness in Marsh's eyes was a direct contrast to the gentleness of his hands as he carried out his tasks. Using duct tape, he bound her hands behind her back, then her feet. Holding up a long scarf, he said, "I'll use this instead of the tape. No need to make this any more uncomfortable than it needs to be."

"I appreciate that. You're sure this Payne guy won't mess with me?"

"Very sure. Silva gave strict instructions that you weren't to be injured or manhandled. That's one of the reasons he sent me to do this. Payne has gotten in trouble before for one thing or another. Has impulse control issues. Silva believes I have the discipline to get this job done without damaging the merchandise."

Sabrina scrunched her nose up at being referred to as merchandise but didn't bother to comment. To Silva that's exactly what she was. And from what Marsh had described, it was how he thought of all women.

He placed the scarf around her neck, but instead of opening the back of the SUV and bundling her in the back, he hesitated.

"What's wrong?"

"I don't know if this will work."

"Do we have a choice?"

"No...at least none that I can come up with."

The doubt in his eyes mirrored her own thoughts, but second guessing themselves would do no good. The game was in play. Payne had been notified that she had been found and had called his boss with the good news. And as Marsh has predicted, Silva had called him to make the pick-up. Retreating and finding another way was not an option.

There was one slight glitch in their scenario. Silva had instructed Marsh to take Sabrina to a small abandoned airstrip in North Florida. They would be met there and he would be given instructions on what to do next. Which meant they still had no idea where Lauren was being held.

She reached for words to reassure him...and herself. "Lauren knows me...she trusts me. Just get me to her and we'll figure a way out. I've got lots of backup so it's not like I'm in this alone. Okay?"

Marsh opened the back of the SUV. Since her hands and feet were already tied, she had to rely on him to lift her up and place her inside. Just as he was about to shut the door, she heard a shout.

Twisting her head, she saw Ian sprinting toward them. The anxiety eased inside her. She hadn't liked how they left things. After he'd left her in bed yesterday morning, he'd barely even looked at her the rest of the day. Last night he hadn't even come to her room.

"Mind if I have a minute with your captive?"

Marsh issued a curt nod to Ian and moved several yards away, giving them privacy.

Ian looked down at Sabrina. She was lying curled up on her side in the trunk, her hands and feet bound. A scarf was tied around her neck that would soon cover her mouth. When she and Marsh arrived at the designated location, she would look like a kidnap victim.

Even though he had never felt less like joking, he winked and gave his best cocky grin. "Comfy?"

"Oh yeah. I'm thinking about traveling like this from now on."

"I'll keep that in mind next time we go on vacation."

"It really will be okay, Ian. I promise."

"Don't make promises you can't keep." Leaning down, he softly kissed her forehead and then gave her a warm, thorough kiss on her luscious mouth. "Stay safe, Sabrina Wilde, or I'll kick your ass."

She snorted. "You and what army, Ian Mackenzie?"

"I believe I can scrounge up a few people who wouldn't mind helping me." Then, even though she wouldn't want to hear it, he had to say the words, "I love you, Sabrina."

"Ian...I..." Her smooth forehead furrowed as she shook her head. "Don't."

"Too late, baby. You're it for me. Better get used to it. It's a permanent thing. Won't go away...and neither will I." He dropped one last kiss on her unsmiling mouth. "See you in a few days."

Before she could say anything else, could tell him not to love her or that he wasn't 'it' for her, he pulled the scarf up and covered her mouth. Satisfied that instead of the sadness his words had caused, temper now gleamed in her eyes, Ian walked away.

The ride to the airstrip was short and uneventful. They had agreed to carry the guise of her capture all the way. The instant Marsh had gotten into the driver's seat, he'd become a different man.

Once he parked, he hauled her out of the back and threw her over his shoulder like he was carrying a bale of hay. She grunted and moaned, none of it fake. By the time she made it to their destination, she would be sore and stiff. Saving Lauren's life was worth it.

Since she was upside down, she saw nothing of the pilot other than his scruffy looking boots. His mocking voice was slightly accented. "Does her face look as good as her ass?"

Marsh's reply was mild, without inflection. "That'll be something you can take up with Silva, Hans. I'm sure the boss would love to talk to you about it."

"Hey, man, I was only joking."

The nervous respect she heard in Hans' voice made her feel better. Marsh had claimed to have a lot of influence with his boss, which hopefully meant any plans Silva had for either Lauren or her would be something he'd mention to Marsh.

Since she needed to maintain her role as unwilling captive, Sabrina did her part. She squirmed and wiggled, kicked her bound legs and felt only a slight amount of guilt when her foot connected with Marsh's groin.

A sharp inhalation of breath and soft curse followed the contact. All guilt feelings disappeared when he slammed his palm against her ass in a stinging slap. "Behave or I'll knock you out again."

She mumbled several vehement curses behind her gag but refrained from kicking him again. Incapacitating her only ally was not a good idea, besides the fact that he'd probably smack her again if she tried.

Marsh climbed up a short flight of stairs and entered the small plane. Dumping Sabrina onto a seat, he buckled her seat belt, then barked, "Stay put."

She glared up at him.

A slimy sounding voice came from the back of the plane. "Well now, that's what I call a handful."

Marsh jerked around and gave the man a nod of greeting. "Your intel was good, Payne. I'll make sure Mr. Silva knows how smooth this went down."

Sabrina couldn't see all of Payne, much of him was in the shadows, but what she could see wasn't reassuring. He appeared to be a behemoth, at least six-six and his bulk put him well over the three hundred pound mark. Payne was definitely not a man she wanted to take on. One swat from him would be certain death.

"Appreciate it, Marsh."

Minutes later, they were speeding down the runway. The instant they were in the air, Marsh pulled out his cellphone. "We're in the air, Mr. Silva. Where would you like us to go?"

Sabrina couldn't hear the other man's words, but the narrowing of Marsh's eyes and the tense twisting of his mouth told her whatever he'd said surprised him, and not in a good way.

"Very well, sir. I'll see you in a couple of days."

Since she was still gagged, asking him any questions wasn't possible. And even if she could speak, she wouldn't have been able to ask in front of Payne. Still, the frown on his face was enough for her to know that something was definitely wrong.

They arrived at night. Where, she had no idea. The trip had taken hours. From the little she had been able to hear, they'd had to go around a thunderstorm. Was that the reason it had taken so long or had they traveled hundreds, maybe thousands of miles?

Other than a couple of trips to the cockpit, Marsh had stayed with her. Thankfully when he did leave, he'd given a telling look to Payne. He hadn't said the words, but his warning was clear: Don't touch the merchandise.

She had been allowed two bathroom breaks, as well as a glass of water and a candy bar. She'd scarfed down the candy, unaccountably grateful for the nourishment. She had no idea what she would face when they landed but figured she'd need all the energy she could get.

When the outside door opened, Sabrina sprang to her feet. After her last bathroom visit, her legs hadn't been retied. Hopefully they'd let her walk out under her own steam. Marsh was there before she could take a step. He gave her a dark look of warning and nodded at her seat.

Sighing her disgust, she fell back into the chair and watched in silence as he taped her ankles together again. He then hauled her to her feet and deftly secured her arms behind her back. More than aware that Payne was watching a few feet away, she thought about giving a performance of resistance.

Before she could come up with something that wouldn't get her in too much trouble, Marsh picked her up and just like before, threw her over his hard, unyielding shoulder. Wordlessly, he carried her off the plane.

She was beyond exhausted and made only a token protest of squirming about. Even though she knew he needed to maintain his front because of Payne, she noticed that when he dumped her in the car trunk and she cursed, a small smile played around his mouth.

From what she had been able to see from her upside-down viewpoint, this airstrip was old and abandoned, too. Not a soul around to help her if things went sour. How many women had been brought to Silva in just this way?

It was dark and cramped in the trunk. She was thirsty, hungry and had a pounding headache. She was, in a word, miserable. She kept herself occupied by concentrating on seeing Lauren and devising their plan of escape.

Marsh would be keeping in touch with Ian and her family, letting them know location and plans, but it was up to Sabrina to create the diversion. She sure as hell hoped that opportunity presented itself immediately upon arrival at their final destination. Otherwise she was going to get decidedly cranky.

At last the car came to a smooth stop and within seconds the trunk popped open. Sabrina pulled in fresh air, grateful to be breathing something besides warm, toxic fumes.

His face set hard and expressionless, Marsh pulled her from the trunk and dropped her on her feet. She was thankful he allowed her to stand still for a moment as her legs were almost numb. As she waited for them to wake up, she took in her surroundings.

They were at a house. Though it was dark and there was only a small porch light burning, she could see that it was a fairly large structure. Was this it then? The place where Lauren had been brought?

But where exactly was this place? The air was warm and fragrant with some kind of flowery smell, yet she couldn't place the scent. And was that the ocean? Yes, she could hear the surf in the distance. Were they in Miami? No, that didn't make sense. Even if they'd had to divert because of a thunderstorm, the flight shouldn't have taken hours.

Surprising her, Marsh reached down and sliced the tape at her ankles with a wicked looking knife. "Let's go." He grabbed her upper arm and pushed her forward.

"Where are we?"

"That's not something you need to know."

Though she knew Marsh could show no weakness or gentleness, his harsh tone and brutal grip on her arm was disconcerting.

The front door opened and hard hands pushed Sabrina forward. She barely caught herself before she fell. Turning, ready to snarl, she was hauled back up on Marsh's shoulders.

"Dammit, put me down. I can frigging walk."

"Shut up before I give you that beating you've been asking for."

Upside down once more, Sabrina couldn't see her surroundings all that well. It appeared to be a large, elegant foyer with marble flooring. The fresh scent of lemons wafted through the air. Was this Silva's house? Did he live here? Was he here now?

"Take her upstairs, third door on the right," a gruff, unfamiliar voice said.

Bouncing on Marsh's shoulders, adding bruises to her bruises, Sabrina gritted her teeth, determined not to make a sound. After what seemed an incredibly long stairway, they were finally headed down a hallway. A lock clicked and then she felt a whoosh of air as the door opened.

Marsh dumped her on the floor and, without another word, walked out. The clicking of the lock was like a final punctuation mark to her captivity.

Her hands still bound, Sabrina struggled to her knees, then to her feet. Hearing a noise behind her, she whirled around and then lost her breath.

"Welcome to your nightmare."

Silva's Yacht

Stationed in her bedroom, Lauren looked out the porthole of her suite and imagined a different life. One that didn't include fearing tomorrow, running from her past, or lying in the present.

What she had suffered at Silva's hands was not a drop in the bucket to what she would endure when he came for her. With Armando dead, the bastard had no reason to let her go or even keep her alive once he tired of her. If she was lucky, perhaps he would kill her quickly, but luck had never been on her side. She'd screwed with fate too many times to expect anything good. He would use her, hurt her, and then that would be it.

A giant light brightened the darkness outside and the sound of a helicopter hovering above told her time was up. Silva had arrived.

Lauren drew a deep breath, did her best to ignore the sobbing sound coming from her lungs. She had known this day would come. Even before Silva's men found her, she had known he would eventually seek her out for retribution. He was an unforgiving man and the blow she'd dealt him would not be forgotten or forgiven.

How many people even knew what she had done? She was guessing as few as possible. A doctor for sure since he would've had to have medical treatment, along with several stitches. Even though it would have meant certain death, she wished for the thousandth time that the knife she'd plunged into his chest that last day hadn't been deflected by a rib. If only she had been able to pierce his cold, black heart.

Footsteps sounded outside her room and Lauren turned around, prepared to face her fate.

Robert unlocked the door and pushed it open, his anticipation a living thing. Ever since he'd let her return to Cruz, he had been plotting to have her back. Her escape from Cruz had been a major setback. How he had dreamed of taking her and making her pay for what she had done to him. It had taken every ounce of his patience not to annihilate Cruz the moment he'd heard of Lauren's disappearance.

Other than the woman in front of him, no one living knew what she had done to him, what he had suffered. He had managed to hide the injury until he could get to his personal physician. It was a convenience that the doctor had croaked not long after that. Made things easier all around.

And here stood the woman who'd dealt him that blow. Her head was cocked arrogantly. That look of insolence had challenged him the first time Cruz had brought her around. Like she believed she was more than she actually was. A part of him had enjoyed her spirit. So few men or women challenged him anymore. Obedience was expected from everyone and as comfortable as that was to him, having someone actually go against him had ignited a spark he hadn't felt in years. But then she had taken it too far. It dug into the pit of his stomach that he hadn't been able to make her pay at that time. But good things come to those who wait. Robert had waited long enough.

"You're looking a little worse for wear, my dear."

"Your men weren't kind when they abducted me."

Though healing, the bruises on her face, stood out in sharp contrast to her pale, lovely skin.

"You shouldn't have resisted so vigorously. I don't like my merchandise damaged. At least not by anyone but me."

He swept his gaze up and down her lovely form, enjoying the way her body shuddered in fear. She made such an enticing picture, like a slender flame in the wind. Only this flame wouldn't be extinguished until he'd had his fill.

"I was told you were unconscious for a time. I do hope you're feeling better. I have plans for you and though it's not necessary for you to feel well, I do want you to stay conscious."

For the first time he saw the flare of panic in her eyes and he knew a moment of triumph. Defiance tempered with terror. What an aphrodisiac!

"I'll die before I let you touch me again."

"Oh, my dear. If you only knew what your challenging words do to me, you wouldn't say such things." He glanced down at his watch. "Unfortunately it's late and I've had a long trip. Once I've had a few hours sleep and something substantial to eat, I'm sure I'll be up for the challenge you seem so willing to offer."

He gave her a small, smug smile and turned to leave. The vase that had been sitting on the table flew by his head, so close that he felt a gust of air before it crashed against the wall beside him.

Without batting an eye, he continued to the door. As he opened it, he threw over his shoulder. "Clean up the mess or you'll be punished worse than you were the last time we were together."

The instant the door closed, he heard a harsh, vehement curse. Yes, he was quite pleased with her.

CHAPTER FIFTEEN

Midnight

Ian paced, checked his watch, and then paced some more. This had been his routine since Sabrina left. Three days of not knowing where she was, or what was happening to her.

In his estimation, they were relying on Holden Marsh way too much. So what if the guy had checked out and was who and what he claimed. That wouldn't mean shit if he wasn't able to control this Silva character. If anything happened to Sabrina… if the bastard put even the slightest scratch on her… He couldn't even finish the thought. Nothing could happen to her.

"You okay?"

Ian glanced over his shoulder at Quinn Braddock. Samantha's fiancé was sprawled in a chair across the room. Though he appeared relaxed, Ian knew those sharp eyes had missed nothing.

He hadn't asked but got the feeling Quinn had been assigned to him. As chief of police, Zach had his hands full taking care of the citizens of Midnight. Brody James had gone back to Mobile to handle some business, and Logan Wright was in the midst of gathering enough equipment to face a full-fledged Armageddon. And Sabrina's sisters were digging deep to find what they could on Silva.

Even though Quinn was in the middle of renovating offices to open his medical practice, he'd apparently put things on hold until this case was over. So in the meantime, Samantha's fiancé had been glued to Ian.

Did they think he would go out on his own?

Okay, maybe at one time he would've. But he trusted Wildefire Security and had complete faith in Sabrina's family. They were as motivated as he was to bringing her home safely.

"I'll be okay as soon as Sabrina's back home."

"I've been there, you know."

Ian nodded, knowing Quinn spoke the truth. Last year, around Thanksgiving, Samantha had been taken, had almost died. Ian had been with Sabrina when Savannah had called and told her what was happening. That event had been one of the biggest reasons Sabrina hadn't told her family about what she'd gone through with Cruz.

He wondered if her family knew how very much she had shielded and protected them.

"You and Samantha went through hell."

Quinn gave an abrupt nod. "The Wilde women are survivors. They may look delicate on the outside, but their steel is bone deep."

Yeah, he'd seen that toughness first hand. He knew what Sabrina Wilde was made of. He also knew she was sometimes too gutsy for her own good.

"She—" The ring of Ian's cellphone caused both men to stand. Showing how on edge everyone in the house was, Savannah and Samantha rushed into the room with Logan right on their heels.

Ian pressed answer and then the speaker keys, allowing everyone to hear.

"We're in," Marsh said. "Sabrina's fine."

Ian glared down at the phone. "What the hell took you so long to contact us?"

"Had a little glitch. Lauren's not here."

"What do you mean she's not there?" Logan growled from the doorway.

"He's got her stashed someplace else."

"Dammit, that's the only reason Bri's there," Samantha said. "We've got to get her out of there before—"

Marsh cut her off. "No, not yet."

"What do you mean not yet? What are you holding back on us, Marsh?"

"Not a damn thing, Mackenzie. I have it on good authority that Silva is with Lauren now. He's due to arrive soon. I believe he'll bring her with him. We need to keep Sabrina here until they arrive."

"And just how long do you plan to wait?"

"As long as it takes."

"Like hell, Marsh," Ian snarled. "She's—"

"Look, she's in absolutely no danger. She's locked in a room… no one can get to her."

Before he could protest again, a gentle hand touched Ian's arm, squeezed gently. "Marsh, it's Savannah. Did Bri tell you anything to say to us?"

"Uh, yeah." Marsh's voice held mild confusion. "She said to tell you 'Roll Tide.'"

A smile curved Savannah's mouth as she looked over at her sister.

Ian would have asked her why they were smiling but Savannah held her finger to her lips and shook her head to keep him quiet.

"What's the location, Marsh?"

"Ensenada, Mexico. Address is 1001 Rico Road. There might be a problem, though."

"What?"

"There are three other women here."

"By choice?" Samantha asked.

"No. Hell no."

"Then we've got our work cut out for us."

"We can bring in more people if we need them," Logan said.

"How many men does Silva have at the house?"

"Three, not counting me. I don't know how many he'll bring when he arrives with Lauren. When I—

"Shit," Marsh said softly, urgently. "Gotta go. Someone's coming. I'll be in touch soon."

The line went dead and for several seconds everyone just looked at each other. Ian glanced over at Sabrina's sisters and broke the silence. "What's the Roll Tide message mean?"

"It's her code," Samantha answered. "Only the three of us know about. If everything's okay, she's to say 'Roll Tide.'

The tension in eased Ian's spine. Such a little thing but he felt a hell of a lot better.

"I'll get online…see if there's a blueprint to the house." Savannah said.

"We'll need a plane," Ian said.

Zach put in. "I got a buddy with a plane in Mobile. He's offered it and his pilot anytime I want to use it. I'll give him a call."

Logan started for the door. "Now that we know it's a private home and we've got more than Lauren and Sabrina to rescue, we may need some different gear. We also need to make sure we can get our weapons into the country without getting caught."

"I can help you with that." Quinn went to follow him. "I have some contacts down there."

"Quinn, I—"

Glancing over his shoulder at Samantha, Quinn shook his head. "Don't even think about it, Sam. We've talked about this already. We're in this together."

Samantha shook her head. "I just wanted—"

"Landsakes, looks like y'all are having a party in here."

Everyone turned to the door where Sabrina's Aunt Gibby stood. Her bright, cheerful statement didn't hide the worry in her eyes. The elderly woman was no fool.

"It's just work, Aunt Gibby," Savannah said. "Did you need something? Is the baby okay?"

"Everything's fine, Savannah Rose. She's sleeping like a lamb. I just came down for a snack and heard what sounded like a pretty intense discussion." Her sharp eyes roamed the room. "Where's Sabrina Sage?"

"She's...uh, she's..." Samantha bit her lip and looked around the room for help.

Knowing how Sabrina and her sisters felt about their aunt, Ian figured Samantha was torn between telling the truth and lying to someone she loved. He helped her out by saying, "She's working away from home right now, Miss Gibby."

"But she's okay?"

"She's just fine, Aunt Gibby." Savannah wrapped an arm around her aunt's shoulders and led her from the room. "Why don't we go grab that snack?"

Showing everyone she wasn't easily fooled, the elderly woman looked over her shoulder. "I trust that she'll be returning home safely and real soon."

The instant Gibby was out of earshot, Samantha gave Ian a grateful smile. "Thanks for the save. I didn't want to lie to her, but my brain froze for a suitable answer."

"No problem. Besides Sabrina would've skinned my hide if her Aunt Gibby became upset." He glanced around the room. "Okay, now that we know our location, let's get to work and make this happen."

CHAPTER SIXTEEN

Ensenada, Mexico

They had been here for months. Three women. Abused. Traumatized. Prisoners.

They lived in an oversized bedroom, slept on cots, shared a bathroom. It was like an old school dormitory. And the stories they'd already shared revealed more about Robert Silva than anything Holden Marsh could have said. These women, for whatever reason, had caught Robert Silva's eye and apparently whatever Silva wanted, Silva took.

The plan was to rescue Lauren. The plan hadn't changed, the number had just increased. No way in hell was she leaving these women behind.

Fully aware of the danger of revealing any information that wasn't absolutely necessary for them to know, Sabrina maintained her role. Until this was over, she was a captive just like them.

Marsh had only been by one time to check on her. He'd been obnoxious and so vulgar, Sabrina had experienced some serious moments of doubt. Could he have fooled them? Was he as evil as he seemed and she was now a victim like these other women?

She'd squashed the doubts. There had been an audience…
it had been all for show. Besides, Holden Marsh had to excel at
deep cover. He'd been inside Silva's organization for almost two
years. The man had more than a convincing way with sleaze.

She had wanted to give a little of her own back simply because
being talked to in that manner was infuriating. However, more
than anything she had wanted to give her sisters a message—their
agreed upon one. So instead of snarling out curses, she'd jumped
on his back and growled her message in his ear.

He'd thrown her down, thankfully on a bed, spewed a couple
more insults and then left. She'd seen the questions in his eyes,
but that didn't matter. Her sisters would ask if she'd said anything
and he would relay the message.

"Do you have a husband, boyfriend, or a lover?"

As Sabrina turned to the woman who'd asked the question,
Ian's handsome face appeared in her mind, his features were
imprinted on her brain. She had traced his face a thousand times
with her fingers and knew that even if she never saw him again,
she would never forget him. Nor would she forget his strong,
solid embrace, forthrightness, and rock solid character. They were
qualities she could look a lifetime for in other men and never find.

"Yes," Sabrina whispered softly. "I do."

"Then he's who you need to think about when you're
being raped."

"Shit, Donna!" Claudia snapped. "What kind of advice
is that?"

"The best I got. She's got a choice of letting what happens to
her rot her insides or think about something else. Either way, it's
going to happen. You know damn well why she's here."

She'd only been here three days but had already gotten
to know the women and their personalities. Donna, with

her strawberry blonde hair and light blue eyes, was the street smart one, doling out biting sarcasm but blending it with a surprising compassion.

Claudia, who had long, black hair and delicately fine features, was the motherly one, who tried to reassure and bolster.

And then there was Ashley. Silky blonde hair, sparkling gray eyes, and the kind of sculptured cheekbones that only models are born with. For whatever reason, Ashley treated the other women as rivals for the same man. She was a prisoner just like they were but had made it clear she planned to stay on Silva's good side.

Sabrina got the idea that Ashley somehow believed Silva would be so pleased with her, he would want her exclusively. Though that seemed odd, Sabrina knew there were all sorts of ways to handle trauma. Perhaps this was just Ashley's.

All the women were beautiful, all between twenty-five and thirty years old. Another thing they had in common that was no surprise—they were all alone in the world—no family. Just like Lauren. And just like Sabrina's cover, Lilah Green.

The accommodations were prison-like in that they were incredibly confining. The women ate together, slept in the same room, spending all of their time with one another. And when Silva was in residence, they were his to do with as he wanted.

Though the women were different in many respects, all three had been surprisingly open about what they were here for and what was expected of them. Because of their openness, she'd questioned them extensively and was glad to hear one theme from all of them. They might be resigned to their fate, but none of them wanted to be here.

She didn't tell them anything about her mission. They would have questions that didn't yet have answers. Neither did she want to give them false hope. None of them were safe yet.

A major worry remained—where was Lauren? Was she being kept in another part of the house? Was she even now being assaulted by Silva and Sabrina was sitting here like an idiot waiting? The thought whirled constantly in her head.

The house was large and though she'd only been in the bedroom, living room and the pool area, she had seen no evidence that another woman was being held. She told herself not to worry…that Marsh had things under control. And she trusted her family and co-workers to know when the time was right. Things would work out.

And when she and Lauren did escape, so would these women.

It was late afternoon when Ian and the team arrived in Ensenada. Keeping a low profile was imperative. According to Marsh, Silva had spies everywhere. If they'd arrived looking like they wanted to kick ass, people would have taken notice. Instead, they looked like a group of men who'd come to fish a little and drink a lot. A buddy bonding time.

The only anomaly to the group was Samantha, but if she stayed low-key, no one should question her presence. Quinn had taken his life into his hands and remarked that she could claim she'd come as their cook. The fire in her eyes had made Ian long for Sabrina so badly he had felt the ache to his soul.

He'd worked his ass off, staying busy so he wouldn't worry about her. She was one of the craftiest, most talented investigators he'd ever known. Undercover work wasn't new to either one of them. But this one worried him more than any other. Robert Silva wasn't just a bad man who needed to pay for his crimes… he was pure evil. He was responsible for multiple murders, the abduction, abuse, and rape of who knew how many women, treating them as if they were less than human.

Sabrina had been up against bad men before but none like Silva.

They hadn't heard anything from Marsh since that first phone call with the location of the house. He wouldn't call back until Silva arrived with Lauren.

Ian hadn't expected to hear any news until that happened, but he had wished for something…anything that would reassure him that Sabrina was okay.

Knowing there was nothing they could do until they got word, he called out, "Once we unload our gear, let's take a look-see around."

With minimal words, they proceeded to empty their vehicles. Several of their weapons were cleverly disguised as fishing gear.

Ian grabbed his duffel bag, along with his weapons bag, and headed toward the beach house they'd rented. They had everything they needed for a successful mission except for the go-ahead.

Ian set his bags down in a bedroom and then roamed through the house. "Nice digs, Braddock."

Quinn nodded. "We got lucky with the location, too. Bunch of guys…" He shot Samantha a wicked grin. "And a good-looking cook renting a house fifteen miles from Silva's house won't attract anyone's attention."

Samantha, who was unloading some of her weapons from a bag, looked up at her fiancé and laughed. "It'd serve you right if I did cook something. Your stomach would never be the same."

"That's what I'm talking about."

Logan, who'd been the quietest of them all, now had a look on his face that could only be described as relieved. He was reading something on his laptop.

"What?" Brody asked.

"Savannah uncovered the blueprints."

A collection of thankful sighs exploded in the room. When they'd left Midnight, Savannah had been pushing through all sorts of firewalls and security blocks to get the blueprints for Silva's house. Hard enough to do that, but she'd also had to avoid sending up any red flags. If Silva got wind of the rescue, they were fried. And Sabrina and Lauren would pay the price.

"Print them out." Ian said. "We'll study them before we head to the house."

Within minutes, they had the schematics spread over the dining room table. The house was large but not so big that it would attract attention of curious sightseers. Two and a half stories of modern architecture of stone, steel, and glass. Four bedrooms on the second floor, one on the first. Since there was a tiny attic and no basement, chances were good that the women were held on the second floor in one or more of the bedrooms. Marsh had been sketchy on details with his first and only phone call. They'd get more when he called back.

Ian took one last look and stepped back. "Let's go take a look."

In one agreement, they loaded back into their vehicles. To anyone who saw them, they were there for fun, fishing, and more than a couple of beers. Only they knew that their purpose had nothing to do with fun and everything to do with saving the lives of five women, including one of their own.

CHAPTER SEVENTEEN

The bedroom door opened and a cold, male voice said, "You got company."

Sabrina looked up from the book she'd been trying to read. The other women had been right about one thing—the waiting was one of the worst parts.

Lauren Kendall stumbled into the room. Honey golden hair tangled, a vicious looking bruise marred her left cheek. She looked so different from the way Sabrina had last seen her, she was almost unrecognizable. But her eyes, golden brown and full of life, were unmistakable.

For the first time in days, Sabrina breathed an easy breath. Marsh had been right—now to get all the women out of here without anyone getting hurt or killed.

"You. Come with me."

Her focus had been on Lauren so Sabrina hadn't noticed that the man who'd shoved Lauren into the room was still there and was pointing at her.

"Me?"

"Don't make me come over there, girl."

Sabrina stiffened her spine. Okay, she had known this would happen. Silva would want to see her, question her. She could only pray that was all he wanted.

As she passed by, Lauren's eyes widened in recognition. Sabrina gave a tiny, almost imperceptible shake of her head in warning. To carry this off, they needed to maintain their roles. Sabrina Wilde and Lauren Kendall did not know each other in this scenario.

The man the other girls had referred to as 'Buck' snapped, "Hands behind your back."

Fighting or protesting would do no good. Besides, until her team arrived, it was pointless. If she resisted, she'd only get hurt. By now Marsh had notified the team that Lauren was here. Anytime they wanted to raid the house was just fine by her.

She complied and was surprised at the gentleness he used in zip tying her wrists. She would like to think his easy handling had something to do with his humanity, but she had a feeling it had more to do with orders from Silva. He wouldn't want his merchandise to be damaged…at least not by anyone but him.

They walked down a long, carpeted hallway and then Buck stopped at a door and gave a short, polite knock. The door swung open and Marsh stood before her. His eyes were cool and dark, his mouth set to grim. Sabrina felt a shiver to her bone. This man was just a little too convincing in his bad guy role.

Marsh backed away and Buck pushed her forward.

"Welcome, Delilah. Or should I call you Lilah?"

She and Marsh had briefly discussed how to handle the meeting with Silva. Since he looked upon women as some sort of subhuman species for his use and enjoyment, Sabrina didn't think it mattered how she acted with him. He would see what he wanted to see.

A man sat behind a massive oak desk. She knew Silva was in his early fifties but had aged well. He was an attractive man—dark hair, a little silver on the sides, dark eyes, good cheekbones. Maybe a little weak in the chin, lips a little too thick. Still, very distinguished looking. He could be a politician...or someone's grandfather.

That thought gave her shivers. Daniel Wilde, Sabrina's grandfather, had been the most honorable and kindest man she'd ever known. He had nothing in common with this lowlife creep.

She raised her chin, defiance stamped on her face. Since she didn't know exactly how to play it, all she could be was who she was. "Why am I here? Who are you?"

He didn't answer, just stared at her as if she were some sort of specimen he was studying.

With her hands tied behind her back, two men behind her, one of them Marsh, she could do nothing but stand there and glare. He probably expected her to cry, beg, or plead. That wasn't going to happen.

"You look nothing like the girl I remember." His eyes never leaving Sabrina, Silva said, "Marsh, you're sure this is the right one?"

"Yes sir. She was in disguise with Walker."

His eyes roamed up and down as if he were considering purchasing livestock and then he gave a disapproving sort of grunt. "Hair's too damn short. Tits half the size of what I'd been led to believe."

Oh there were so many things she would like to say to this pervert. However, if he didn't like her looks, maybe she could at least escape his attentions. His next words divested her of that hope.

"I do like her legs though and her face is exquisite. Armando liked her mouth and I can see why."

Remembering what Cruz wanted her to do with her mouth, Sabrina felt a shudder run through her. Reverting to her standby when she was afraid, she deflected with biting sarcasm. "So this is the only way you can get women? Kidnap them? You lowlife, scum sucking, disgusting piece of crap."

She expected anger, possibly retribution, but the light in his eyes said something different. He got off on the spirited ones. Is that why he was obsessed with Lauren?

"Tsk. Tsk," Silva said mildly. "Such common language from such a lovely young woman." He opened his desk drawer, pulled something from it and threw it behind Sabrina. "Marsh, if you would be so kind?"

Before she knew what was happening, a large hand smacked duct tape over her mouth.

Silva grinned, revealing slightly yellowing teeth. "That's much better. I'll have your mouth uncovered when it's time for it to be put to use."

She refused to shudder again or show the slightest amount of fear.

"So, Lilah, you intrigued me from the moment I saw you, but you've caused me some aggravation as well. Since you're a woman, that's certainly no surprise. It comes with the territory from your kind. However, it does tend to put me in a sour mood."

Since she couldn't respond verbally, she allowed her eyes to speak for her. Besides, what would she said? Sorry I escaped from a kidnapping? Please forgive me for trying to save my life?

Surprising her, Silva ordered, "Untie her hands."

In seconds, the zip ties were removed.

"Take off your clothes."

She froze, stopped breathing. She was dressed in jeans and a T-shirt. It's what she'd been wearing when she arrived and she had no plans to take them off until she was home. No way in hell was she going to allow this bastard to touch her. He'd have to kill her first.

Maintaining a tough demeanor when your mouth is covered and your knees are shaking wasn't easy. Sabrina reminded herself that she had worn bravado as a second skin for many years. She could damn well do this.

The sound of a chair rolling on the floor pulled her from her self-lecture. Silva stood, leaned over his desk and barked, "Do what I said. Now!"

Instead of taking her clothes off, she made use of her free hands to rip the tape from her mouth. "No way in hell, you freaking pervert."

"Why you little—"

"Mr. Silva."

Never had she been happier to hear Holden Marsh's voice.

Without moving his gaze from Sabrina, Silva said, "You have a problem with my request, Mr. Marsh?"

"Not all, sir. She's yours to enjoy as you see fit. It's just the men are getting a little restless. One of your public performances might put them in a better frame of mind."

A slick coat of dread spread throughout her body.

"That's a brilliant suggestion, Marsh. And as defiant as this bit of fluff seems to be, she'll make excellent entertainment." He waved his hand as if he were some kind of emperor. "Set it up. Two o'clock this afternoon, in the main parlor."

"Yes sir."

A smile spread over Silva's face, transforming it from attractive to demonically evil. Sabrina saw in him the man who had killed, raped, and destroyed lives without conscience.

"Take her back to her room. Tell the other girls to bathe and prepare her for a performance. They know what I expect."

A hand grasped her arm to pull her around. When she whirled, she glared up at Marsh. What she saw didn't reassure her. He looked almost as evil as Silva.

Hard hands pushed her forward toward the open door. On legs that were shaking now in relief, she was grateful to make it to the door without collapsing. Time enough to do that when she got out of Silva's sight.

As she reached the door, she heard Silva's voice as he apparently answered a phone. The urgency in the man's voice made her want to stop and listen.

"What do you mean she— Slow down, dammit, and tell me—"

She was shoved out the door and as it closed behind her, she heard a vicious curse and the sound of breaking glass. Whatever news Silva just received had put him in a violent temper. She just hoped to hell the rescue team arrived before she was forced to face that violence.

"Here. You didn't eat much when we came in."

Ian twisted around from the window he'd been staring through for the past couple of hours and took the turkey sandwich Samantha held out to him. Instead of telling her that any food he tried to eat stuck in his throat, he just gave her a nod of thanks.

Returning his gaze to the window, he said quietly, "I can't help but worry about her."

"She's going to be okay. Bri always lands on her feet."

He didn't bother to dispute her. It was true—Sabrina did have an amazing ability to extricate herself from sticky situations. But there were things her sisters didn't know. Cases she'd been involved with that had come close to ending her life. What he had told her their last morning together was the stuff of his nightmares. One of these days her luck wouldn't hold, he wasn't going to be there to save her, and that bullet she'd been dodging would finally hit its target. The thought of the light dimming in her bright beautiful eyes tore at his gut.

No. Just no. That would not happen on his watch. He'd damn well make sure of it.

After doing a long distance observation and perimeter search, the team had returned to the house, grabbed some food, and reviewed their plan. Now all they could do was wait to hear from Marsh.

"Did she take wild chances when she was a kid, too?"

"A few." Samantha grimaced. "After our parents' deaths, we all changed in some way. Savvy buried herself in books, I buried myself in every school activity or social event I could. And Bri…" She swallowed hard.

"What? How did Sabrina change?"

"She shut down completely the first few days after it happened. Couldn't talk…wouldn't talk. Not to anyone. Not Savvy, not me. It was like something had died inside her."

Her mouth tilted in a sad little smile. "She had always been the most mischievous of us. Had the wildest ideas and schemes but they were always done in fun, kind of lighthearted. You know?"

Yes he did know. He'd seen occasional glimpses of that lightheartedness. And then, as if she remembered something, a shadow would come over her, like a cloud passing over the sun, and the façade would be back in place.

"After their deaths, she buried her true self beneath a veneer of toughness…an attitude…" The struggle to explain something she didn't understand apparent in her expression. "I don't know. It's like she started acting as if she didn't give a damn. And the thing is, I think it's because she cared so damn much. Even though it almost destroyed Savvy and me, I think Mama and Daddy's deaths affected Bri even more. Like it killed a part of her, too.

"We thought, or at least we'd hoped, that when she met Tyler, we'd get the old Bri back. For a while we did. Not the lighthearted

Bri we'd known, but some of the darkness seemed to have been lifted from her. Then, well, you know what happened."

A familiar rage engulfed Ian at the mention of Finley's name. "First dead man I wish I could bring back to life so I could put him in the ground myself."

"Believe me, we all felt the same way. She'd always been so distrustful of people…always looking for a hidden agenda. And then when she finally lowers her guard…"

"The asshole proves her theory that people can't be trusted."

"Exactly. But you've been so good for her, Ian. Savvy and I had almost decided that she'd never trust another man again."

"I wish I could get her to trust me with her heart."

"Don't give up on her. You're exactly what she needs. Someone who loves her for who she is. You know her darkness as well as her light."

Yeah, he knew her. And knowing her as well as he did, he had little hope she would ever change her mind about their relationship. Sabrina in many ways was still a mystery. She had secrets she wouldn't share, demons that haunted her, day and night. It was hard to stay optimistic about a future with her when she refused to trust him with the deepest parts of herself.

The cellphone lying on the coffee table blared a loud chime. His heart leaping to his throat, Ian stalked over and pressed the answer key. "Mackenzie."

Marsh's tone was urgent, his words clipped. "Thirty minutes."

Ian looked up at the eager, determined faces of the rescue party. "Let's go."

CHAPTER EIGHTEEN

"What are you doing here?"

Lauren's harsh whisper brought Sabrina's head around. After being shoved back into the bedroom by Buck with the gruff words "Boss says get her ready," Sabrina had been staring at the door, waiting. For what, she didn't know. But something had happened, or was about to happen. The phone call Silva received when she'd been going out the door had infuriated him. Did it have anything to do with her? With Lauren?

Sabrina didn't know if she needed to find out more or wait for the team to arrive. Had Silva somehow been alerted to what was about to go down? What if Silva had men waiting for the rescue team? It could be a slaughter.

No, she had to go with her gut, which told her that Holden Marsh was legit. If something had changed, he would let her know. She had to trust her that.

Turning, she gave Lauren a quick nod of approval, kept her voice low. "Good to see you."

"What's going on?" Lauren whispered. "How on earth did he get you, too?"

"Are you okay?" Claudia asked. "Why are you back so soon?"

The other women crowded around Sabrina and Lauren. Claudia and Donna wore expressions of concern. The suspicious expression on Ashley's face made Sabrina cautious in her answer.

"I don't know. He got a phone call and they brought me back here."

No need to tell them about Silva's plans to entertain his men with her later. She had every hope that the rescue team would be here soon. And if not, she'd find a way, no matter what she had to do, to make sure Silva never got his hands on her.

"You two know each other?" Donna asked.

Sabrina hesitated, her eyes darting to Lauren with questions. What had Lauren told the women while she was gone? Had she blown Sabrina's cover? Maintaining their roles until this was over was the only way to ensure everyone's safety.

Showing that she did comprehend a little of the situation, Lauren said, "I thought she looked familiar, but no, I don't know her."

Claudia touched Sabrina's arm. "Come on into the bathroom. We need to get you ready. He doesn't like it if you're not prepared for him on time."

Refusing to even consider what preparing for him entailed, Sabrina pulled away. "I'm not doing a damn thing to get ready for that asshole."

Three sets of eyes went wide with fear and worry.

"But you have to," Donna said. "He'll make it hurt worse if you're not prepared."

Desperately wanting to tell them that soon they'd never have to worry about Silva ever again, Sabrina just shook her head again.

It was obvious they weren't all right with her decision, but other than to forcibly make her go through whatever preparations Silva deemed necessary, they could do nothing.

While Claudia, Donna, and Ashley gathered on the other side of the room, whispering, Sabrina took the time to talk with Lauren. Still wanting to maintain that they were strangers to each other, Sabrina kept her distance and her eyes focused elsewhere. Her voice stayed low, without inflection. "So, how have you been?"

At Lauren's soft snort, Sabrina spared the other woman a glance. A glittering light of amusement gleamed in Lauren's tired, bloodshot eyes. "Oh you know, read a few books, saw a couple of good movies, got kidnapped by a psychopath. Same old, same old. How about you?"

Appreciating the woman's sense of humor, Sabrina allowed herself a small, stiff smile. "Pretty much the same."

Lauren shot a quick glance over at the women across the room and lowered her voice even more. "What are you doing here? How did he get you?"

"Would you believe I came willingly?"

"Hell no." Breath shuddered through her. "Are you… Did you…" Tears filled her eyes. "Are you here for me?"

"Yeah, I am."

"Oh God, thank you." She closed her eyes in relief but opened them quickly again. "How are we going to get out of here? Do you have help? We can't just walk out the door." And then, with a definite wobble in her voice, she asked, "Does Logan know?"

"Logan knows. He's in on this, as is the rest of the Wildefire team. I don't know exactly how this is going to go down. Be ready for anything but know that we're getting out of here soon."

"What about them?" Lauren nodded toward the other women.

"They don't know yet, but they're coming, too. No way in hell are we leaving them behind."

Lauren sat down on the opposite end of the bed and wrapped her arms around herself. "I don't know what I'm going to say to Logan."

Even though the other woman had been through some tough times, Sabrina couldn't forget the deep pain in Logan's eyes when Lauren had disappeared without any explanation. "Hmm, 'I'm sorry' comes to mind."

"I am sorry. I just…" She shook her head. "I don't know how to explain why I ran when I don't really understand it myself. I think I just got scared that he was too good to be true. Trust is hard for me."

That was something they had in common and since it struck a little too close to home, Sabrina didn't offer any sage advice. "He's never stopped looking for you…since you left."

Lauren swallowed audibly. "Thank you for telling me that. It helps."

"I hope you guys can work things out. He's a good man."

"Yes, he is. Is that how you knew Silva had me? Logan found out somehow?"

She was sure that Lauren could keep the secret, but she didn't intend to risk anyone's safety by revealing Holden Marsh's undercover role. Lauren only needed to know that there were people working to get them out.

"I'll explain everything once we're out of here."

"Silva won't come quietly. He's a powerful man."

Apprehending Silva wasn't even part of the equation, but explaining that to Lauren would only bring about more questions. Sabrina just said vaguely, "We'll get out of here…that's a promise."

"We've come to a decision."

Sabrina stood, whirled around. She'd been so focused on her discussion with Lauren, she hadn't noticed that the other women had finished their own chatting. Sabrina watched warily as they circled around her. The intent in their expressions was easy to read. This was an ambush…for her own good, of course.

"Look, I know you were given orders, but no way in hell am I going to get ready for that creep. So just get over it. Got that?"

The move shouldn't have surprised her, but it did. A pillowcase covered her head. Someone grabbed her arms and pushed her forward.

"Oh for heaven's sake. Seriously?" Digging in her heels, Sabrina refused to budge.

"Don't make it hard on yourself." She recognized Claudia's voice, which held a distinct hint of tears.

She really didn't want to hurt the women. They were scared. And if they didn't do as they were told, they would most likely be punished. However, she had to be prepared to aid in the rescue when it went down. That certainly couldn't include whatever kind of grooming ritual these women intended to perform on her.

Wrenching her arms out of their grasps, she jerked the pillowcase from her head. "I'm going to tie all three of you up if you don't leave me alone."

"We're doing this for your own good," Ashley snapped.

Claudia nodded. "She's right. I once forgot to shave my legs and he got really mad."

Torn between sadness and amusement, Sabrina backed out of their reach. "I don't care if my legs rival Sasquatch's in hairiness, I am not going to prepare myself for that slug. So back off. Now!"

Claudia and Donna backed away, apparently taking her at her word. Sabrina only got a glimpse of the determined light in Ashley's eyes an instant before the woman attacked. Leaping onto Sabrina's back, she pushed her to the floor and tried to straddle her.

Sabrina rolled, flipping the woman over, facedown onto the carpet. Straddling her back, she twisted Ashley's arms behind her. "I really don't want to hurt you, but you're half an inch from pissing me off."

Ashley squealed and lurched up, trying to throw Sabrina. "Let me go, you bitch."

"Not until you settle down."

"It'll serve you right if he gives you a good beating for being so disobedient."

"Yeah, well, he can just shove his—"

The sound of a man clearing his throat had all eyes turning to the door.

Arms folded, his back leaning against the doorframe as if he hadn't a care in the world, stood the most beautiful sight imaginable. That sensuous mouth she'd kissed thousands of times was turned up in a big, teasing grin.

"Now if you were only in your underwear and pillow feathers were flying around you, my fantasy would be complete."

Sabrina blew a strand of hair from her eyes. "What are you doing here?"

"Giving you a lift home. But if you want to finish up, don't let me stop you. I'll be glad to wait." His grin grew bigger. "And watch."

Releasing the still struggling woman, Sabrina got to her feet. "Where's Silva?"

"Apparently he had an emergency at home and had to leave. Took all of his men but one. And that man is out of commission for a few hours."

Breath whooshed out of her. After all the worrying and planning, they were going to be able to walk out of the house without bloodshed.

"What's going on?" Donna asked.

Sabrina turned back to the women who'd given up hope of ever escaping from Robert Silva. Never had she been happier to deliver good news. "Ladies, you're going home."

CHAPTER NINETEEN

Chicago
Silva's Estate

"I don't want to hear another damn excuse! I want to know how they got away from you."

"I don't know, Mr. Silva…honest, I don't. Mrs. Silva went into the salon, just like she's done every third Thursday for the past ten years."

"And you didn't think it strange that she took my four children with her, plus the damn nanny?"

"No sir. She does that a lot."

Knowing an explosion inside him was imminent, Robert stalked away before he could do bodily harm to the idiot standing before him. Oh the man would be punished…no doubt about that, but not yet. Not until Robert had all the information necessary.

"What did the people inside the salon tell you?"

"That Mrs. Silva had cancelled her appointment two days before. No one expected her to come in and when she did, only the receptionist saw her. She stated…" The man glanced down at his notes, apparently wanting to make sure he got the words correct. Robert noted with some satisfaction that his hand was trembling.

"Her words were: "We're in the city for some shopping, but my little ones need to go potty. Is it okay to use your facilities?"

He raised worried eyes back to Robert. "They were given permission and all of them went to the back. The receptionist said she got busy and didn't notice that they never came out. She assumed they had and she'd missed them."

"And?" Robert said with lethal quietness.

"A camera shows them going out the backdoor to the alley behind the building. There's no camera in the alleyway so there's no way to know how they escaped." He swallowed hard and amended, "I mean...left."

"I see."

"Mr. Silva, sir...I deeply apologize. I know it's my responsibility to keep an eye on your family and I screwed up."

"What about the trackers inside my wife?"

"Since I didn't know she was gone for a couple of hours, by the time I checked the monitor, the trackers had already stopped functioning. They must've been removed and destroyed right there in the alleyway."

He truly didn't know who he was angrier with—Erica, who had known from the first day of their engagement that running from him would mean dire consequences, or the man Robert had charged with making sure she never had the chance to run.

She had to have been planning this for a long time. When he'd first gotten the call, he had assumed she left because of their last encounter when she had asked to come with him and he had shown her once again what her purpose was. But disappearing without a trace, finding someone to remove the trackers, having money to do such things, would have required substantial planning. While she had been enjoying the wealth and status of being married to one of the most powerful men in the world, the bitch had been plotting to leave him.

"Who has she seen, where has she been over the last month? I want a complete list of her activities, including all of her friends and associates."

"No place different, Mr. Silva. I send you her weekly agenda, just like you told me to. She's done nothing different."

Hell, he didn't keep up with those things. He usually took a thirty second perusal of her agenda and deleted it. He didn't care where she went or what she did as long as nothing negative reflected back on him. "Send them to me again."

"Yes, sir."

"What about her friends, any new ones?"

"She really doesn't have any friends, sir."

That was because she was as boring and useless as a wad of chewed gum. But she was his, dammit.

"What about phone calls?"

"I—"

"What?"

"When I was going through her receipts a couple of weeks ago, I noticed she'd purchased something at an electronics store. When I questioned her, she said it was a battery operated toy for your son. She showed me the toy."

"And?"

"When she disappeared, I called the store to verify that the toy was the only thing she purchased. It wasn't. Apparently she used a credit card for the toy but also paid cash for a prepaid cellphone."

Just as he'd figured, she'd had help. No way could she have done this on her own. Not when Robert had ensured that she never had a dime in currency.

"Do you enjoy your job, Antonio?"

Another hard swallow. "Yes sir, very much, sir. I'll do anything to keep it."

"The only way you'll be able to keep it is to find my wife and children. Do you understand this?"

"Yes sir. I'll do whatever I have to do to find them."

"Excellent. And just in case you need extra incentive to ensure your success, I took the liberty of providing it."

Before Antonio could ask him what that might be, Robert pressed a buzzer on his desk. Marsh entered the room.

"Is it done?" Robert asked.

"Yes sir."

"Show Antonio the photographs."

Marsh withdrew a stack from his coat pocket and handed them to Antonio.

The color drained from the man's face. His eyes wide and filled with fear, he whispered hoarsely, "This is my grandmother."

"Yes it is, Antonio. The only family you have left. The woman who raised you. The only one who loves you. If you don't find my family, you lose yours. Understand?"

Instead of agreeing, Antonio turned to Marsh. "Please don't hurt her. She's an old woman. She's never done anything to anyone."

"It's not Marsh you need to be begging, it's me. But begging will do you no good." He leaned forward and whispered softly, "Find my family, Antonio, or I'll have Marsh cut her up into little pieces and stuff them down your throat. Understand?"

"Yes sir…yes sir."

"Now get out of here before I decide to kill you where you stand."

Showing that he wasn't a complete idiot, Antonio ran.

Robert walked slowly behind his desk and slumped into his chair, suddenly weary to the bone. Most of his men wouldn't be allowed to see his fatigue, but Marsh had proven his trustworthiness.

"The old woman give you any problem?"

Marsh gave a cool smirk. "She's ninety-three years old. Not a whole hell of a lot she could do."

"I don't want her dead until it's time."

"We'll keep a close eye on her. If she looks like she's about to keel over, we'll get her some help."

"I'm putting all my available men on the search, but I want you to head it up."

"Yes sir."

"Bring my family back to me, Marsh, and there will be a considerable reward for you."

"I'll do my best, Mr. Silva."

"Update me daily. You're dismissed."

Robert's attention was distracted by the ringing cellphone on his desk. If he had been paying attention, he would have wondered about the satisfied smile on Marsh's face as the man walked out the door.

CHAPTER TWENTY

Midnight

This was what freedom felt like…something Sabrina would never take for granted again. For months she had worried that the mysterious man who had tortured and killed Cruz would find her and somehow hurt her family. Now that worry was gone. And not only that, Lauren had been found. Plus three other women had escaped Robert Silva's brutality.

It wasn't a perfect situation. No one would dispute that. Silva was still a free man, still able to kidnap, rape, and torture. Still manufacturing and selling illegal drugs. Able to do all manner of evil deeds. But Marsh had said that he was close to bringing the man to justice. Since he hadn't steered them wrong about anything else, Sabrina had to believe him on this. Someday soon, Robert Silva would get his just deserts.

And now everything could return to normal. She could stop worrying about bringing danger to her family, trouble to her town. If she wanted, she could sleep past dawn, not have to prowl the town morning and night. When a case came their way that pulled her out of town, she could take it without worry or guilt. And when the weekend came, she could go to Tallahassee and be with Ian without fear that her family wouldn't be here when she got back.

It was an irrational fear, deeply rooted in what had happened to her parents. Just because she realized where the fear came from didn't mean it went away. She'd lived with this terror for nineteen years. Most times she could squash it until just a glimmer followed her around wherever she went—a constant reminder that in the blink of an eye everything could change…everything could be lost. But for the past few months, that fear had been an all-consuming fire, just waiting to expand and destroy everything she held most dear.

"I'm loaded up. Guess I'd better get on the road."

Ian stood in the doorway, tall, broad-shouldered and handsome. Her white knight. The man she depended on for so very much.

For some odd reason she couldn't explain, she didn't want to see him go. They'd been lovers for several years. She'd said goodbye to him numerous times, but this time the impending separation, no matter how short-lived, made her ache inside.

"Do you have to leave right away? Can you sit for a spell?"

"Of course."

He settled beside her on the sofa, took her hand. "What's got you so melancholy looking? Everything turned out even better than we anticipated."

"You're right. Lauren is safe, back with Logan."

"And hopefully will stick around this time."

From the reunion Sabrina had witnessed at Silva's house, she was almost sure that Lauren Kendall's days of running were finally over. The woman had thrown herself into Logan's arms as if she'd never let him go. And there'd been a determined light in Logan's eyes. One that said he would make sure Lauren had no cause to want to run ever again.

Sabrina turned Ian's hand over, noting both the strength and elegance of it. Her fingers gently traced a light scar that ran up the length of his arm. Most of them were only noticeable if one looked closely. How many times had she touched these scars, thought about how she might never have known him if his injuries had been worse? How empty her life would have been.

"Sabrina...sweetheart? What's wrong?"

Unable and unwilling to put a name to her gloomy mood, she shook her head and did what she'd always done—deflected. "Think we'll ever hear from Marsh again?"

"Maybe. Once Silva finally gets put away."

A shiver zipped up her spine. "Can't be soon enough for me."

"At least once he's arrested there'll be plenty of people who'll be glad to testify. The testimonies of Claudia, Donna, and Ashley alone should be enough to put him away for a couple of lifetimes."

"You think they'll be okay?"

"They have a better chance now than they did with Silva, that's for sure."

"I just feel like I should've done more for them."

"Like what? You helped rescue them, brought them to Mobile, put them up in a hotel, gave them money to travel back to their homes and offered to pay for counseling." He touched her cheek, softly, gently, "Sweetheart, you've done more than enough."

The women had been heartbreakingly grateful. Seeing their relief and happiness had made every moment of fear or discomfort worthwhile. Two of them wanted to return to their home states—Claudia to Texas, Ashley to Oregon. Donna had decided to stay in Mobile for a few days until she figured out what she wanted to do. Sabrina had offered to help her find a job, but she had turned her down, saying she wanted to stand on her own for now.

Whatever the women ultimately decided to do, Ian was right. At least now they had a chance.

"It was fun working with you on this. I miss that."

"I do, too. Working with the entire Wildefire Security Agency was great. You've got a good team."

"You could be a part of it, you know. You'd make a wonderful addition to the team."

The words were out before she could stop them. Though they were impulsive, they were true. Ian would be an asset to their agency. She knew what his answer would be before he opened his mouth.

"I appreciate the offer, but I've worked hard to establish myself in Tallahassee."

She gave an awkward shrug, self-conscious for having made the offer. She never used to be so needy. "It was just a thought."

Ian searched Sabrina's face for several seconds. Try as he might, he couldn't gauge her mood. Most times he could read her well enough, even when he didn't always understand her. Today though, she had a vulnerable, almost nervous air about her. And knowing her as he did, she wouldn't tell him if he asked what was going on.

He took the hand that still held his and kissed it, his mouth lingering on her soft skin, savoring her delicate fragrance. The urge to bundle her up and take her with him was a living thing. Leaving Sabrina even for a few days always felt like a slash to his heart. When she was in one of these rare vulnerable moods, he felt the pain even more so.

"I know you'll be busy this week, catching up from being gone for so long, but how bout I come to your place this weekend? Maybe stay a few extra days."

Her words made him smile. She finally felt safe leaving Midnight, leaving her family on their own.

"I haven't seen my mom and dad in a few weeks so I thought I'd go for a quick visit. Come with me."

Perhaps it was unfair of him, but he'd deliberately put her in a difficult spot. She couldn't claim she needed to stay in Midnight, couldn't say she couldn't spare the time. She had no viable excuse. Still, he wasn't surprised when she gave him one.

"Maybe some other time. You need to spend some time with your family without me tagging along."

"So that's the reason you won't come with me...because you'd be in the way? Cut the bullshit, Sabrina. At least be willing to tell the truth. Being around my family makes you uncomfortable for one reason only—they want to know when we're going to make our relationship permanent and that's not something you want to talk about...or hell, even think about."

"That's not true, Ian."

With deliberate slowness, he pulled his hand from hers and stood. And since he was way too tempted to grab her and give her a good, hard shake, he took several long steps away from her.

"Lying doesn't look good on you, Sabrina. Don't start now."

"I'm not lying. It's just—"

Her struggle couldn't have been more apparent. The need to come up with something other than the bald-faced truth—that she didn't want a permanent commitment with him.

"Dammit all, I am not Tyler Finley."

"This has nothing to do with Tyler. I'm just not ready to make a long-term commitment. I don't know why we can't continue the way we are. We're good together this way."

"Yes, we are, but here's the problem. I want to spend the rest of my life with you, not just the weekends or the odd holiday. I love you, Sabrina…everything about you, even the things that drive me crazy. You're the most courageous, intelligent, strong-willed, stubborn, talented, maddening, beautiful creature I've ever met. I want the right to wake up to your smile every morning, have you sleep in my arms every night."

"We can still do that. I… If you can't come to work here, maybe I could move back to Tallahassee…work from there. I could talk to Savvy and Sammie. See how they feel about it."

"Stop lying to both of us." He took a breath. "I'm thirty-three years old, Sabrina. I've found the love of my life, the woman I want to marry, have children with, have a life with, and grow old with. You just need to decide if you want that, too."

"So, is this an ultimatum?"

"It's a statement of fact, nothing more." His laugh was a hollow sound. "Putting that look on your face when I tell you I love you is the last thing I want. It just makes me damn sad."

He went to the doorway. When he turned back to look at her, his heart almost broke. She looked even more vulnerable… so damn lost.

"I'll call you when I get home."

"I'm sorry I can't be what you need me to be, Ian. I really am."

He growled his frustration. She still didn't get it. "I don't need you to be anyone other than who you are. Maybe that's the problem—you think you need to be someone else. You don't."

He turned and walked away.

Sorrow and regret clogged her throat as she listened to Ian's vehicle start up and pull out of the drive. Every muscle, every cell in her body urged her to run after him. She fought the urge and stayed seated, unmoving. She couldn't go after him, couldn't make promises she wasn't sure she could keep. She wasn't a good bet for anything permanent. Nothing lasted forever. Why couldn't he understand that, accept what she could give? Why did things have to be so damn complicated?

He had been right and wrong about Tyler Finley. Her inability to commit had everything and nothing to do with her former fiancé who'd betrayed her in the worst possible way. She had taken his death hard, but thanks to her loving family she'd been on the road to accepting it as an unavoidable tragedy. When she'd learned the truth—that the man she'd loved had never really existed, that it had all been a lie—that he'd been using her to gain access to her money, she had accepted a painful reality. She didn't deserve happiness. Not after what she had done.

If only she could make Ian understand without having to tell him the truth. Not committing to him had nothing to do with her lack of feelings for him and everything to do with her need to protect both of them from future heartache.

"Bri, what's wrong?"

She jerked at the sound of Savvy's voice. She hadn't heard anything other than the sound of Ian's Jeep driving away.

"Nothing's wrong. Why?"

"Well...maybe because you have tears streaming down your face and you're gripping that pillow like it's your lifeline."

Oh hell, she hadn't realized she was crying either. What was up with that? She never cried. Never.

Wiping the tears with the back of her hand, she gave her best fake smile. "Guess it's all kind of hit me at once. I just need to get some sleep, eat a good meal or two, then I'll be right as rain."

"If you cried every time you were exhausted, you'd be swimming in tears year round." She sat beside Sabrina, took one of her hands that was still clutching the pillow. "Talk to me, sweetie. Tell me what's wrong."

"Nothing new, really. Ian just wants what I can't give him."

"And why can't you, Bri?" Before she could answer, Savvy shook her head, stopping her. "Don't say it's because you don't love him because I know you do. I've seen your face when he walks into a room. It lights up like a thousand stars. He makes you happy. He loves you, Bri. I know what love looks like. It's written all over his face. And yours.

"So tell me, Sabrina Sage Wilde, why can't you allow yourself the happiness that's clearly within your reach?"

Sabrina almost said the words. For the first time since that awful, terrible event, she almost told her sister the real reason she couldn't commit, the terrible truth of why she didn't deserve happiness, would never deserve happiness. And if she said them, she would be driving a wedge between her and her sisters that could never be breached. It would be an insurmountable, desolate barrier that nothing, not even their love for her could heal.

No. She couldn't do it. She could face down psychopaths and trained killers. She had stared death in the face several times and not flinched. But she couldn't live without her sisters' love. If they knew the truth, there would be no way to come back from that. She would lose them. She had lost so much already…she couldn't lose them, too.

"Guess I'm just not the marrying kind of girl. After Tyler, who could blame me?"

"You give Finley way too much power over your life if you continue to allow him to hurt you."

"You're right. Tyler Finley means nothing anymore other than remembering a really bad decision. It's just my track record when it comes to guys isn't the greatest."

"Are you lumping Ian in with other guys?"

"No, that was a stupid thing to say. Of course I'm not. I just can't—" She took a breath, tried again. "I just don't think a happy ever after is in my future. Not like you and Sammie."

"But why, Bri?"

Saying she didn't deserve that kind of happiness was a sure way to fire up her sister. And knowing Savvy, she'd go grab Sammie so they could gang up on her. Having them tell her how wonderful she was, and how she deserved all sorts of happiness would not go over well with her today. Having a meltdown was definitely not on her agenda.

"I'm just being silly." She went to her feet. "Want to go to Faye's and see what's going on in town. It's been forever since we've all gone there together. I'll go call Sammie."

"Bri," Savvy said softly, "don't make the same mistakes I did. Zach and I were apart for ten years because we were both too stubborn and prideful to admit our feelings. None of us are promised tomorrow. If Mama's and Daddy's deaths taught us anything, it's to never take tomorrow for granted."

Mentioning their parents' deaths was like pouring salt into an open, festering wound. She couldn't breathe, literally could not draw a breath.

Sabrina managed a hoarse "I'll call Sammie about dinner" and fled the room.

C

CHAPTER TWENTY-ONE

Ensenada, Mexico

For the second time in less than forty-eight hours, Robert was standing in an empty house demanding to know what the hell happened. True, he had left only one man in charge, but that should have been enough. They were just women. Weak, spineless creatures. And these five were weaker than most. One man should have been more than enough.

It was a conspiracy. Had to be. Two escapes in less than two days by women who probably couldn't balance their checking account—if any man had ever been foolish enough to allow them to have one.

The man left behind to guard the women, Lionel Wilson, was nervous and had every reason to be. Robert wouldn't allow this infraction to pass. He did, however, want the full story before he disposed of the idiot.

"Okay, Lionel, let's go through it once more, shall we?"

"Yes, sir, Mr. Silva." The man gave an audible, nervous swallow. "After you left, sir, I peeked in on them, just to make sure everything was okay. They were talking to each other in groups."

"What kind of groups?"

"Uh…I don't know what you mean. Just regular groups, I guess."

Really, Lionel would be lucky to see the next five minutes. Robert took another patient breath. "How were they grouped, Lionel? Who was talking to whom?"

"Well, uh…let's see. Claudia, Donna and Ashley were talking in one corner. Those two new girls…can't remember their names. They were talking to each other."

"All right. And then?"

"I closed and locked the door, like always. Came back downstairs and…"

"And what?" Robert asked softly.

"Well, I'd been awake most of the night, so I guess I fell asleep on the couch. When I woke up, I—" What little color he'd had in his face drained as his voice wobbled. "I woke up to find that my hands and feet were tied."

"You're telling me that somehow, someone tied you down without you even waking up?"

"I must've been drugged or something, Mr. Silva. That's the only explanation."

"And how were you drugged?"

"The…uh, I…uh."

Apparently realizing that Robert was on the verge of killing the man with his bare hands, Marsh interrupted to ask, "Why did it take you so long to contact Mr. Silva?"

"Well, it took me a while to get untied. Then, I did a thorough search inside and outside the house, just to make sure they weren't still around. That took a while, too."

Robert cocked his head as if in wonder. "A full day?"

"Yes, sir. I thought maybe I could take a ride through town. You know, just to see if maybe they'd been seen."

A vice was squeezing his forehead and Robert was sure his brain would explode any minute. "You went through town asking people about five runaway slaves?"

"Oh no sir, I was real discreet."

Thankfully Marsh took up the questioning again. "And you couldn't find them anywhere. Correct?"

Lionel nodded at Marsh, then turned to Robert again. "I'm real sorry, Mr. Silva."

The stupid prick had no idea just how sorry he was going to be. As much as Robert wanted to grab the letter opener from his desk and jab it into Lionel's eye, he refused to lower himself to such pettiness.

"You're fired, Lionel. Marsh, please escort this man out."

As Robert turned his back on the moron, he caught Marsh's eye and gave a slight nod. The acknowledgement was on the other man's face. He knew what to do and how to take care of it discreetly.

Lionel would pay dearly for allowing the whores to escape.

Midnight

A Wilde family gathering was often chaotic but always entertaining, especially when Aunt Gibby was added to the mix. The elderly woman had been a constant in Sabrina's and her sisters' lives for as long as they could remember.

They sat at a long, narrow table in the middle of Faye's Diner. Zach was still in his uniform and the picture of him, looking so strong and unyielding, yet holding his infant daughter in his arms as if she were made of spun glass brought a lump to Sabrina's throat. Savvy sat beside him, practically glowing as she looked at her husband and daughter.

On the opposite side were Sammie and Quinn, who in between bites of Faye's delicious chicken and dumplings, kept whispering to each other as if they were teenagers. The occasional soft laughter from Sammie and responding husky chuckle from Quinn made Sabrina smile. Less than a year ago, Sammie had almost died and Quinn had been going through his own personal hell. To see them so happy and settled was a joy.

"Now what's got you smiling so sad-like these days, Sabrina Sage?"

Turning to Gibby, Sabrina couldn't help but be cheered. Though she was in her late seventies, Gibby had the gleeful demeanor of a mischievous child.

"Not sad at all, Aunt Gibby. Just happy to see how settled and content Savvy and Sammie are."

"And wondering when that's going to happen for you? I believe Ian would make you a fine husband. He's a good upstanding man with honor and integrity. He's nothing like that rapscallion Tyler Finley."

Oh no, she would not have another conversation about this today. "How's Fred doing? Has he grown much?"

"Why he's gained ten pounds if he's gained an ounce. And his paws? I swan, they're bigger than my hands."

"I'm glad he found a home with you."

"Never thought I'd have a dog inside the house. Oscar and Samson aren't exactly dog people, but after a few tense days filled with some pretty nasty meowing, they accepted him just fine."

Sabrina grinned at her aunt's words. Oscar and Samson were cats. The fact that she had described them as not being dog people was so very Gibby. Fred had definitely found his forever home.

When Sabrina had spotted the poor, malnourished mixed breed puppy wandering down the road a few months back, she hadn't been able to resist picking him up. Though it was obvious the poor guy didn't have a home, she'd taken him to the vet. After a few days of care and searching for an owner, the vet's office had called with the news that he was now healthy and apparently belonged to no one. The first person Sabrina called on was Aunt Gibby, who'd taken one look at the puppy and promptly fallen in love.

A tall shadow loomed over them. "Miss Gibby, here's a nice, juicy bone I wrapped up for Fred. It should take him a day or two to gnaw this one down." Faye handed Gibby an aluminum foiled wrapped bundle. "I also included some shrimp and catfish bites so Oscar and Samson won't get jealous."

"Thank you kindly, Faye. He devoured the last one you gave him so fast, the cats pouted for days. They'll be thrilled with their own treats."

"How's he doing?"

While Gibby regaled Faye with pet stories, Inez Peebles came to sit beside Savvy and admired the baby.

Sabrina gazed around the table and then her eyes moved to the rest of the diner. The restaurant was bustling, filled to the brim with Midnight residents who enjoyed gossip almost as much as they enjoyed Faye's chicken and dumplings, shrimp and cheese grits, or her fried green tomatoes.

Sabrina had known most of these people her entire life. Often incredibly generous, occasionally irritating, and always amazingly nosy, they were her extended family. With the exception of just a few, she loved them all. At that thought, something settled inside her. This was good. This was her life, her family. Maybe she didn't have everything her heart desired, but she had more than many people did…and certainly more than she deserved.

Had Ian arrived home yet? After what they'd said to each other, were things going to be awkward, uncomfortable between them? They'd had spats before but none that had cut so close to the bone…to the heart of their feelings for one another. The disappointment in his eyes, the sadness on his face, would be an image she'd carry in her mind for a long time. If only...

She shook her head, exasperated with herself. There were way too many 'if onlys' in her life and didn't solve one damn problem.

A bell chimed, jerking her out of her thoughts and alerting everyone of a new customer. All eyes went to the front door and a long awkward silence followed, washing over the entire restaurant. A long time Midnight resident, one she and her family most certainly did not love, strolled toward them.

The determined expression on Ralph Henson's sour face was enough to let everyone know something was about to happen.

Zach went to his feet and stood in front of Savvy and their baby, shielding them from Henson.

"I got a right, same as anyone else, to be here."

"As long as you stay away from my family, I've got no problem with you being in any public place."

Before Henson could respond, Quinn went to stand beside Zach. And Sammie and Sabrina stood on either side of them, a family united, ready to protect and defend what was theirs.

"Well now," Henson sneered, "that's quite a picture you men make. A thief and a murderer. You Wilde girls sure haven't done very well for yourselves."

Ugly, malice-filled eyes targeted Sabrina. "Maybe you can find yourself a rapist, little girlie. Then you Wilde girls will have a full set."

Sabrina took a step forward, snarling, "You lowlife scum sucking piece of—"

"Henson," Faye's voice boomed like thunder. "You either sit your boney butt down at the counter and order a meal like decent folk or you forget about ever coming back in here again."

It was no surprise to anyone when the man snapped his mouth shut and seated himself at the counter. While Henson might be willing to risk getting his butt kicked, he wasn't about to take the chance of getting banned from Faye's.

As if there had been no drama, Sabrina and her family settled back down at the table and resumed their meal. For just a couple seconds more, a pregnant silence permeated the room as if the onlookers were expecting something else to occur. When it was apparent that the fireworks had ended, the noise level increased as everyone discussed what had just happened.

"I'm sorry, you guys," Zach said.

"It's not your fault, Zach," Gibby said. "Ralph Henson was born mean and he'll die mean. And in between the two, he'll do his best to make other folks as miserable as he is. Don't you pay him no mind."

Zach gave a grim nod. "Thank you, Aunt Gibby." He gave Savvy a reassuring smile that didn't erase the worry in his eyes.

Sabrina ground her teeth till her jaw hurt. Years ago, Ralph Henson had done his best to destroy a teenaged Zach. And now instead of acting like a decent person who might want to have some kind of relationship with his only grandchild, he was behaving like the ass he was.

Some day Ralph Henson would reap what he sowed. Sabrina could only pray that the fallout wouldn't hurt Zach and Savvy.

Chapter Twenty-Two

Tallahassee, Florida

Ian knew he was behaving like a jerk. Problem was he didn't know how to stop. Other than a quick phone call to let Sabrina know he'd made it home safely, he hadn't talked to her in almost three weeks. She'd called him several times and left messages. He hadn't returned the calls.

He took a swig of his ice-cold beer and stared up at the night sky where millions of scattered stars lit up the heavens. Today's temperature had been a scorching ninety-seven. Tonight's humid eighty degrees wasn't much better, but for the life of him, Ian couldn't work up the energy to go inside like a sane man and cool off.

Seemed like the dog days of summer had arrived a helluva lot earlier than usual.

As if by psychic connection, Ian heard a clip-clop of claws on the tile an instant before twenty-seven pounds of Bassett Hound plopped into his lap. Grunting slightly, Ian watched as Jack circled a couple of times to get things just right and then settled down with a gusty sigh.

Rubbing a silky, floppy ear, Ian breathed out his own sigh. "We're quite the pair, aren't we, Jack? Two bachelors pining after the same girl."

Although he and Jack lived together and had a good, affectionate bond, when Sabrina was around, the dog didn't know Ian existed. For him it was all about Sabrina. Just one of the many things he and Jack had in common.

"You think I should suck it up and call her, don't you?"

The only answer was an impolite doggy snore.

"At least one of us can sleep."

Dropping his head back onto the cushion of the lounger, Ian resumed his star gazing. Maybe the answer was up there because he sure didn't have one down here. He and Sabrina had been going like this for years now. And he had no reason to believe anything would ever change.

From the moment he'd met her, Ian had been entranced. He had liked her sense of humor as well as her dedication to the job, which seemed to mirror his own. They had soon realized that they made a great team, first as friends, then as partners, and not too long after that, as lovers.

There was something inside Sabrina that glowed. Some kind of inner light that radiated brightness and warmth. Ian didn't have a poet like bone in his body, but Sabrina made him wish he did. He wanted to write sonnets, poems…hell, a whole damn book about what she did to him, the way he felt about her, what she meant to him.

But Sabrina didn't want to hear any of those things from him. She wanted to keep things the way they were. He wanted more…a lot more. Seeing her only on the weekends wasn't doing it for him anymore. He wanted it all.

Sure she'd had a rough experience. Getting your heart crushed wasn't easy to get over. Sabrina had been young and vulnerable, easy pickings for a slimeball like Tyler Finley. Not only had the slug seen an easy mark, he had likely enjoyed someone as lovely and innocent as Sabrina falling for him.

Losing her parents at a young age and in such a traumatic way had most definitely made a major impact on her life. Because of that, Sabrina had issues long before Finley slithered his way into Midnight.

There was more, though. Had to be. Sabrina was tough and nobody's fool, but she had something inside her, something that ate at her...something that just would not let her go.

If nothing else, her nightmares proved that. Not only did they torture her almost every night, they were heartbreaking in their simplicity. She didn't wake up screaming. She didn't shout or jump from the bed. Nothing dramatic. What she did do was worse in Ian's estimation. He would rather she scream or shout as if she were doing battle. At least then he could be glad that she was fighting against whatever was hurting her. Instead, she whimpered like a beaten animal. She would wake with tears streaming down her face and the most heartbreaking sadness in her eyes.

How many times had he tried to get her to talk about them? Too numerous to count. She refused to discuss them. Ian had just learned to hold her until she either fell back asleep or she stopping shaking.

Her sisters didn't know about them. Just in the brief conversations he'd had with both of them, he'd figured that out. How very alone she must have felt all those years to be suffering this way. She hadn't even shared them with the two people she was the closest to and trusted the most.

Ian wished he could heal her hurts, fix everything in her life that had gone wrong. But not only could he not do this, Sabrina would cut him off at the knees if he even tried. Never in his lifetime had he met someone so vulnerable who was also so stubbornly strong and independent to a fault.

No, all he could do was love her, be there for her, and hope to hell that someday she would let her guard down long enough for him to help her heal.

The cellphone lying on the table beside him played her ringtone. Ian grabbed it before he could talk himself out of not answering.

"Ian? Hey! I'm so glad you answered. I've missed you."

"I've missed you, too."

"Everything okay? Why haven't you called me back?"

Was everything okay? That would be a big fat no, but there was no point in arguing about the same old thing.

"Everything's fine. Just been busy with a new case."

"You're working something new? Tell me about it."

This had always been their way—talking work instead of feelings.

It was so damn good to hear her voice, he couldn't resist. "Remember that murder case where the guy was accused of killing his boss and two co-workers when they were on a company retreat?"

"Of course. It was all over the news for months. But I thought that had already gone to trial."

"It has but Pearson Bell, the man's attorney called and hired me. He thinks it was a set up."

"Seriously? How? Why?"

He could just see her, probably curled in a chair, wearing one of her many football jerseys for pajamas. Since it was late, after ten o'clock, she'd smell sweet and fresh because she always showered in the evenings before going to bed. Had she used her tangerine lotion or was that only when he was with her?

There was nothing he enjoyed more than holding a softly fragrant and silky Sabrina in his arms. At the thought of her sweet, sexy flesh, a strong surge of arousal blanked his mind of every thought but the need to have her here with him. To taste, to devour…

"Ian…you there?"

He shook himself out of his lust-filled fantasy. "Yeah, sorry. So anyway, there's new evidence that there was a power struggle inside the firm, lot of office politics but on a higher scale."

"Did you get to talk to the guy…what was his name, Harlan Mills, wasn't it?"

As if nothing had happened to interrupt their harmony, Ian fell into their natural rhythm of discussing a case, describing his meeting, the facts he'd uncovered, and once again, he appreciated her input. One of Sabrina's many talents was her ability to feel a case. Where he could be analytical and focus on facts and evidence, Sabrina saw the emotion behind the facts. They had made a damn good team.

"Enough about me. What about you? Any new cases for Wildfire Security?"

"Nothing big. A couple of minor ones that got handled pretty quickly. We're taking a look at a new case in Birmingham. Sammie and Brody are there now."

Ian frowned at that news. Was she still hesitant about leaving town? "Why didn't you go?"

"I was supposed to but Donna called and wanted to talk. I went to Mobile, stayed there a few days."

"She having trouble getting back to real life?"

"Seems like it. At least more so than Claudia and Ashley. I've heard from both of them. They're back home, trying to resume their lives. Even though they won't see justice done until Silva is put away, they seem to be adjusting.

"I'm worried about Donna, though. I offered again to bring her back to Midnight to stay here at the house. Thought maybe a small town environment might be good for her. She refused."

"You can only do so much."

"Yeah, I know."

"You coming to Tallahassee soon?"

He heard the soft little catch of her breath and knew she'd been worried that things had changed between them, because of their argument. He regretted not calling her. Sabrina gave what she could and the last thing he wanted to do was make her feel insecure.

"Tomorrow okay? Unless something comes up, I can be there by four."

"Sounds great, but I've got a five-thirty appointment."

"Then I'll be there waiting for you when you get home. It'll give Jack and me a chance for some playtime." Her voice went sexy, teasing. "Then when you get home, we'll have our own playtime."

"I'll hold you to that."

They went on to talk about other things, their voices going softer and more intimate as he told her how much he wanted to hold her, kiss her, taste her. By the time the call ended, Ian was missing her more than ever and wishing with everything within him that she wanted him just as much.

Ensenada, Mexico

"I can't tell you how happy I am that you came home, my dear. I've missed you terribly." With a deliberate, gentle touch, Robert pushed a strand of hair off the woman's face. "You know, you were always my favorite."

A nervous smile trembled on her lips as her eyes gleamed with hopefulness. He wanted to make sure she felt comfortable and welcomed. That she had no cause whatsoever to regret coming back to him. He would make promises, see to her comfort, feed and clothe her, give her only the finest of everything. And then, when he was sure he had gleaned every ounce of information from her, he would make her suffer for having the audacity to leave him in the first place.

"Thank you, sir. I…um…missed you, too."

"Are you comfortable? Do you need anything?"

Ensconced on the sofa, wearing a cashmere robe he'd purchased for one of his mistresses, the woman held a frothy umbrella drink and nibbled on caviar. Maybe if she'd been brighter she would have realized that Robert was never nice without an ulterior motive. She had information and he was a patient enough man to enjoy this little game he played. Perhaps he'd use a different kind of coercion later on, one that wouldn't be near as comfortable for his houseguest. For now it was actually quite delightful to watch her pretend like she had some kind of value as a human being.

She took an unladylike gulp of her drink, swallowed loudly, sighed gustily and said, "No sir…I'm mean, yes sir, I'm real comfortable. And everything tastes real good."

"Excellent. You be sure to let me know if there's anything you need. All right?"

Thoroughly enjoying the woman's incredible stupidity, Robert waited for her nod before continuing. He leaned forward and gave her his most intimate and conspiratorial smile. "Now, tell me exactly how it happened, and don't leave anything out."

"Well…her real name is Sabrina Wilde. And—" She bit her lip as if in a moment of regret.

Robert took her hand and squeezed it gently, wanting to reassure her. If it became necessary he would gladly beat the truth out of her. For right now, he would play the gentle, forgiving master.

"It's okay, sugar, you can tell me."

"She lives in Alabama, in a town called Midnight."

CHAPTER TWENTY-THREE

Chicago

Holden Marsh had just about had his fill. Shit would never shine no matter how deeply it was scrubbed. Robert Silva would continue his evil until he was taken down for good. Holden had known this going in, but it didn't make the job any easier to bear. Lately it was all he could do to get up in the mornings. It was made worse by the fact that if he could get away with it, he'd put a gun to the bastard's head and relieve the world of one less scumbag.

That kind of corroded thinking was the reason he knew this had to end soon. He wasn't a coldblooded killer and he'd bent his ethics and smothered his conscience on this job more than anything else he'd ever done in his life. If this didn't end soon, it would end him.

For a short while, he'd had a reprieve. Working with Sabrina, Mackenzie, and Wildfire Security to rescue Lauren Kendall had been damn fun. Maybe that's why he hadn't put a bullet into Silva. Not just because the rescue had been accomplished without bloodshed. It'd felt damned good to do something worthwhile and clean for a change.

Arranging for Erica Silva and her children to escape had been a little more complicated. Even with another undercover agent posing as nanny to Silva's children, it had taken longer than he had anticipated to pull it off.

When he'd learned what Silva's wife had gone through to ensure their getaway, he couldn't believe her courage. Erica had worried that her husband was catching on. That he knew what she was planning. What she had done right before Silva had left Chicago was something Holden could barely fathom. She had asked to go with her husband on his trip, believing if he suspected she was trying to leave him, her request would eliminate his suspicion. She had known exactly how he would react. The woman had barely been able to walk upright for several days.

But now they could all breathe easier. Erica and her minor children were in a safe house in another state far away from her husband's influence and wrath. When the time came to testify against the man, she would be more than willing to spill the bastard's secrets.

He had followed up those two successful rescue missions with a final, game-winning trifecta. Lionel Wilson, Silva's former employee, had been delivered to Holden's handler at the DEA. Lionel had a long and seedy history with Silva, but he was more than happy to testify against the man who'd ordered his death. Lionel would still go to prison, but he was alive and breathing. That wouldn't have happened if the DEA hadn't intervened.

Silva had ordered several murders in the last few months. Murders that Holden had been ordered to carry out. A few had been unavoidable, adding more black marks to Holden's soul. So far he had saved more lives than he had taken and that was a win in his book.

Being ordered to kidnap and kill Antonio's ninety-three year old grandmother had put a hole in the pit of his stomach. Fortunately the old woman was still spry and had her wits about her. When she'd been told what was going down, she had taken great pains to look as terrified and pitiful as she could for the camera. Antonio would see his grandmother again, however, he would likely be standing behind prison bars when that happened.

But Holden still didn't have what his superiors wanted, felt they had to have to get a solid conviction—irrefutable, damning evidence of Robert Silva's warehouses where a dozen highly addictive and dangerous drugs were manufactured and distributed throughout the world. Holden knew there were at least three—one in the US and two in South America—though he suspected there were several more. Despite the fact that Holden had been with Silva almost two years, he'd yet to be invited to the inner circle of Silva's drug enterprise.

The invitation was imminent. Holden Marsh had more than proven his worth to his employer. How much longer would he have to wait and just what kind of crap would he have to do before the invitation came and this could end?

Hell, he didn't even know where Silva was this minute. The man had withdrawn to a private retreat to lick his wounds. He'd left ten nights ago with little more than a muttered, "Call me when you find my family."

And now everything was back to a holding pattern. Something had to break and soon.

That thought had barely entered his head when his phone rang.

And Holden's world imploded.

He listened. Grunted his agreement. Gave praise, congratulations. Even offered a couple of theories of what might have happened. All the while, his mind whirled with all the things he needed to do. Finally, able to end the call, Holden dropped the phone on the chair.

"Un-freaking-believable."

The woman was going to die—that was a given. But just how many more people would be killed because of her stupidity? He had tons to get done, but first he had to alert the one person Silva would likely want dead more than anyone else.

Long strides had him in his bedroom in seconds. As he pulled his duffle bag from his closet, he grabbed one of his burner phones and keyed in a number.

She answered with suspicion in her voice, most likely because she didn't recognize the number. And because her instincts were good.

"Sabrina, it's Marsh."

Her voice changed, became relaxed, friendly. "Hey, how are—"

"We've got a problem."

He told her what he knew which wasn't a lot. Fortunately she was a smart woman and could fill in any blank spaces. She knew Silva would be coming for her, along with anyone else she cared about.

They didn't waste time talking. He wished her luck, feeling like shit that he'd put her in this position.

He dumped clothes and toiletries into the bag, taking only what he had to have. If Silva had this place searched, he didn't want it to look as though he'd cleaned the apartment out and left.

Not that Silva suspected him yet. There was no reason to. Still, Holden was too experienced and had been through too much to take anything for granted. If any shit went down, he would be prepared.

Within minutes he was out the door, closing it without a backward look. On the way to his car, his eyes on alert for threats, he placed another call. Sabrina would make the same call...maybe already had, but the man needed to know a few other things.

When the phone was answered on the first ring, Holden didn't waste time with pleasantries. "Mackenzie, Sabrina's in danger."

Tallahassee

In the two-minute phone conversation with Marsh, Ian packed his clothes. Once he ended the call, he took the time to grab a half-dozen weapons from a stash he kept in the closet of his spare bedroom. Then because he knew she might need the comfort, he grabbed Jack, a bag of dog food, and they were off.

As he sped out of the driveway, he punched a speed-dial number, but it wasn't Sabrina he called.

"Zach, have you talked to Sabrina?"

"No…not today. Why? Wait…looks like she's on the other line."

"Okay, talk to her but call me right back. We need to make plans."

Zach didn't bother asking what the hell was going on, which Ian appreciated. Every second counted.

They should have kept closer tabs on the women. Yeah, Sabrina had done a lot for them, but one thing they hadn't counted on was one of the women actually returning to Silva. Who the hell does that?

Ashley had actually seemed to be the most grateful of the three women they'd rescued. Her claims of having a couple of distant cousins in Portland were true…Ian himself had checked them out. Apparently whatever had happened with them had caused her to believe she was better off being a sex slave to Silva. How was that even remotely possible?

Marsh didn't know what Silva had planned. Whatever it was, Ian would be there to face it head on with the rest of the Wildes.

His cellphone rang with Sabrina's ringtone and Ian pressed the button on his steering wheel. "Sabrina."

"Ian...you've heard?"

"Yeah, Marsh called me. I'm on the way."

"I can't believe she did this. How could she go back to him? He'll kill her after he's gotten what he wants."

"I don't know, but she made her decision. We just need to do everything we can to insure everyone else stays safe."

"Agreed. Here's where we are so far. I've called Donna and Claudia. They can't believe it either, but Brody's already making arrangements for their safety. Donna is still in Mobile, so she's covered. He's sending one of his men to Houston to protect Claudia.

"Savvy and I are about to leave. We're taking Aunt Gibby and Camille Sage to Mobile. Brody has someone to protect them."

"Savannah isn't staying with them?"

"She said she wasn't about to abandon us. Camille Sage is on formula now so Aunt Gibby should be fine with her. She and Zach had a big blow-up and aren't speaking to each other."

"That's not true," Savannah said in the background. "We had a lively discussion and I'm sure when I get back, he'll have had the chance to calm down and see reason."

As protective as Zach was of his wife, Ian doubted that, but he wasn't surprised at Savannah's decision. The Wildes stuck together, no matter what.

"What about Lauren?" Ian asked.

"Logan is taking her to the safe house we used when we were protecting her before. One of his men will see to her protection."

Her voice went softer and he knew she didn't want anyone else to hear her. "I really messed up, Ian."

Leave it to Sabrina to take responsibility for someone else's mistakes. "No you didn't."

"If I hadn't pursued Cruz, none of this would have happened."

"And you never would have known that Silva had kidnapped Lauren. You saved her life, Sabrina. And three other women. Just because one was too screwed up to appreciate her freedom is not your fault. You gave four women a chance…one of them made a choice that she didn't want to stay safe. That's on her, not you."

"If anything happens to my family…" Her voice went thick with tears. "They're my everything, Ian."

"Nothing's going to happen to them, baby. I promise."

"We're having a family meeting tonight at seven. You'll be here in time for that, won't you?"

"Yes. I should be there not long after you arrive back from Mobile."

"Good. I—Okay, gotta go help Savvy get the car loaded. I'll see you soon. Right?"

The vulnerability and uncertainty in her voice sounded so unlike the self-assured Sabrina. Ian wished with all his might he could be with her now. "I'll see you soon, I promise."

For the thousandth time since she'd left home, Sabrina checked her phone for missed calls, voice mails, or texts. Zach had said he would call if he spotted anything suspicious.

Dammit, she was stronger than this but couldn't stop herself from compulsively checking just to make sure she hadn't missed a message. She had to do better. Earlier, she had almost lost it with Ian. No matter what he said, she'd gotten them into this situation. It was up to her to get them out.

"Bri, for the last time, this is not your fault."

Savvy's reassurance couldn't diminish the knot in her gut.

"I keep telling myself that, but I'm the one who brought this asshole into our lives."

"Technically Lauren did that when she came to us asking for our help. When we took this venture on we knew it would put us in the crosshairs of some very bad people. It goes with the territory."

"I know. And the rational part of me is saying deal with it and move on."

"And the other part?"

She glanced over at her sister Savvy, who she loved more than life. "The other part says gather my loved ones together and head for the hills. I couldn't bear it if anyone was hurt because of this."

"We'll be fine, Bri. As long as we stick together, the Wildes can't be defeated."

Even with the brave words and encouraging smile, Savvy's red, swollen eyes told a different tale. Saying goodbye even for only a few days to her daughter had been gut- wrenching for her sister.

"Are you sure you don't want to go back, be with Camille and Aunt Gibby?"

"Of course I want to be with them, but they'll be fine. Aunt Gibby is great with the baby. And I'm not about to let my family face this monster without me."

"And you and Zach? Are you guys going to be okay? He seemed pretty steamed."

"We made a vow to face every adversity together. When he calms down, he'll remember that."

The two-lane highway stretched out before them led to Midnight. One of only two roads into town. It wouldn't be easy, but they could be monitored, watched night and day to prevent Silva and his thugs coming into her town. But that was only if they used the roads. What if they came through the woods or pastureland? There were hundreds of places they could enter. Not every location could be monitored and protected.

"How are we going to keep them out, Savvy? There're just a few of us. Who knows how many men Silva will have with him."

"We'll make do, Bri. We always have. This goon will not defeat us. Besides, Silva isn't just going to drive into town and start trouble. He's evaded prosecution all these years. No way is he going to allow a personal grudge to become public."

Sabrina had firsthand knowledge of how Robert Silva handled his personal grudges. He had people to do his dirty work for him so his hands could stay clean.

"Shouldn't we warn the rest of the town? Just in case?"

"I mentioned that to Zach. He said he might call a special town meeting to put people on alert. He's going to talk to the town council about it tonight."

"What about—" Sabrina's heart twisted with sadness as she spotted a large object in the middle of the road. She was too far away to tell what kind of animal it was, but judging by the size, it was either a deer or maybe a large dog. Poor innocent creatures had no defense against mankind.

Easing her foot off the accelerator, she slowed her car down as she approached. She was within twenty yards when she realized it was neither a deer nor dog. It was a human being.

Savvy gasped beside her, recognizing the same thing. "Bri...? Is that what I think it is?"

Ten yards from the body, she stopped. The highway was free of traffic this time of day. People who worked outside Midnight hadn't made it home yet.

Pulling her gaze away from the bloodied body in the road, she took in her surroundings. Thick, dense forest on both sides. Anyone could be hiding anywhere. If she got out, she'd be easy pickings for a sniper.

Sabrina took her gun from the console beside her. Savvy pulled hers from her purse.

Though the body faced away from her, she could tell it was a woman and she was blonde. There were no visible signs of life but no way could she not check.

Sabrina pulled on the door handle. "Call Zach. It's probably too late to save her, but tell him to bring Quinn just in case."

"We're already sitting ducks here, Bri. If you get out, you're just making it too damn easy."

"Maybe, but I don't think Silva wants it easy, at least not yet."

"And if it's a trap?"

"Hell, Savvy, if he's got a sniper out there somewhere, we'd both be dead right now."

With that, she pushed open the door and got out of the car. She took the few steps to the body, walked around it and then expelled a long, sad sigh. The woman's face was bloodied and bruised, but Sabrina easily recognized Ashley.

Although she already knew by the unfocused, glassy look in the woman's eyes, Sabrina pressed her fingers against her neck, searching for a pulse. Her skin was cold, icy, almost as if she'd been in a freezer before she'd been dumped here. Silva had most likely had her killed not long after she returned and then put her on ice to preserve the body.

Cursing the brutal bastard, Sabrina gently turned the dead woman over onto her back and saw that Ashley's body wasn't the only message he'd sent. There was a typewritten letter attached to Ashley's blouse.

Hello Sabrina. Yes, I do know that's your name. Thanks to Ashley here, I know all there is to know about Sabrina Wilde. What an interesting and resourceful woman you are. Almost makes me think you're one of the precious few with tits and a brain.

But I digress.

You've inconvenienced me, Sabrina, and I'm too busy of a man to take that lightly. Therefore, recompense is due. You have twenty-four hours to comply by surrendering yourself.

If you don't comply, there will be consequences. Just how important is your family to you?

There was no signature. She didn't need one. Besides, Silva wasn't about to implicate himself. Nothing linked him to this letter or even Ashley's murder. If she accused him of murder, he would laugh.

The sound of a siren told her that Zach and Quinn were on their way. Sabrina stood, holding the letter in her hand. Silva wasn't going to stop until he was either dead or he got what he wanted. She just needed to decide what she was going to do about it.

Chapter Twenty-Four

It was going on dusk when Ian approached Midnight's city limits. He was pleased to see a roadblock about a quarter mile from the town. Bart Odom, one of Zach's deputies, was a stoic sentinel standing beside his police car, his lights whirling a warning. No one was getting into Midnight via the roadways without first being checked out by the police department. Unfortunately there were a lot of other ways to get into town.

Sliding his window down, Ian said, "How's it going, Bart?"

Bart gave a nod. "Evening, Ian. It's been fairly steady. Folks coming home from work or shopping. Wanting to know what's going on."

"What are you telling them?"

"What Zach told me to say. Just doing a routine check. Most everyone's buying it…none of 'em looked real pleased. We'll have to come up with a better reason soon."

"And more people to guard the road."

"You got that right. If that asshole wants into town, just one of us standing against him isn't going to get it done. Zach said we've got a few hours before that'll happen."

"How's he know that?"

"Got a letter with the body."

That was news. Sabrina had texted him about Ashley's body. She hadn't mentioned a letter.

"I'll head on up to the house. You need to check inside my vehicle?"

"Yeah. I'm sure you're on the up and up, but Zach'll tear me a new one if I don't check everybody."

"That's no problem. I appreciate you being thorough."

The big man swept his flashlight into Ian's Wrangler. "This is my town. Ain't nobody coming in and harming me or mine."

After being cleared to go, Ian drove slowly through the downtown area, not surprised that everything looked as normal as always. Cars and trucks were parked in front of Faye's Diner, as always doing a steady business this time of day. A couple of places, an insurance office and some kind of children's store, were still open. Several people strolled down the sidewalk around the town square enjoying the cooling temperature. A teenaged couple sat in front of the large Mimosa tree fountain, most likely throwing pennies into the water and making wishes.

Everything looked peaceful and serene—a typical summer evening in Midnight. Ian had an ominous feeling that things were soon going to change.

The instant he turned into the tree-lined drive that led to the Wilde mansion that uneasiness increased. Lights blazed throughout the house, cars were parked sideways in the drive, preventing other cars from entering.

He pulled onto the side of the road, in front of the mansion and got out. The sight of Sabrina running toward him worried the hell out of him. Had something else happened?

He'd barely exited his vehicle before Sabrina was at his side. "What's wrong? What's happened?"

Instead of answering, Sabrina flew into his arms and held on tight. Having never been the clingy sort before, she felt a minor shock at her behavior. Going on full meltdown, especially right now, would not only be bizarre but also stupid. She had to stay strong.

"Sweetheart?"

Allowing herself one more moment of comfort, she breathed in Ian's scent and then spoke against his neck. "Nothing else has happened. I was just worried about you. You took longer than I thought you would to get here. And I couldn't get you on your cellphone."

"Sorry about that. I was going to bring Jack with me, then decided if there was trouble, I didn't want to take the risk of him getting hurt. I dropped him off at the sitter's house. That put me behind. And you know there are a lot of dead zones between here and Tallahassee. Hard as hell to get a signal."

He was right of course. And she had known that but the wild panic she'd been feeling since finding Ashley's body wouldn't settle. Until everyone she loved was either within her grasp or she knew their whereabouts, her chaotic fears wouldn't rest. But now, Ian was here. He was safe. She could take a breath, slow down and finally get her thoughts together.

She pulled away, straightened her spine and settled herself down. It was time to make some decisions.

"Everyone's gathered in the living room. We've got sandwiches and stuff if you're hungry."

Ian grabbed his bags from the back of his Jeep. Handing her the lightest one, he carried the other one and then hand in hand, walked with her into the house.

"Have you heard anything more from Marsh?" Ian asked.

"No. I don't know if that's a good thing or bad. No news isn't always good news."

Ian stopped abruptly and pulled her around to face him. "Talk to me."

How could she tell him, make him understand her fears? "It's as if my nightmares are coming true. I've put my family in danger again."

His eyes narrowed in confusion, speculation. "What do you mean, again?"

She wanted to slap her hand over her mouth. Existing on a dozen cups of coffee, minimal food, and razor-edged nerves had made her careless. She had to get herself together or she couldn't do what needed to be done.

"You know what I mean. I put my family in jeopardy when I went after Cruz. And now this."

The doubtful expression told her he wasn't buying it for a minute. Ian, better than anyone, knew she'd been having nightmares long before she'd ever heard of Armando Cruz.

"Is that what your nightmares are about? Putting your family at risk?"

His quiet, gentle voice invited her to open up…share her burden. She couldn't. This secret, this shame, had been hers since she was ten years old. It wasn't one she could ever share.

"After what happened to my parents, who wouldn't have nightmares?"

Grabbing her shoulders, he shook her gently and then leaned his forehead against hers. "Hear this. You did nothing to cause this. If we hadn't gone after Lauren, she'd likely be dead."

"I know but—"

His voice hardened. "But nothing, Sabrina. Snap out of the useless, self-indulgent guilt and let's figure out how to deal with this problem. Together."

The words were harsh but much needed. Ian was right. Lamenting over poor choices did nothing. She could wallow in guilt till the cows came home and it wouldn't solve a damn thing.

"You're right." She took in a breath, let it out slowly and then straightened her shoulders. "Let's figure out a way to kick Robert Silva's scrawny ass."

Ian dropped down into an oversized chair in the living room. The room was large with plenty of seating, but more chairs had been added. Apparently others would be joining them soon. For now, it was Sabrina and her sisters, Zach, Quinn, Brody, Logan, and now Ian.

After giving a grim nod to the room in general, Ian asked, "I understand there was a letter with the body?"

Sabrina handed him a piece of paper. "We put the original in an evidence bag. This is a copy."

Ian's blood turned cold. "The guy's off his rocker."

"Yeah," Quinn agreed. "That's why he's so damned dangerous."

Zach stood in the middle of the room, taking charge as the Chief of Police. "Now that we're all here, let's update everyone so we're on the same page. Aunt Gibby and Camille Sage are under armed guard in Mobile. Lauren is in Magnolia Springs, also under armed guard.

"I've got my two deputies guarding both entrances into town, but we all know if Silva wants in, that's not going to stop him." His gaze swept around the room, meeting each person's eyes. "We need help."

"What about law enforcement from the surrounding towns?" Ian asked.

"I've contacted them, but they're about as short staffed as we are here in Midnight. They've offered assistance if something goes down. Having their people come over and guard the town for preventative measures isn't going to happen."

"Then where do you propose to get more help?"

"I'm going to call a town meeting and explain what's going on."

"How do you think that's going to go over?" Logan asked.

"Hard to say. It'll scare some of them for sure, which isn't all bad. Fear's a healthy thing sometimes. But Midnight residents come together when one of their own is threatened."

"I agree." Quinn put his arm around Samantha's shoulders, his voice thick as he continued, "If it wasn't for them, Sam and I might not be here. I don't know which one of them saved our lives that night, but it doesn't matter. When they heard Sam was in trouble, they were determined to save her."

"There is another option," Sabrina said.

Noticing the stubborn tilt to her chin, Ian already knew where she was headed but asked anyway, "And that would be?"

"We do what the letter says. I go with him. You guys follow or put a tracker on me and we—"

Ian didn't even bother to let her finish her sentence. "I think I speak for everyone here when I say hell no. And even if I don't speak for everyone, believe this—I will hogtie you and have Zach throw you in jail before I let you near that bastard again."

Fire in her eyes, she surged to her feet. "I believe Zach would have issues with you telling him who to put in jail."

"Don't be too sure of that, Sabrina," Zach said, "I'd let him do that if I thought it'd keep you safe."

Sabrina turned her gaze to her sisters, as if expecting them to back her up. Since their expressions were identical to his and Zach's, she dropped back into her chair. "Okay, fine. We'll have a town meeting, alert them to what's going on, but that can't be a long-term solution. This man has got to be stopped."

"Agreed," Zach said. "I've talked to Marsh. He's going to try to convince his people to move on Silva. Even though they want more evidence to be able to put him away for good, based upon this new threat, he's confident they'll change their minds."

"And until then, we wait and watch each other's backs," Brody said.

"Exactly." Zach stood. "I'm going to meet with the town council tonight...let them know what's going on, about the plans for a town meeting. Tomorrow morning, after school starts, I'll use the tornado and hurricane warning system. Folks know to tune into our emergency channel on the radio. I'll announce a meeting at the town hall for nine o'clock. We won't get everyone, but we'll get enough so word will spread fast. With Midnight's grapevine being what it is, within an hour, everyone will know."

"You know not everyone's going to be onboard with this," Savannah said.

His eyes went cold with determination. "Leave those few to me."

CHAPTER TWENTY-FIVE

A thick silence permeated the interior of Ian's SUV. He hadn't said anything to her since that insulting 'hogtie you' statement and damned if she was going to act as if everything was okay.

She and Ian were taking the nine to midnight shift on the other end of town. Sabrina had always enjoyed their surveillance gigs together. You could learn a lot about a person when there was nothing to do but listen to crickets chirp and wait for something to happen. She'd done plenty of lone surveillance jobs and definitely preferred having company. Tonight was the exception.

Oddly enough, she and Ian rarely argued. She could count on one hand when they'd been really angry with each other. She gave most of that credit to Ian. He was an easygoing, even-tempered man who might get frustrated about something but rarely lost his cool.

Sabrina knew she was the opposite and did her best to moderate her responses because of Ian's calming ways. Losing her temper with Ian around often made her feel like a bratty child who didn't get her way. She hated that feeling.

So now, instead of yelling at him for his highhanded, infuriating remark, she would take the high road and stay quiet.

As they drove through the downtown area, she kept her eyes open for anything unusual or out of place. Coming up on nine o'clock meant most businesses other than a couple of gas stations were closed. Faye's still had a couple of stragglers inside. Knowing Faye, the woman would have them out the door within the next few minutes. All was quiet, peaceful. She prayed it stayed that way. Midnight and its colorful, quaint, and sometimes zany characters meant so much to her. Having anything, especially the evil of Robert Silva, invade it would be so wrong.

They pulled off the road about a quarter mile out of town and Ian turned off his headlights. The peace of the night flowed around them…the only sounds the typical summertime chorus of crickets, frogs, and the occasional owl.

"Okay, so maybe the 'hogtie' comment was a little over the top."

"Yes, it was."

"I'm sorry." Then ruining a perfectly good apology, he added, "Doesn't mean I won't do it, though."

Sabrina huffed out an exasperated breath. "Oh for heaven's sake, Ian. It's not like I haven't done anything dangerous before. I know how to take care of myself."

"Yes you do, but you've never had to deal with someone who is intent on doing harm to you immediately. Silva has a personal grudge against you now. This isn't like before, when he merely wanted you as his captive. He'll want to make you pay for humiliating him. He knows who you are…knows about you and your family. Whatever contingency plan you had, he'd be ready for it."

"Okay…fine. It was just an idea."

"A stupid one."

She ground her teeth, refusing to get into a pointless argument. Especially when everything he said was the truth.

"I called my folks to let them know what's going on. No details but enough for them to be on alert."

Sabrina closed her eyes. She'd been so caught up in her own world, her own drama, she hadn't given any thought that Ian's association with her might well endanger his family, too.

"I'm so sorry, Ian. I didn't even consider they could be in danger, too."

Rough, callused fingers trailed tenderly down her cheek and then his big hand cupped her jaw, turning her face toward him. "The entire world isn't your responsibility to save, sweetheart. There are others who can pick up the slack."

"No, but I should have—"

"You've got more than enough on your plate. Other people can take care of things, too."

She shook her head. "I'm the one who started this train wreck."

Releasing her, Ian straightened in his seat. Looking out the windshield, he asked quietly, "Have you ever thought about getting counseling, Sabrina?"

So startled by the question, she stared at his profile for several seconds before finally finding her voice. "Counseling for what?"

Ian heard the defensiveness in her tone and when he turned to look at her, saw the fear in her eyes. Emotions tightened his chest. There was nothing he wanted to do more than hold her, reassure her that everything would be okay. If he could slay every dragon for her, calm every one of her fears, he would. But that wasn't something Sabrina would allow or want. And the damnable thing about that was, her self-sufficiency was one of the reasons he loved her so much. She was fiercely independent, yet felt things so deeply, allowed them to touch her so hard, that her emotions made her intensely vulnerable.

Her childhood trauma had shaped her and made her who she was, just as it had her sisters. But Sabrina's pain seemed deeply rooted, much more than Savannah's or Samantha's. Admittedly he knew Sabrina better than he knew her sisters, but they both appeared more grounded…less damaged.

"You were ten years old when you thought your father murdered your mother and then killed himself. The death of one parent is traumatic enough. You lost both your parents and under horrific circumstances."

"I don't need you telling me how I lost my parents, Ian. I lived it. I know exactly what happened to them."

"I'm not trying to start an argument. I'm just saying that you could still have residual trauma from that event. Not unlike PTSD. Maybe if you—"

"And maybe you need to mind your own damn business."

He fought the familiar anger. Every time he tried to dig deeper, she shut him down. If he didn't care so damn much, he wouldn't even try.

"You are my business. Whether you want to admit it or not, I'm not just your occasional lay."

He heard a gasp, knew he had shocked her.

"What the hell? Why would you say something so idiotic?"

The fury trembling in her voice told him he'd pissed her off, too. Good. He'd take a pissed off Sabrina over a terrified or guilty one any day of the week.

"I have never thought of you that way, Ian, and you damn well know it. We have a good relationship. Why do you have to muck it up with touchy-feely stuff?"

"Because that touch-feely stuff is what makes a relationship worthwhile."

Ian heard mocking laughter in his mind. If any of his former army buddies could hear him now, pansy-assed pussy would be the kindest insult they'd throw at him. Still, he continued, "Sex without those feelings is meaningless. Physical gratification and nothing more."

"I have feelings for you, Ian. You know I do."

"Hell, yeah, I know you do. In fact, I believe you love me. You're just too scared to admit it."

He found immense satisfaction in telling her this since he had grave doubts she had ever even admitted it to herself. And as he expected, she took exception to his declaration.

She sputtered, "You're a...a pompous, egotistical ass."

Ian fought a grin as he noted that she didn't deny his statement. That was indeed progress.

"Yes, I can be pompous and egotistical. And quite often an ass but I—"

All amusement disappeared, all chatter stopped. Headlights appeared in the distance, coming toward Midnight and at a high rate of speed.

She was a freaking idiot for coming back here. Not only because Silva would be delighted to kidnap and torture her again, but also because Logan was going to have a major meltdown when he found out.

On top of that, this was totally unlike her. She ran away from trouble, she didn't run to it. Okay, for whatever reason, trouble seemed to find her anyway, but she had never sought it out. And now, she was not only seeking it, she wanted to face it head-on. Maybe that's what being in love meant—being able to face your fears.

Logan loved her. As impossible as that seemed, she was finally willing to accept that possibility. After all the screw-ups, miscues, and downright stupid decisions, she'd found a man who knew her backward and forward and still loved her. That was more than just a surprise...it was a bona fide miracle.

The fact that she didn't deserve his love made it all the more miraculous. She had used him and run from him. And what does he do? He rescues her and forgives her. Who does that?

Yes, he'd yelled at her. Told her what an idiot she was for running, for being scared. For getting kidnapped by Silva. All the things he'd said were true. Even as they'd hurt her, there wasn't a single accusation she could deny. And then, when he'd had her in tears, a bundle of misery and regret, he'd shouted again. This time he'd told her he loved her and that she damned well better get used to it because he intended to love her for the rest of his life.

Who does that? Logan Wright, that's who.

So, despite every instinct telling to run the other way, here she was, back in Midnight because, dammit, she was tired of running. Tired of being alone. Tired of looking out only for herself. Logan had given her his love and in spite of their history he trusted her not to run away. When he found out she'd left, no doubt he would believe she had disappeared on him again.

It was time to show him, but even more importantly, it was time to show herself, that Lauren Kendall was through running away. She might still be running, but this time, it was to the man she loved.

Didn't mean he wasn't going to be royally pissed at her, though.

Sabrina stood on the side of the road with Ian beside her. They were both armed. The car pulling to a stop beside them might well be a Midnight resident, which meant she and Ian were going to have explain why they were stopping traffic going into town. If, however, this person wasn't a resident, then they'd be the ones explaining.

Her flashlight highlighted a familiar face. *Oh crap.*

"What the hell are you doing here, Lauren?"

A mutinous look in her eyes, Lauren tilted her chin slightly in a gesture that felt altogether too familiar. Sabrina knew that look because she'd seen it on her own face.

"I'm here to help."

"Logan left you in Magnolia Springs for a reason. If Silva finds you—"

"I'm safer here, surrounded by you guys than I am with just one guard."

Surprising Sabrina, Ian's only comment was, "Where's your bodyguard?"

"He's studiously guarding me, just like Logan asked him to."

"Apparently not," Ian said dryly, "seeing as you're here and all."

Lauren flashed a nervous smile. "I'm a good escape artist. I left a note so he wouldn't worry. Besides, I—"

Sabrina's cellphone rang. She barely got out her name before Logan growled, "Lauren's headed your way."

"She just got here."

"Hold her there." Logan ended the call abruptly, but not before Sabrina heard him say softly, "Damn foolish woman."

"Guess the shit's about to hit the proverbial fan."

Despite the seriousness of the situation, Sabrina had to fight a smile. "You don't sound too worried."

"Please." Lauren gave a slight eye-roll. "I've been through worse than Logan Wright's fearsome temper."

Apparently Logan had been on his way when he made the call. Headlights coming from Midnight pierced the darkness. Sabrina looked back at Lauren and noticed that despite her brave words, she was nervously biting her lip.

Logan's car stopped several feet away. The instant he got out of his vehicle, Lauren got out of hers.

Instead of yelling—which is what Sabrina would have expected of him—or even marching over to her, he did something extraordinarily surprising. He stood in front of his car and held out his arms. With a soft, gulping sob, Lauren took off. Logan met her halfway and caught her up in his arms. Holding her fiercely, he covered her face in kisses.

Sabrina didn't know why a hollow ache appeared in her chest. She was glad for them. Heaven knew Lauren deserved happiness and she really liked Logan, who was one of the good guys. But for some unknown reason, she had to turn away from the emotional reunion.

In an effort to break the odd tension that now surrounded them, she was about to say something glib to Ian when she noted the expression on his face mirrored her own thoughts. He looked both envious and a little wistful.

The ache in her chest grew.

CHAPTER TWENTY-SIX

Alone on the stage, Zach stood at a podium, waiting for everyone to be seated and the room to quiet down.

"Okay, if everybody will find a seat, we'll get started." Pointing to a section, Zach added, "There are a couple empty chairs up front here."

Ian stood in the back of the small auditorium watching. The police chief had been right. The severe weather alarm and radio announcement had done their job, bringing the residents to the town hall. The main room probably held close to three hundred people and it was standing room only. About half that number stood outside the doors, waiting to hear what was going on. Their expressions ranged from curiosity, to irritation, to alarm.

This could either go well or become a monumental shit storm.

"Would everyone please take any available seats so we can get started?" Zach called out again.

"What's going on, Chief Tanner?" A man shouted from the middle of the crowd. Before Zach could react, another voice yelled, "Yeah, what's up, Zach? I got crops that need tending to."

Ian noted with approval that in typical Zach style he wasn't drawn into speaking until he was ready. Last night when Ian and Sabrina had finished their shift and returned to the Wilde house, they'd learned the results of Zach's impromptu city council meeting. Not everyone was happy with the way the police chief wanted to handle the situation. Apparently a couple of the council members wanted to wait and see what happened, believing if the town was told that trouble might be coming, citizens would panic.

Zach had argued and won, saying that the town had a right to know that they could be in danger. Ian agreed but knew that Zach was walking a fine line between informing the public so they could be prepared and scaring them so much they'd assume everyone was a threat. Midnight wasn't immune from the impulsive or crazy.

Sabrina and Savannah, as well as Logan and Brody, were standing on the outer edges of the room, strategically placed. They were there to add confidence and lend support if for some reason the crowd got rowdy. Samantha and Quinn were taking their shifts at the city limits, as was one of Zach's deputies. Bart, Midnight's other deputy, stood at the town hall entrance in case there was trouble.

"Thank y'all for coming," Zach said. "I know it's an inconvenience to disrupt your day like this, but the city council and I believe it's best that you stay informed when it comes to the goings-on in this town."

"So what's this about, Zach?" a man shouted from the back. "Sarah Jane's got a doctor's appointment in Mobile. We need to get going soon."

"I'll get right to the point, then," Zach said. "We have information that makes us believe there's a credible threat to the town."

"What kind of threat?" a woman called out.

"There's a man, a criminal, who has insinuated that he will harm residents of the town. We are fully prepared to handle any threats, but I felt…we felt it would be best to inform everyone so you can be on guard."

More questions came from various citizens in the crowd: "What does this man want?"

"Why would he threaten us?"

"Why can't you arrest him if he's made a threat?"

"All excellent questions and I'll address each one. However, one thing I want to caution you about. Do not assume that just because you don't recognize someone that they are here to harm you or your loved ones. If you see anyone unfamiliar or remotely suspicious, contact the police department and do not engage. Am I clear on that? The last thing we need is for the public to take the law into its own hands."

There were rumblings, grumblings, but thankfully no one challenged Zach on that issue. And he was so right. Midnight sure as hell didn't need a town of vigilantes.

"This man believes he is above the law. At this time, he can't be arrested because we have no reliable evidence to support the threat."

"Well then how do you know he wants to hurt any of us?"

This was a touchy topic and Ian watched as Zach skirted around how he knew about the threats. They didn't need to know that the threat had been delivered, attached to a dead body.

"We received a letter. He didn't sign his name, but we know who he is."

"How do you know? Who is it? None of this makes any sense."

"It's related to a case Wildefire Security took on several weeks ago. We—"

"I told you...didn't I tell you that bringing that kind of business into our town was going to cause problems. Invite evil into our midst? Well, here's my proof."

Standing in the middle of the room, a sour-faced, mulish looking Ralph Henson scanned the crowd as he made his 'I told you so' statement. No doubt about it, the man was looking to make trouble.

"The Wildefire Security Agency is not responsible for bringing anything but commerce and jobs into this town." Zach's expression went fierce as his eyes skewered Henson. "I believe everyone here will agree that evil has been in Midnight a long time."

Henson slumped back into his seat, looking somewhat crestfallen that he hadn't received the support from others that he apparently had been hoping for.

Zach's gaze scanned the crowd again as he continued, "As far as what this man wants…it's not completely clear. We hope to bring him to justice soon. However, we felt it necessary to give you notice so you can be vigilant. We look out for our own in this town. Always have. Let's continue to do that." He paused a breath and then "Any other questions?"

As Zach fielded a few more questions about what residents should look for, Ian let his eyes wander around the room. Brody and Logan were on either side of the back door. Savannah stood by the stage, close to her husband.

Ian's heartbeat picked up cadence when he noted that Sabrina was no longer standing on the left side of the room. When Zach had started talking, she'd been directly across from Savannah. Leaving her post before the meeting ended was unprofessional and completely out of character for her.

Where the hell had she gone?

Sabrina raced to her car she'd parked in front of the town hall. Her breath was coming so fast she knew she would hyperventilate if she didn't slow down. Thankfully she hadn't locked the door and was able to throw herself behind the wheel. In seconds she was backing out of the parking space and speeding down the highway.

Her hands were shaking so hard, she couldn't hold a phone in her hands much less dial a number. Grateful for her voice-activated phone, she pressed a button on her steering wheel. "Call Sammie."

Heart-pounding seconds passed before her sister answered. "Hey Bri, is the meeting over?"

"Almost. Zach wanted me to ask that you and Quinn come to the town hall. I'm headed your way to take over."

"Why? What's up?"

"I'm not sure. He just asked me to call you."

"Are you by yourself?"

"Ian's right behind me. You guys come on ahead. I'm seconds away from you."

Thankfully her sister trusted her enough to say, "Okay. We'll head that way."

Blowing out an explosive breath, Sabrina tried to get her thoughts together. What now? It wasn't as if she'd had a choice in the matter. She just needed to figure out what she was going to do to get herself out of this without getting dead.

She spotted Quinn's SUV approaching her from the opposite direction. Forcing a smile to her frozen lips, she smiled and waved to Quinn and to Sammie who sat on the passenger side. They wouldn't suspect anything until they got to the town hall and learned that Zach hadn't requested their presence. By then it would be too late. Silva would already have her.

CHAPTER TWENTY-SEVEN

Sabrina wasn't answering her phone. Ian had looked everywhere for her, including the women's restroom. After a hasty apology to the two ladies who screamed at him when he barged in, he'd made a mad dash outside. Something was going on.

He was in the middle of calling Savannah's cellphone to see if she knew Sabrina's whereabouts when he got to the sidewalk and spotted Quinn's SUV. Samantha got out and strode rapidly toward the entrance as if on a mission. Quinn proceeded toward an empty parking spot a few yards down the road.

Frowning, Ian ran to the area where Quinn was about to park and shouted, "What are you guys doing here?"

Quinn slid the passenger side window down. "Sam got a call from Sabrina. Said Zach wanted us to come here. She took our post. Said you were right behind her."

Ian wrenched open the passenger door of the SUV and dove inside. "Drive back to the checkpoint."

Thankfully Quinn required no explanation as he made a quick u-turn and sped back toward the checkpoint.

Ian hit redial for Sabrina, already knowing it would do no good. What in the hell was she thinking?

"You want to tell me what's going on?" Quinn asked.

"Sabrina disappeared from the meeting. She's not answering my calls and she tells you that Zach needed you at the meeting. Which, as far as I could see, he didn't. That leads me to only one conclusion."

"Shit. She wouldn't be that reckless, would she?"

Ian cut his eyes over at the man. "You have no idea."

They were almost to the location Ian and Sabrina had parked last night when he saw her. She'd parked her car on the side of the road and was walking down the middle of the highway, headed away from town. What the hell?

Quinn veered sharply to go around her, and then pulled to a jerking stop, blocking her.

Ian was out and running toward her before the vehicle even stopped. "What the hell are you doing?"

"Get out of here, Ian. I don't have a choice."

"Like hell, you don't. Get in the car this second."

Her face was bloodless, her eyes dark pools of anguish. "I can't. I just can't." She skirted around Quinn's vehicle and started running.

Ian went after her. "Dammit, Sabrina. Don't do this!"

A large black Hummer moved toward them at a high rate of speed. Ian had one option and took it. Going airborne, he tackled her, managing to maneuver mid-air so he could take the brunt of the fall.

She fought him like a lioness protecting her cubs—kicking, punching, scratching, screaming at him to let her go. Ian blocked every blow, but dammit, she wouldn't stop. Unable to control her almost manic movements, he clipped her on the chin. The instant her body went limp, he was on his feet with an unconscious Sabrina in his arms and dove into Quinn's waiting vehicle. They sped away.

The Hummer that had been racing toward them skidded to a stop.

Ian twisted around to watch what would happen. The Hummer remained motionless, but what got his attention was the driver, a man they had all trusted—Holden Marsh.

Sabrina returned to consciousness slowly. The mumble of voices a distant sound, obscured by the pounding in her head. She moved slightly and moaned at the ache in her jaw.

"Don't move too fast. I tried not to hit you too hard, but you'll have a headache."

Ian. Of course he would come after her. Why did… The memory of what had occurred jolted her consciousness and she shot up. Agony sent her back down to her pillow as waves of nausea roiled in her stomach. She closed her eyes and spoke between clenched teeth. "Zach and Savvy…he's going to kill them."

"We're fine, Bri." Savvy's face appeared before her, tears glistening in her worried eyes. "How could you put yourself in danger like that?"

The relief at seeing Savvy, knowing she and Zach were safe, was almost overwhelming. If there was ever a time she wanted to ignore her 'no tears' mantra, it was at this moment.

"Why, Bri?" Savvy asked again.

"I had no choice. They texted me and attached a video. It was live feed. They were going to shoot you both if I didn't come."

"Yeah. We know. We checked your phone."

Ian's hard voice told her he still didn't think what she'd done was correct. Well, tough shit. She'd had to make a split second decision. What else could she have done?

"Then you know I did what I had to do."

"Bullshit, Sabrina," Ian snapped. "You should've told us what was going on."

"I—"

"Here." Quinn appeared before her, handing her a small white pill, along with a glass of water. "This'll help with the pain."

"No, I don't want to sleep. I need to talk…figure out what we're going to do."

"It won't put you out…just ease the ache."

She thanked him with a half-hearted smile, put the pill on her tongue and then gulped down the water.

Easing her head back onto the pillow, Sabrina eyes roamed around the room. It seemed the gang was all here and every one of them had the same exact expression—concern and anger mixed with bafflement.

"Look, I know it looked crazy, but I didn't have a choice. The video of Zach speaking was live feed. The bastard was there in the audience filming. The text said that if I didn't get to the checkpoint, alone, within five minutes, both Zach and Savannah would die."

"We know, Bri," Savvy said. "We've all seen it."

"Well then, why is everyone staring at me as if what I did was crazy?"

"Oh, I don't know…" Ian's voice was thick with sarcasm. "Could it be because you almost got yourself killed?"

"Oh for the love of…" Sabrina expelled a giant, exasperated sigh. "What the hell was I supposed to do? Call a Wildefire meeting so we could discuss our options? I went with my gut."

"What were you going to do once they had you, Bri," Sammie asked. "Did you think about that?"

Of course she hadn't. She'd had one thought only. Imagining Zach being shot. Knowing Savvy would see that and then she would be shot, too? Even now, when she had time to think about it, she still couldn't come up with a better solution. Saving her sister and brother-in-law was the only thing that counted.

"Did you find the guy who sent me the recording? Was it one of Silva's men?"

"We found him and no, it wasn't one of his men," Zach said. "Quinn called and told us what was going down. Based on the location of the recording, we pinpointed where the camera was and found the guy. It was Sid Everhart's kid, Trenton."

Sabrina shook her head. "That makes no sense. He's barely sixteen years old. Why would he—"

"He didn't know what he was doing. Said he was getting gas at a service station about ten miles out of town yesterday when some guy approached him. He asked him if he lived in Midnight. When the kid said yes, the guy gave him fifty bucks to text him if anything interesting happened in Midnight. Trenton texted the guy about this morning's radio announcement and meeting. He was told if he recorded it, he'd get another fifty.

"I've got him sitting in jail right now. His dad's with him and he's none too pleased."

So it had all been for nothing. They hadn't had guns on Zach and Savvy as she'd feared. Her eyes roamed around the room again, seeing the confirmation of her thoughts in everyone's eyes. "Guess I panicked."

"And almost got yourself killed." Ian's grim voice told her she would get no sympathy from him.

Arguing would do no good. She'd done what she thought she had to do. "So what's the plan? I am so ready to kick Silva's ass." She ruined the tough statement by having to cover her mouth from a yawn and then almost cried aloud at the pain in jaw.

She didn't know who she was the most irritated with—Ian because of his inflexibility, Quinn for giving her a pill that obviously was going put her out, or herself for causing a near disaster.

She concentrated on the easiest of the three and glared at Quinn. "I thought you said those pills wouldn't make me sleepy."

His mouth twitched as if he fought a smile. "They shouldn't unless you're already exhausted. Based on those shadows beneath your eyes, I'd say the answer is obvious."

Sabrina shook her head. "I don't have time for a nap. I'll sleep when this is over."

"Will you? Or will you stay awake to keep from having nightmares?"

Sabrina turned the full focus of her glare to Ian. How dare he mention her nightmares. The last thing she wanted was for her sisters to start asking questions about what kept her up at night.

"When did your nightmares start back, Bri?" Savvy asked. "Are they the same ones you used to have or new ones?"

All eyes focused on her. Everyone's but Ian's held concern, compassion. His held a challenge. Would she tell the truth? That her nightmares had never stopped. And after she'd learned the truth about how her parents had died, they'd become worse and more evil. Of course she couldn't say that.

"Ian's exaggerating. Besides don't you think we should be focusing on Silva and what he's going to do next?"

Sammie sat on the edge of the bed and brushed a gentle hand over Sabrina's hair. "You need to get some rest, sweetie. You're exhausted."

"I'm not sleepy." She was thankful that everyone politely ignored another yawn. She hurriedly covered her mouth.

"Get some sleep," Savvy said and dropped a kiss on her forehead. "Thanks for watching my back, sis. I love you."

Despite her protestations, she simply couldn't keep her eyes open any longer. Deciding she'd be able to think more clearly when the clouds of exhaustion disappeared from her brain, Sabrina closed her eyes. And when she woke, she and Ian were going to have a serious discussion on boundaries. How dare he reveal—

Sleep claimed her before she could finish her thought. But once again, a peaceful rest was not to be hers as she plunged hell pit deep into an all too familiar nightmare.

Ian kissed Sabrina's forehead. She was already asleep and he hoped like hell she wouldn't wake for several hours. He'd never known anyone who could exist on so little sleep. He'd done it in the army but that'd been a necessity to stay alive.

He followed the crowd out of Sabrina's room and headed down to the living room where most of their meetings had been. Samantha and Savannah held back to walk with him. He knew what was coming. A part of him felt guilty for exposing her nightmares, another part was glad that they were out in the open. How had her sisters not known?

Savannah grabbed his arm. "Tell us about Bri's nightmares."

"That's up to Sabrina to tell you."

Samantha stood beside her sister. "You're the one who opened the door, Ian. You risked Bri's wrath to let us know."

Wrath was a good word for it. She was furious with him though she'd done her best to act only slightly irritated. But he'd seen the betrayal in her eyes. Right now, that couldn't matter. Sabrina might never understand that his love for her went far deeper than his need to keep the peace between them. She needed help. He hoped, with her sisters' support, she would see that.

"I risked her anger because you two need to know what she's going through. It's up to her if she wants to tell you more."

"She had them for years after our parents' deaths. We all did to some degree." Savannah shared a worried look with Samantha. "Ours stopped...we thought hers had, too."

Samantha snorted. "That's because she told us they had."

"She probably didn't want us to worry."

Ian held his tongue. Though not worrying her sisters might have been part of it, that wasn't all. He'd heard too much, held her too often after a bad one to believe that concern for her sisters' feelings was the only reason she didn't tell them.

They entered the living room where Zach and Quinn were pouring coffee and chowing down on the food that April had picked up at Faye's. With everything that was going on, no one had taken the time to eat.

Ian grabbed a ham biscuit, swallowed half of it in one bite and then washed it down with a cold glass of orange juice. "So who's going to make the call to Marsh?"

Zach took one last gulp of his coffee. "I will. And he better have a damn good explanation."

"You think he's been playing us?" Quinn asked.

Zach placed the cellphone on the table. "I don't know jack-shit anymore, but I do know I'm tired of playing it his way. We could've easily lost Sabrina today." He punched in a number and then hit the speaker button.

Marsh answered on the first ring. "That was a close one."

"You want to tell us what the hell is going on?" Zach said. "You were coming after Sabrina to take her to Silva?"

"I was trying to prevent her from being taken." An explosive sigh almost rattled the phone. "Listen, the man's gone off his rocker. I figured he would but not this bad. He's a control freak and has lost control on several fronts. I expected erratic behavior, but I think he's about to lose it completely."

"Maybe you'd better tell us what else he's lost control of."

"His wife and kids have disappeared."

"Someone took them?"

"No…not exactly. They're in a safe place."

"Your doing?" Ian asked.

"A member of my team. She was inside…undercover, too."

"Why didn't you tell us about her…about these other things that are happening?" Savannah asked.

"There was no need. Your part should've been over. Would've been over if Ashley hadn't come back to him."

"Fair enough, but it's gotten out of control," Ian growled. "Sabrina could have been taken today."

"I agree," Zach said. "And I'm not going to have my family or my town terrorized. This has to end."

"Look, I just need a couple more days. Besides, you have no viable proof that Silva is even remotely related to Ashley's death or the threat against Sabrina. It's your word against his. It wouldn't have a chance in hell of standing up in court. We need more."

"Maybe so, but between my contacts, as well as Zach's and my sisters', we can make it uncomfortable for him," Savannah said.

"And it'll get you nowhere. You'll either piss him off or most likely amuse him. Have patience. My people—"

"Your people have two days," Zach warned. "After that, we'll do what we have to do."

After a long, tense silence, Marsh expelled another harsh breath. "I'll let them know. How's Sabrina doing? Looked like you clocked her hard, Mackenzie."

Ian's stomach turned. He'd have that memory in his head forever. "She's fine. She's resting now."

"I really didn't expect to see her running down the middle of the road, ready to give herself willingly to Silva. Girl's got some grit."

Yes she did, Ian thought, but unfortunately she also had a wild, impulsive streak that overcame commonsense far too often.

"Her family means a lot to her." Lame words for the powerful emotions he knew she felt about her family. They were everything to her.

"I'll do my best to see that no one else gets hurt. Sorry it's come down to this."

"Do what you can," Zach said, "and do it fast."

"Will do. I'll let you know of any new developments."

The instant the call ended, Zach was up and issuing orders. "We're not going to wait around while Marsh and his people get their ducks in a row. We've got to be proactive. Be ready for whatever might come our way."

"And that's why you should use every weapon you have, which includes me."

Ian frowned over at Samantha. "What are you talking about?"

It was apparent that Quinn already knew what his fiancé meant because he stood, shaking his head slowly. "Hell, no, not in my lifetime."

"Or mine."

All eyes turned to the doorway where a determined looking Sabrina stood. The blooming bruise on her cheek stood out in stark contrast to her too pale face. "Pretending to be me is not an option, Sammie. If it becomes necessary to go after Silva that way, then it'll be me playing me."

More frustrated than he'd been in ages at the stubborn woman he loved, Ian glowered at her. "I thought you were going to sleep."

The defensive shrug she gave told him what her words wouldn't. She'd had another nightmare.

"No one's going after Silva," Zach said. "It that understood? We'll find another way without putting anyone at risk."

"What are we going to do then?" Both Savannah and Samantha went to stand beside Sabrina. It was a united front of Wilde women.

Zach glared at his wife while Quinn shot daggers at his fiancé. Ian joined the two men, his determined gaze focused on Sabrina. She would not be putting herself out as the sacrificial lamb again. This shit had to stop.

Little did they know that as the Wilde women faced the men who loved them, another man had already decided their fate.

CHAPTER TWENTY-EIGHT

Chicago
Silva's estate

Robert paced back and forth in his office. His breath came in spurts and pants, his skin was clammy and cool. He was alone. Having his men see his fear would make him look weak. They needed to see his strength, his unwavering resolve. And that was why he'd ordered everyone out because dammit, he was afraid.

Someone was trying to destroy him. Not that it was an unusual occurrence. He'd been living outside the law and avoiding legal consequences for as long as he could remember. It was his birthright. Inheriting the family businesses and making them thrive was an obligation he took seriously. His grandfather and father had been skilled but somewhat backward when it came to branching out. They'd both been eliminated by competitors. Robert didn't intend for that to happen to him.

He had taken what his family had made and expanded, quadrupling his wealth. He'd worked too long and too damn hard to allow someone to destroy what he had created.

Who was the culprit? He had thousands of employees all over the world. He wasn't well liked, but he was respected and feared, which was much more important. Yet someone, somewhere didn't fear him enough. That someone had to be stopped.

His troubles had begun with that private investigator, Sabrina Wilde. She had obviously helped set this up. Who was she working with? No way in hell was she doing this alone.

He should've had the bitch killed instead of bringing her to his home to play. She'd been a sweet little treat. One he'd intended to enjoy before he made her disappear permanently. That had been his mistake, but one he would rectify. He would bring her here, make her reveal the traitor, and then eliminate her.

Losing his pets was an inconvenience. The women were unimportant and easily replaceable. Besides one of them had come back to him and he'd showed her exactly what she was worth.

And Lauren? He'd have another chance at her someday. No one could stop Robert Silva when he set his mind on his goal.

The disappearance of Erica and his children was another matter—a gravely serious one. More than an inconvenience or minor irritation, it was an embarrassment. If a man couldn't control his family, then how could he be expected to oversee a multi-billion dollar business? His reputation was at stake. He had to get them back.

Robert continued to pace back and forth, his temper rising with each step. How dare anyone do this to him. He was Robert Silva, feared by all, revered by many. He had contacts. Paid people high up in the government to look out for him. And not just this government, but several others as well. He could leave the States right now...take his business to a half-dozen other countries where he would be welcomed with open arms. Did the idiots think he had no contingency plan? No way out? He would show them. Would show them all. He was Robert Silva. No one got the best of him. No. One.

The timid knock on the door was an irritant. Any other time, he would've refused to answer until the man's fist was bloody and he'd learned his lesson. Today he had bigger fish to fry.

"Enter!" Robert said in his most commanding voice.

The door opened as timidly as the knock had sounded. Who was this insipid little wimp? He had a mind to shoot the spineless creature the minute he showed himself. How had he hired such a weak—

Lewis French stuck his big head inside. His pock marked face, with its giant pug off-kilter nose, droopy eyes, and extra thick lips, was both repulsive and intimidating. He was one of Robert's toughest men. The mournful expression on his ugly face told Robert something dire had happened.

Dread washing through him, Robert barked, "What's wrong?"

"Two of your warehouses, the one in Detroit, the other in Colombia have been raided."

Robert fell back into a chair, vaguely glad there had been one to catch him. Those warehouses were two of his largest. A new product shipment had been due to go out this afternoon.

His mouth felt numb, his limbs frozen. "Did they...." He swallowed to clear his dust dry throat and croaked, "Had the shipments left yet?"

Sorrow in his eyes, Lewis shook his head. "They got it all. I'm sorry, sir."

A tidal wave of fury roared through him, sweeping away the numbness and shock. Only a handful of his employees knew about those two warehouse locations. Even the warehouse managers didn't know the real name of their employer. He held this information as close to his chest as any tightfisted poker player. Which one of those six men had given him up?

Lewis cleared his throat. "There's something else."

Hell, what could be worse than this? Almost half his empire had been seized. He wasn't ruined, but he was damn well bruised and bloodied.

"What else?"

"One of your contacts called. I took the message cause you didn't want to be disturbed. He wouldn't wait until I got you so you could talk to him. I—"

"Get to the point, man!"

"A warrant is being issued for your arrest."

Shock brought Robert to his feet. "That's not possible. Just not possible. I've got too many people looking out for me to even let that happen."

"Some people are talking, sir. Revealing secrets."

"People? What people?"

"Your wife."

So that's what had happened to the bitch. He felt a trace amount of humor. "She doesn't know a damn thing. If that's all they got, then there's nothing—"

"They have more, sir. Said there were two men that were talking, too—Frederic Richie and Lionel Wilson."

Those two men were supposed to be dead. He had ordered their deaths himself. And one man was supposed to carry out both executions.

Robert gripped the edge of his desk, and with great effort forced a mild tone. "Ask Marsh to come in, would you?"

Two minutes later, Marsh entered as cockily as he always did. That had been one of the reasons Robert had trusted the man so much. He didn't show the fear that most of his other employees showed. Robert had liked that arrogance...trusted it. Thought with that kind of attitude there'd be no way the man would ever betray him.

"You wanted to see me?" Marsh said.

Robert leaned back in his chair, let his eyes roam up and down. The man was not only a traitor, he'd gotten lazy. The bulk beneath Marsh's shirt was much thicker than when he'd first started working for him. The idea that this man believed he was so safe that he even allowed himself to get sloppy and out of shape was an added insult.

"I have one question for you. Did you sell me out to the highest bidder or are you an undercover cop?"

Surprise, then alarm flickered in the other man's expression. If Robert weren't so infuriated by the bastard's betrayal, he might have enjoyed the moment.

"I'm not sure what you're talking about, Mr. Silva. I've neither sold you out nor am I a cop."

"Then tell me why Lionel and Frederic are talking to the authorities instead of feeding the fishes? And how did the Feds get to my wife?"

If he'd had any doubts before, they were immediately washed away by the grim knowledge in Marsh's eyes. "I see someone's been talking."

"You're not going to deny it again?"

"What's the point?" Apparently hoping to distract him, Marsh said, "You'll be in jail before nightfall" and went for his gun.

Already prepared, Robert fired three shots into the traitor's chest. An expression of anguish passed over Marsh's face before he fell, thudding like thunder to the floor.

Robert allowed himself a quiet moment of joy. The traitor was dead.

And now he had one more thing to handle before he left the country. One more small but important task to see to…tie up one last loose end before he disappeared completely.

They would never see him coming.

Midnight

Ian sat across from Sabrina and watched as she consumed a decent if skimpy meal. One scrambled egg and a half slice of toast wasn't much, but it was more than he'd seen her eat in the last two days so he decided to call this progress and move on. He had agreed to talk to her, but only if she ate. The forceful way she was shoveling food into her mouth wasn't from her enjoyment of the meal. She had an agenda and wanted to get on with it.

She washed down the small meal with the last of her orange juice and slammed the glass onto the table so hard Ian was surprised it didn't crack.

"Now can we talk?"

He nodded. "Of course."

"You had no right to tell them about my nightmares."

He cocked his head questioningly. "You've got a maniac who wants to kidnap, torture, and murder you. A town that's on edge. And your primary concern is that your sisters found out you still have nightmares about your parents? Why? What is it about your nightmares you don't want your sisters to know? Do you not think they'd understand?"

"They don't need anything else to worry about."

"Contrary to what you may believe, I don't think your nightmares are near as concerning to them as is your need to hide them." He grasped her hand in his and squeezed gently. "What is it you're hiding, sweetheart? Tell me. Let me help you."

She pulled her hand from his and stood. "I think we need a break, Ian."

Blowing out a frustrated breath, Ian went to his feet. "Fine. Let's go for a walk. It'll be good to get some sun on your face. We've got watch in a couple of hours. We can—"

Ian cut off his words when Sabrina started shaking her head. "What?"

"I mean a break from each other. When this is over, I think it'd be a good idea if we didn't see each other for a while."

He had underestimated her fear. Not only did she not want her sisters to know about her nightmares, she feared Ian digging deeper into them.

"I see."

"You deserve someone who can offer you more. I'm not that person."

"So we're breaking up?"

She raised that stubborn chin of hers, hid her thoughts behind the familiar belligerent façade. "Yes."

Ian had a lot he wanted to say, could say, but damned if he wasn't tired of trying. Instead of challenging her, he turned and walked away.

Sabrina gripped the back of her chair. She couldn't breathe. The ache in her chest was too great. Everything within her told her to call out his name, tell him she didn't mean what she said. Do or say anything to fix what she had broken. Frozen in place, unable to act, she watched as he strode out of the room without another word.

Tears blurred her vision. Blinking rapidly, she fisted her hands and willed the moisture away. Crying didn't solve one damned thing. She might be a coward, but she was no crybaby. Did crying bring her mother and father back? Erase her sins? Hell no.

Ian deserved someone who could commit. Someone not screwed up from the past. Someone who would love and appreciate him for the amazing man he was. That person couldn't be her. She might want that happiness with all her heart but she couldn't grab it…didn't deserve it. A girl who'd caused her parents deaths didn't deserve happiness.

"Bri…come quick."

Sabrina whirled around to see both Sammie and Savvy standing at the doorway. The worry in their eyes pushed her grief aside.

She followed as they went into the living room where Zach, Quinn, Brody, and Logan stood in the middle of the room as if frozen in place.

"What's wrong?"

"Listen," Zach whispered. "You hear that?"

Sabrina held her breath and strained to hear. A whirring noise. Sounded like a… "Helicopter," she said softly.

Zach's radio sputtered and crackled a warning. "Chief?" Bart Odom's voice, pitched high with excitement, came through slightly garbled. "We got trouble coming. It's headed to your house."

A roaring noise boomed outside, above the house. What the hell? Was Silva brazen enough to land a helicopter in their front yard? Was he that crazy?

The whirring noise ended and the sounds of men shouting out orders followed.

Hell yes, he was that crazy. They were under siege.

Sabrina ran to the window. Like a giant prehistoric bird, the helicopter sat in the middle of their peaceful, beautiful yard. Only last week, they'd played tag football in the very spot where a half dozen men, armed to the teeth, swarmed around the helicopter. And in the midst of that lethal swarm was Robert Silva.

"Listen up," Zach called out from behind her, "they've jammed the cellphones. I got a call into my office before I got cut off. An emergency broadcast will instruct folks to stay in their homes. We'll have some help coming from surrounding towns, but until reinforcements arrive, we're on our own." He held up a box. "I've got five walkie-talkies. Frequency's too low for the jammers to mess with them. Grab one and your weapons. Cover the house, front and back. Don't shoot until absolutely necessary or on my say so. Got it?"

Everyone else went into action while Sabrina's eyes frantically searched the room. One very important person was missing from their group. "Where's Ian?"

CHAPTER TWENTY-NINE

There was a fine line between having balls of steel and being stupid-assed crazy. Robert Silva had taken a giant leap across that line today.

Just how the hell did Silva expect to get away with this? Flying in a helicopter full of armed men as if he could just massacre an entire town? Marsh had said Silva was losing it…gone off the deep-end. In Ian's opinion, the man was well beyond deep-end and was head over ass bat shit crazy.

Crouched behind a giant Juniper, Ian pulled out his cellphone and hit Zach's speed-dial number. Nothing happened. He checked the read out. Shit. No signal. Silva had likely brought jammers to the party.

Had Zach been able to get a call off before the phones went down? Was help on the way or were they on their own? If Zach had gotten a call out, every law enforcement agency within a hundreds miles was probably on their way. Should he take Silva down now or hope that the cavalry arrived before somebody did something even more insane?

Could he take that chance? Sabrina was in that house, along with a lot of good people he cared about. The answer was a no brainer. No way in hell was he going to wait. Silva was going down.

The asshole was easy enough to spot. Not too many men showed up in an Italian suit and silk tie to commit kidnapping or mass murder. With his dark hair slicked back and thousand dollar shoes on his no doubt manicured feet, he looked like he was going to some kind of freaking business meeting. He obviously believed his men would protect him.

Six men armed with military grade weapons surrounded Silva. Ian counted three…no four with MP5s. Looked like the other two had AK-47s. Silva was an anomaly with a Glock in one hand and a bullhorn in the other.

They all stared at the house without moving, as if they were waiting for something.

Dammit, the bigger guys were in the back, covering Silva's ass. Ian didn't have a clear shot from here. Staying low, he ran a few yards to the right. It was summertime and the yard was filled with all kinds of leafy bushes and trees. A man could stay hidden and take his time till he was ready to engage.

Halfway to his destination, Ian came to a screeching halt. Another man occupied the same place Ian had been heading. And he was most definitely not one of Silva's men. If he wasn't mistaken, it was Neal Benfield, the pharmacist from Tatum's Drug Store.

Not wanting to startle the man since he was holding a shotgun, he said in a quiet whisper, "Benfield, what are you doing here?"

With his white beard, round glasses, and rotund belly, the pharmacist looked like he should be dressed in red and ho-ho-hoing, not expertly holding a shotgun on seven armed and dangerous criminals.

"Heard about the trouble here. Damned idiot thinks he can come to our town and shoot people willy-nilly? He's got another thing coming." He jerked his head toward a large bush only a few feet away. "There are more of us."

"How many?"

"Twenty...maybe thirty by now. We came on foot."

Ian couldn't contain his smile. Silva was in for some major surprises. Bastard hadn't counted on having to fight an entire town, most of whom could shoot a gun a helluva lot better than he or his men. On the other hand, neither Silva nor his men would hesitate to put a bullet through any of these people.

Ian needed to get to Silva and end this before the bloodshed began.

"I'm going to neutralize the main asshole. Can you cover me?"

"Sure thing. Which one is he?"

"The man in the middle. You can barely see him because of the goons surrounding him."

Benfield stretched his neck to see. "Yeah...yeah. I see him. I—Wait, is he wearing a suit and tie? Is he crazy or what?"

"I vote crazy." Ian said and took off.

He came across several more Midnight residents, five men and two women, before he made it to the other side of the yard. None of them surprised him more than Faye Grissom who was holding a semi-automatic shotgun like a pro and looking as though she could bring down the entire group by herself.

Crouching behind another large bush, Ian had no trouble getting a bead on the back of Silva's head. He would only get one opportunity to take him down. It was fifty-fifty what would happen after that. The men would either fire back or they'd surrender. Just how loyal were they? From what he knew about the man, Silva didn't exactly sound like the kind of leader who inspired loyalty. Would they give up to keep from being killed?

Either way, he had—

Silva raised his bullhorn. "Send out Sabrina Wilde and no one has to get hurt."

"Get the hell out of here while you're still breathing, Silva!" Zach shouted.

One of the goons moved, blocking Ian's clear shot. Shit.

A gun blasted. The living room window shattered.

Ian waited...waited. Not moving his eyes from his target. A clear shot would come again. He ignored the thudding of his heart. That was one shot. No one would've been at the window. No one was hurt. Sabrina was safe. Concentrate. Focus. Wait.

One of the goons moved, Ian squeezed the trigger.

Silva's men dispersed. A volley of shots rang out. Windows shattered, wood splintered. An unearthly noise erupted. The entire grounds became a battlefield as Silva's men fired at the house. Bullets whizzed from all angles. The citizens of Midnight shot at Silva's men from behind. Sabrina and the rest of the mansion's residents returned fire from the front.

Dammit, the hired guns didn't know their boss was down. They would continue to shoot until they were told to stop or they were dead. Ian ran to Silva who was flopping around on the ground like a landed fish.

Though a huge part of Ian wished he'd killed the bastard, Silva was alive on purpose. Imagining him in prison for the rest of his life was too tempting an image to pass up.

Grabbing Silva by an arm, Ian jerked him to his feet and pressed his gun to the man's head. "Tell your men to back off or you're a dead man."

Showing that he wasn't completely insane, Silva shouted, "Stop!"

It took several seconds before the firing finally ended. The quiet after the storm was almost as powerful as gunfire, a shock to the senses.

It took every bit of his control not to fire a bullet into Silva's head as Ian took in the devastation. The mansion was riddled with bullet holes. All the windows were shattered. The hanging baskets on the porch looked as though they'd exploded, leaving dirt and broken flowers scattered everywhere.

Material things, they could be fixed. But if anyone was hurt?

"If Sabrina or anyone in that house has one scratch on them, you're a dead man."

"So what do you intend to do?" Silva asked. "One man against my army? Your odds suck."

"One man?" Ian barked out a laugh. "Try an entire town, asshole. Okay guys, let's show them what Midnight, Alabama is made of."

One by one, men and several women came out from behind trees and bushes. Benfield had been wrong about the number. There were at least fifty people here and all loaded for bear.

"Now the smart thing to do is tell your men to drop their weapons and surrender."

"I am a Silva. We do not surrender."

"And here I was thinking you're not altogether stupid." His gun still at Silva's head, Ian glanced around. The armed goons had dropped their guns and were holding their hands in the air. At least two citizens of Midnight covered each one.

"Looks like your hired guns are a little smarter than you."

"You think you're so smart, Mr. Mackenzie. I have contacts and friends you could never fathom. You'll be the one in jail for holding an innocent man against his will."

Ian grinned. "That right? We'll just see about that."

Silva slumped, moaned dramatically. "I need medical assistance. My shoulder is injured."

"And believe me, it was my pleasure."

The front door opened. Zach walked out with a gun in his hand and a furious look on his face. He spotted Ian holding Silva, along with the other residents of Midnight with their guns on Silva's men.

"Looks like you caught yourself a puny one, Mackenzie."

He wanted to laugh at the joke but had to know one thing first. "Where's Sabrina?"

"She's right behind me."

His hold on Silva tight, Ian couldn't look away from the door. The instant Sabrina emerged, he began to breathe again.

Sabrina raced toward Ian, who stood beside an arrogant and harried looking Silva. Before she reached him, she did a once over of Ian's body, ensuring he was safe. The angry words she'd hurled at him earlier completely forgotten. She could easily have lost him today. And one thing she realized in the midst of the barrage of bullets—when she hadn't known if he was injured or dead—she couldn't bear to lose Ian.

"Everyone okay?" Ian asked.

"Yeah. A lot of damage, but nothing that can't be fixed." She cut her eyes over to Silva. "I cannot wait to see you behind bars."

"You'll have a long wait, I assure you. Or did you think your friend Holden Marsh would be helping you?"

"What are you talking about?"

"Simply put, I relocated three of my bullets into the traitor's chest before I arrived here."

Oh no. Poor Marsh. Instead of being able to be the one who finally put him away, Silva had killed him.

"Son of a bitch," Ian snarled. "Then you'll be punished for his murder, too."

"You have no idea who you're dealing with. My attorneys will have me out of jail before nightfall."

The oily smugness in Silva's voice made Sabrina want to vomit. No way in hell would the asshole get away this time.

"Now, if you don't mind, I need medical attention. I've been shot."

She couldn't argue with that. With the blood soaking his suit jacket, she was surprised he was still standing. Ian's grasp on him kept him upright.

Buddy Lawson from Midnight's volunteer fire department rolled a stretcher toward them. Ian pushed Silva onto the stretcher and using the handcuffs Zach threw him, cuffed both the man's wrists to the railing.

Midnight's deputies, along with Brody and Logan, handcuffed Silva's men. In the middle of Zach reciting Miranda rights to them, a familiar noise came from above. For the second time in less than an hour, the thundering flutter of helicopter blades filled the air.

All eyes went to the sky and then watched as a silver helicopter landed on the street in front of the mansion. Five men jumped out. Another one got out much more slowly but was easily recognizable.

Sabrina grinned. "Looks like you might've made a mistake about those bullets, Silva."

"That's not possible." Silva tried to get up and cursed when he realized how bound he was to the stretcher.

Holden Marsh walked toward them. "Everyone okay?"

"Yeah," Sabrina said. "Glad to see you are, too. Silva said you were dead."

"That's because Mr. Silva can't hit the broad side of a barn."

"That's not true. I hit you, you bastard. I know I did."

Marsh touched his chest and grimaced. "You hit Kevlar, you idiot. Broke a couple of ribs. Bullet proof vests come in damn handy when dealing with murderous assholes." He glanced at a man standing a few feet behind him. "Isn't that right, Walker?"

"Yeah. Thankfully."

Sabrina gasped and turned at the sound of a familiar voice.

"Hi, Sabrina." Ryan Walker gave her a crooked grin. "Sorry about what happened."

She shook her head. "Wow. Now I'm the one who's questioning herself. I saw you die."

"No," Marsh said, "what you saw was a fake execution. Silva ordered Walker's death. And since I kind of like the guy, I let him know what was going down."

"You could've let me know, too."

"Sorry," Walker said, "but I did tell you to be prepared for anything."

"You son of a bitch."

The snarl came not from Silva but from Ian.

"Ian…don't."

Ignoring her, he continued to glare at the two men. "You let Cruz put his filthy hands on her, almost sexually assault her. And you did nothing to stop it."

Walker eyes went glacial. "I killed the bastard. We had to let it play out or we never would have convinced Silva that we were both still with him." His expression softened slightly when he looked at Sabrina. "That was the reason Marsh came in so soon. Silva would have been glad to let it play out longer, but we put a stop to it as soon as we could."

She believed him but still resented not being told upfront. It would have saved her several bad moments.

"Don't blame Walker," Marsh said. "We were operating on need to know only."

"Your concept of need to know items needs to be changed," Ian said. "You scared the shit out of her for no reason."

"Ian, it's fine. Really." Sabrina patted Ian's tense arm soothingly and then nodded at both Walker and Marsh. "I am glad both of you are okay. And the entire town of Midnight is glad this is over." She paused and added, "It is over, isn't it?"

"Yeah," Marsh said. He jerked his head forward. "Let's get out of the crowd and I'll tell you everything I can."

Sabrina glanced down at Silva lying on the stretcher, pale and defeated, powerless and weak. It was a beautiful sight.

Perhaps it was small of her but couldn't resist flashing him a bright smile and saying, "See you in court, asshole."

Turning away before he could respond, she went with Ian, Marsh and Walker to the edge of the yard. On the way, she nodded and smiled her thanks to the Midnight residents who'd come to their aid. She vowed never to complain about their nosiness ever again. Without them, this wouldn't have turned out near as well.

As she listened to Marsh and Walker discuss the various charges Silva would receive, Sabrina took a moment to look around. The house was a wreck. Almost every window was broken. Bullet holes were scattered like pockmarks along the front siding. Shattered flowerpots, dirt, and broken flower petals covered the front porch. Yes it was a mess, but everything could be fixed, repaired, replaced. Nothing of great significance had been harmed.

Her eyes searched out her loved ones. Savvy and Sammie stood with Lauren, talking with several of Midnight's residents. Quinn was moving from one injured man to the next, checking their wounds. Zach and his deputies, along with Logan and Brody, were seeing to the arrest of Silva's men. All were here and accounted for. That was what mattered. Everything else paled in comparison.

"Sorry about this," Marsh was saying. "I didn't know until it was too late that the asshole was headed here."

Sabrina was too relieved at the outcome to be angry. "You said he'd gone over the deep end. I don't think any of us expected he'd do anything this outrageous."

"He seems to think he'll get out of it," Ian said.

Marsh snorted. "We've got an army of people ready to testify to make sure that doesn't happen. Plus, we found two of his warehouses. It's just a matter of time before we get them all. There's no doubt this time…the bastard is going down."

Sabrina glanced over to where Silva was being treated. The paramedics were slowly rolling the stretcher across the yard, headed toward the ambulance.

Ralph Henson stood talking with a group of men. Odd, she hadn't even noticed he was here. She turned to say something to Ian about it and then stopped, studied. Something was off…wasn't right. Henson was holding his gun low at his side, loosely, carelessly. The stretcher passed by Henson and Silva took advantage of the other man's stupidity.

As if in slow motion, Sabrina watched the man's arm swing toward them. She managed to shout, "Gun!" an instant before Silva fired.

And Ian, as always, put her safety above his. Throwing himself forward, he caught her in his arms, pushed her to the ground and lay on top of her, shielding her.

The ground slammed into her back. From a distance she heard shouting and multiple shots as chaos erupted. A deafening silence followed.

The body on top of her was a dead weight, utterly still.

"Ian?" she whispered."

No answer.

Oh God, no, no, no.

Suddenly she was free as someone lifted Ian from her and laid him on the ground. Blood poured from the wound that had gone into his back and straight through the other side. Sabrina crawled over to him. Her heart shattered. His face was pale, still. He was unmoving, unconscious. Oh God, was he breathing?

"Move, Sabrina. Let me see to him."

She scooted out of the way for Quinn to get to him but refused to release Ian's hand. Unable to take her eyes away from him, a prayer, a mantra formed in her mind: *Please not, Ian. Please don't take him, too.*

CHAPTER THIRTY

Ian blinked heavy eyes open. He was groggy, sore, and unaccountably angry for some reason. What had happened? Confusion dissolved as memory kicked in, panic quickly followed—Robert Silva and a gun. *Sabrina!*

Hearing a slight sound, he shifted his head and his gaze fell upon a beautiful sight. Sabrina—thank you, God, healthy and safe. The expression on her too pale face was one of sadness, her beautiful eyes dark with worry. Then he remembered one other fact. Ah hell, he'd been shot.

"So what's the verdict?"

"Hey!" She popped up from her chair, radiance replacing her darkness. "How are you feeling?"

"Like someone shot me. And I sure as hell hope somebody took care of that asshole who did."

"That's something you don't have to worry about. Silva is dead."

"I should've killed him when I had the chance. What happened? I remember seeing him pointing the gun toward you. That's about it."

"That's because you were being the hero again. Saving my ass."

"And what a pretty one it is, too."

Instead of smiling, tears glimmered in her eyes. "I thought I'd lost you."

"Takes a bigger gun than that to take down a tough skinned guy like me."

"Yeah. That's why you were unconscious for almost twenty-four hours."

"Hey, you'll spoil my tough guy image if that gets around." He glanced down at the large bandage covering his chest. "So what's the damage?"

"Surprisingly minimal. Quinn said if you're going to get shot in the back, you picked the perfect spot. No organs or arteries hit or even nicked. It was a through and through."

"Good to know there's a perfect place. I'll keep that in mind for the future."

"Seriously, Ian. You could've been killed."

"But I wasn't. I—" A sick thought came to him. "A through and through? Were you hit?"

She gave a slight shrug. "My shoulder. Barely a scrape. I didn't even know it until we got to the hospital. It's nothing."

"Let me see."

Unbuttoning her shirt, she lowered the material so he could see the small bandage on her shoulder.

"Does it hurt?"

"Not even a little. Didn't even need stitches."

"I'm pissed you were hurt that much."

"I'm perfectly fine."

He moved slightly, grimaced at the deep throb in his back and chest. He'd take the pain though. She was safe...that's what counted. "Everyone else is okay, too?"

"Yes. I don't know if Silva was aiming for me, Marsh or Walker. It might not have mattered to him. He just wanted to kill at least one of us."

He'd seen Silva's eyes when he'd turned that gun to aim. He would have killed Sabrina. Ian didn't doubt that for a minute.

"And who's the lucky one who got to kill Silva?"

"Hard to say. An instant after Silva fired, five people shot him. Zach, two of Marsh's men, plus Logan and Brody." She gave a sad smile. "Logan's really hoping his bullet was the one that counted."

"Can't blame him for that. What about Marsh? Is he pissed off that Silva is dead?"

"Actually I think he might've been relieved. He's been by twice to check on you. Feels all sorts of guilt for not making sure Silva was secure."

"He should've been. I put handcuffs on the bastard myself."

"They took one off to administer the IV."

"And who was the brainiac that gave him the chance to grab a gun?"

"That would be none other than the slimy slug Ralph Henson. He was holding his gun loosely in his hand. All Silva had to do was reach out and grab it as he went by on the stretcher.

"Zach's going to do his best to charge Henson with something. Aiding and abetting. Or maybe reckless endangerment. Said the charges probably wouldn't stick, but it'll give the idiot a few bad moments."

Ian glanced around at the surprisingly spacious hospital room. "So where am I?"

"Memorial Hospital in Mobile. Marsh's helicopter flew you here. He and Walker stayed behind to clean up the mess. Quinn and I came with you."

"And the rest of your family? They're okay?"

"Right as rain and thrilled to have this over. Zach and Savvy have already taken Camille Sage and Aunt Gibby back to Midnight. Sammie and Quinn are overseeing the repairs to the mansion. Logan and Lauren went away for a much needed vacation. And Brody is already looking at a new case."

"And I slept through it all."

She grinned. "Yes you did, you slacker." She went from amusement to somber in a flash. "Seriously, Ian, you scared me. I thought I'd lost you."

Now wasn't the time to mention what happened just minutes before Silva arrived. She had told him they were over, finished. That conversation could wait for another day. He was hurting, sleepy, and he had Sabrina looking at him as if she never wanted to let him go. For now he'd drift away with that image in his mind. Reality would come soon enough.

It was a week before Sabrina was comfortable letting Ian out of her sight for more than a few minutes. Quinn, as well as Ian's doctors, had assured her that he should recover without even a hint of residual damage. Even now, she couldn't get the image of a bloodied, unconscious Ian out of her mind. She had come so close to losing him.

They hadn't yet talked about what had happened before Silva had arrived and all hell had broken loose. She was sure he hadn't forgotten it. Hadn't forgotten that she had broken up with him… told him to go find happiness somewhere else. The stupid words she'd spouted echoed in her mind. When she closed her eyes, she could still see the hurt on his face.

She hadn't meant them. They were said for self-protection, not because she wanted to end it with him. And now she was faced with a dilemma. How could she reverse those words and get back what she had only just realized she wanted more than anything?

For the first few days after his injury, he'd slept a lot. Two days ago he'd been released from the hospital and she had insisted that he come home with her. He'd been about to say no. She'd seen it in his face, but then Savvy and Sammie, along with Zach and Quinn, had shown up and insisted he come back to Midnight and stay. She hadn't planned it, but the entire Wilde family ganging up on him had worked. He had agreed.

Yesterday he had walked outside, around the house. Soon he would want to leave. If she didn't say something soon—fix what she'd broken—he might leave like she'd asked him to and never look back.

As frightened as she was to reveal her emotions, she was even more scared of losing him.

Sabrina went to the bedroom where he'd been staying. She was ready to cut herself open and bleed herself dry if that's what it took. The room was empty. Not only that—his luggage was gone.

Running from the room, she sped down the stairs and caught him as he was coming out of the kitchen. He was holding a cup of coffee in one hand and a biscuit in the other. She was so glad to see him, she skidded to a stop and gave him a brilliant smile.

His mouth full of half a biscuit, he mumbled, "Uh oh. The way you're looking at me makes me think these biscuits were for something else."

"Oh no. I made them this morning. For you. I'm just happy to see you eat them."

"Good." He grinned and added, "Especially since this is my third one."

Feeling decidedly giddy now that she'd found him, she let her eyes roam over his body. "You should eat a few more. I think you've lost weight."

"Once my mom sees me, I'm sure she'll remedy that."

A reminder that his luggage was missing.

"You're leaving?"

He finished the rest of his biscuit in one swallow, washed it down with a long gulp of coffee, and nodded. "I talked to Quinn last night. He told me to check with my regular doctor in a couple of weeks, just to make sure everything was okay. But he said I was good to go."

Uncertainty replaced the giddy feeling. "You don't have to leave. I mean, it's not like you have to get back to work anytime soon, is it? You don't have any cases pending. Besides, you're still not fully recovered."

"No, but I need to see my family. It took a whole lot of persuading to convince them not to come to the hospital in Mobile. I know my mom. She needs to see for herself that I'm okay. The last thing you need is a horde of Mackenzies on your doorstep."

If there was one thing Sabrina understood, it was the love of family. Even if Ian's family was the most overwhelming one she'd ever been around. "I know you need to see them. I just…I was wondering…"

"Something wrong?"

She took in a breath and then let it explode from her with words, "I've been thinking."

"About what?"

"About us. About what I said…before. I don't want to take a break. This incident with Silva reminded me how good we are together."

"You mean working together?"

"No…well, yes. Working together but also romantically… as…um, lovers." She inwardly winced at the incredibly awkward and unromantic words. Words were one of Ian's gifts—being able to say sweet, sexy things. Phrases that either turned her heart over or turned her body into an overheated mass of desire. Sabrina wasn't good with them. Her feelings always felt too raw and powerful to communicate verbally.

He cocked his head, his brow wrinkled as if he were working a difficult puzzle. "So you want to go back to the way things were before this all happened?"

Nodding, her tense muscles loosening in relief, she was grateful he understood what she meant without her having to come out with something more touchy-feely.

"So we'd be like before? See each other on weekends. Go on vacations together. Spend all holidays here, with your family."

"Well, with the exception of Thanksgiving and Christmas, since I know you'd rather spend those holidays with yours."

"With nothing changing from what we had before."

A little taken aback by his cool tone, she frowned. "I thought you were okay with our relationship."

"There's one aspect of our relationship I've never been okay with."

"What?"

"The fact that you didn't want more than what we had."

"That's not true. Just because I don't say the words or we don't have a marriage certificate, doesn't mean I don't have strong feelings."

"I don't need the words, Sabrina. And contrary to what you might think, I don't need the paperwork either. But what I do need is you…all of you. Not just the parts you're willing to give me."

"I don't know what you're talking about."

The disappointment in his eyes shattered her heart. Ian had looked at her in many ways before, but she didn't know if he'd ever looked at her like this. For the first time ever, she felt as if she'd really let him down.

She took a breath, scrambled for the right words to make everything okay again. "I've been more open and honest with you than anyone else in my life."

"I believe you. That's what makes it so damn sad."

"Excuse me?"

"There's a line you can't cross, Sabrina. You've got so many secrets inside you...so many things you keep from me. From your sisters. Your family may be okay with that, but I'm not."

She snorted. "Don't be ridiculous. People don't tell each other everything. I'm sure you have plenty of things you've kept from me."

"Actually, I don't. But if there were something you wanted to know, you can be damned sure I'd tell you. And you know why? Because I trust you. I know you'd never take what I confide in you and use it against me. But you don't have the same trust in me, do you?"

"It has nothing to do with trust. I just can't..." She couldn't go on. How could she make him understand why she kept secrets without telling him what they were?

"You've got a lot of baggage. Something I've known for a long time, but I'd always hoped that someday you'd trust me enough to open up and share everything with me. I no longer have that hope."

"So what are you saying?"

"I'm saying goodbye, Sabrina. This just isn't going to work. I would kill for you, die for you. Hell, I'd even become an Alabama fan for you."

His brief attempt at humor was belied by the pain and sadness in his beautiful eyes. "I love you more than life, sweetheart, but I can't be with you. Not like before. Until you're free of the baggage that constantly shadows your every step and prevents you from being able to move forward, we can't be together."

The hurt was tremendous, the pain overwhelming…immense. She opened her mouth, tried and failed to speak. Her entire body trembled with emotions she'd successfully smothered for years.

"I don't want to hurt you."

Too late for that…too damn late. "So you want everything—my heart, my body, my thoughts. You ask for too much, Ian. Too damn much."

"I'm not asking for anything I'm not willing to give you myself."

She held out her hands to him, as close to begging as she'd ever been in her life. "This is all I have to give you. All I can give you."

"It's not enough."

"Fine." She drew in a shaky, jagged breath. "If you can't be satisfied with that, then you're right, we are over."

He raised a hand and touched her cheek in a brief, gentle caress. "Be happy, Sabrina."

With those words, Ian turned and walked out the door.

Sabrina didn't know how long she stood there. In a dim part of her mind, she remembered hearing an engine start-up and his vehicle drive away.

It could've been minutes or hours later that Sammie came to the door and said, "Hey, we're headed to Faye's for lunch. You and Ian want to join us?"

"Ian's gone."

"Gone? Wow, he must be feeling better. Will he be back this weekend or are you going to his house?"

"Neither." She straightened her spine, stood straight and determined beneath the crushing blow of pain. "We ended things."

"Ended things? What are you talking about? Why would you break up? That makes no sense."

Sabrina glared at her sister. "It makes perfect sense. Not everybody deserves a happy ever-after."

"Maybe not, but you guys sure as hell do."

Sabrina stomped past her sister, wanting only to get alone somewhere and deal privately with the devastation. "Ian does. I don't."

"What? Wait! Bri!"

But she couldn't wait. If she said one more word, all that emotion she'd stored up for years would explode and there would be no sign of Sabrina Wilde any longer. God only knew what would be left if she ever let that happen.

With each mile he drove, Ian's chest tightened a little more. By the time he got home, he wondered if he'd still be breathing. Telling himself he'd done the right thing wasn't helping. But hell, what else could he have done? Sabrina wasn't going to change. Pretending otherwise was pointless.

When she had told him she didn't want to end things, he'd had a momentary rush of extreme happiness. Maybe all the shit they'd gone through the last few months had been worthwhile. Maybe at last it'd broken that barrier she'd shielded herself with for so long. And then she'd kept talking and he had realized that nothing had changed at all.

He had no doubt that she loved him. Sabrina wasn't the type of woman to sleep around. Opening herself up…being sexual with someone meant being vulnerable to them. If she didn't care for him deeply she never would have been with him. But that didn't solve their problems. For Sabrina, intimacy could only go so far. She couldn't open up completely and because of that, refused to make a deeper commitment.

The last of Midnight disappeared in his rearview mirror and Ian felt the pain like a knife had entered soul and was slowly but surely shredding it apart. As if his guts were hanging from his body and he was bleeding out without any idea how to stop the flow.

Saying goodbye to her was a million times more painful than anything else he'd ever done. Doing the right thing used to be simpler. A man protected and provided for his loved ones. A man served his country. A man told the truth. A man stood up for what he believed in. Those were the good things in life… the right things.

And a man said goodbye to a future with the woman he loved because she saw no real future for them. Yeah, it'd been the right thing to do.

Today the right thing felt like death.

CHAPTER THIRTY-ONE

Sabrina sat on the edge of the bed and stared unseeingly at the floor. She was so infuriated with herself she wanted to scream. Her eyes burned with weariness, her mind blurred from exhaustion. And here she sat, like a knot on a log, unable to do the necessary thing.

What a coward she had become. She was afraid, literally terrified. Like a little kid who feared monsters under her bed or in the closet, she was afraid to go to sleep. Afraid to dream. This wasn't a new thing for her. She'd learned to exist on a minimum of sleep, but that was when staying awake hadn't been so damned painful. But now, because reality seriously sucked, she wanted to escape into sleep. And yet she feared it, too.

It had been two weeks since Ian had left her. He hadn't tried to contact her. He had said they were over, finished. As he'd shown many times in the past—Ian Mackenzie was a man of his word.

She couldn't blame him for ending things. How many times had he tried to get her to commit? Tried to get her to reveal the reasons for her nightmares. Dozens. Each time she had pushed him away, refusing to allow herself the happiness or the peace that came from total sharing...total commitment.

The man had been more than patient. He knew what he wanted. And he was tired of waiting for it.

Sabrina knew what she wanted too…she just couldn't take it. How do you take something you didn't deserve? How do you allow yourself heaven when you only deserved hell?

The knock on her bedroom door shook her out of her misery. Even though a knock in the middle of the night was never a good sign, she welcomed the reprieve. Before she could take a breath to even call out, "Come in" her bedroom door swung open and both her sisters were standing there.

Sabrina sprang to her feet. "What's wrong?"

"We need to talk," Savvy said.

The narrow-eyed look of determination on her both her sisters' faces had Sabrina's heart thudding. She glanced at her bedside clock. "At one-fifteen in the morning? Can't this wait until tomorrow?"

"No, it can't," Sammie said coolly. "This discussion is long overdue. Nineteen years to be exact."

The thundering in her chest drowned out Savvy's words, but Sabrina easily read "Damn straight" on her lips.

Wrapping her arms around herself was an obvious sign of self-protection and comfort. Sabrina knew better than to show that kind of weakness. She felt as if she were standing at the top of a skyscraper, teetering on the edge. One wrong move and she would topple a thousand floors to a hard, unforgiving sidewalk. Everything in her life would be splattered…revealed. She wouldn't be able to hide any longer. The truth would be out. They would know.

She tried for a reasonable, calm tone. "Listen. I don't really feel up to talking right now. I'm tired and really need to get some sleep. Can't we—"

"Don't give us that, Bri," Savvy snapped. "If we leave now, you'll be gone before daylight."

"Now where would I go?"

"Hell if we know." Sammie's eyes took on a challenging gleam. "You used to run to Ian. I don't know where you'll go now."

Oh, that had been a low blow. Even though it was the truth. She would be gone tomorrow. And yes, if she hadn't ruined things with Ian, she'd be on his doorstep by dawn. When had she become so predictable...so readable?

"You'll do anything to avoid talking to us," Savvy added. "This stops here."

Her breath was coming faster, harsher. If she didn't slow it down, she'd be in a full-fledged panic attack. And wouldn't that put the petrified cherry on top of her shit sundae?

She swallowed...took a silent, calming breath. Okay, she could do this. She'd been deflecting, deferring, avoiding for years. This was no different. She just had to find her cool again. This could still be turned around.

She cocked her head, arched a brow, even added a sneer to her mouth for extra emphasis. "I've managed to piss both of you off and all without saying or doing a damned thing. That's a new one, even for me."

"Oh you've said and done plenty, Bri. That's the problem. You've said and done so much, we completely missed what you were really saying."

"Good gosh, Sammie. You do know that makes no sense. Right?"

"None of this makes sense, Bri," Savvy said. "That's what's so puzzling."

"What?"

"Two nights ago, I walked by your bedroom. I heard you crying."

Sabrina snorted. "You know better than that. Crying's not my thing. It was probably the television."

"It was you, Bri. I knocked on the door and when no one answered, I walked in. You were asleep…and you were crying."

Even though Sabrina avoided tears like a plague of locusts, on numerous occasions she'd woken with a wet face. Having her emotions betray her while she was unconscious was frustrating, but she had yet to figure out how to stop them.

Still maintaining her cool façade, she lifted her shoulders in a careless gesture. "I'm sure you're mistaken about that, but so what if I was? Ian and I broke up. Is that not reason enough to cry?"

"Absolutely it's a good reason to cry. Except you weren't crying about Ian. You were crying about Mama and Daddy. You called for them, several times."

Could a person wither and die just from sheer misery? She had a feeling she was about to find out. Sabrina eyed the door behind her sisters. Could she skirt around them and escape? Dare she chance it?

And then what, Sabrina? Avoid your sisters for the rest of your life?

Spine stiff as an iron rod, she snapped, "So? I have nightmares about mama and daddy from time to time. Don't tell me you don't, Savvy. Or you don't, Sammie."

"Maybe we do, Bri. But it's doubtful that we say I'm sorry over and over again."

Oh Lord, no. Please. Not now. Not tonight. Not like this.

Hands on her hips, Savvy advanced into the room. It took every bit of courage for Sabrina to stand her ground and not back away.

"No answer, Bri? Maybe this'll help. Let me ask you a series of questions. If you answer honestly, I think we can get to the bottom of this fairly quickly."

"You're no longer a prosecutor, Savvy, and I sure as hell am not on trial."

Savvy went on as if Sabrina hadn't said a word. "What do you have nightmares about? Why do you cry out to Mama and Daddy, asking for their forgiveness? What on earth would they need to forgive?"

A knife to her chest couldn't hurt worse. This was it. This was what she had been avoiding for so long. What she never wanted her sisters to know.

No! There was still a way to get out of this. Think, dammit. Think!

"Nightmares don't make sense. You know that."

Sammie's mouth twisted with a wry smile. "Good try on the deflection, but it's a no go. What are your nightmares about, Bri?"

Fine. She could do pissed off about as well as anyone. "That's nobody's damn business. Not yours. Not Savvy's. Not Ian's. My thoughts, nightmares, dreams, are my own. They are none of your fucking concern. You got that?"

Tears blurred Savvy's eyes and Sabrina hadn't known she could feel any worse. She tried again, hating herself for lying but unable to do anything else. "Really, guys. It's nothing. Let it go. Please?"

"We want to help you, Bri. I'm sorry we didn't notice before, but we're noticing now."

Oh for heaven's sake. "I don't want you to notice anything, Savvy. I want you to leave, both of you. Right now."

"No," her sisters said in unison.

"Come on, Bri," Sammie said. "We love you. Whatever is bothering you, we want to help."

"You can't help me. Neither of you can." Realizing she'd admitted something she hadn't intended, she added a quick amendment, "I don't need help."

Sammie sauntered toward her, her smile as phony as Sabrina's often was. "Well then, let's just talk. Have a little girl chat like the old days."

"We can talk after we all get some sleep."

Savvy shook her head. "But you won't sleep, will you, Bri? Or if you do, it'll be in between nightmares."

"This is ridiculous." Grabbing her pillow, she skirted around her sisters and headed to the door. "I'll go find another bedroom to sleep in that doesn't have nosy, interfering sisters."

"Nosy, interfering sisters who love you more than anything," Sammie said.

"Please, Bri. Let us help you," Savvy pleaded. "There's nothing you could say or do that will stop us from loving you."

Sabrina jerked to a stop. The tears in her sisters' voices slashed through her heart, crumbling her resolve. She was hurting them when it was the last thing in the world she ever wanted to do.

Gripping the doorjamb, fingers strained tight, her nails digging so deep into the wood she vaguely wondered if she were leaving indentions. She could no longer live this lie. No longer keep the truth from them. No matter what happened, she had to reveal her greatest shame…greatest sin.

God. Oh God, oh God. Please help me do this. Please.

Turning, she faced the two people who meant more than life to her. Tears she had refused to shed for years streamed down her face. The violent tremble of her mouth barely allowed her to form the words she had held inside her for so long.

"I'm responsible for Mama's and Daddy's deaths."

She felt as if she were a stranger, standing outside her body, watching events unfold. Watching her sisters absorb the awful, terrible truth.

Shocked silence followed her confession. Finally, Sammie broke the stillness. "What the hell are you talking about?" With Savvy immediately adding, "Why on earth would you believe you had anything to do with their deaths?"

Of course none of this made sense to them. It was nineteen years ago. She and her sisters had been ten years old. They hadn't even been in Midnight when the murders occurred. How could one little girl cause such destruction?

Now that she'd forced the words from her mouth, she noticed a calming, numb-like feeling settle throughout her body. That was it... they now knew the worst possible thing about their sister. Anything else would be anticlimactic—the explanation was a mere formality.

"Do you remember the day we left for camp?"

When both her sisters nodded, she continued, "Do you remember I didn't want to go? I wanted to stay home and go to Miranda Kershaw's birthday party."

"I kind of remember that," Savvy turned to Sammie, who stood beside her, and talked slowly as if remembering. "All three of us were invited, but I think you and I were more excited to go on a camping trip than to a birthday party."

"I vaguely remember. Mama had built up the idea of summer camp so much in my mind, I couldn't wait to leave."

She shared a frown of confusion with Savvy before turning her gaze back to Sabrina. "But what does this have to do with their murders?"

Without even being aware of it happening, both her sisters had each grabbed one of her arms and led her back into the bedroom.

Sabrina found herself being pushed down on the sofa. As soon as she was seated, her sisters sat on either side of her.

"Tell us," Sammie said.

Taking in a breath, Sabrina revealed her deepest shame. "Mama and I were butting heads—like we sometimes did."

Both sisters nodded. Daddy had once said that Sabrina had popped from her mama's belly disagreeing with them. And while that was an overstatement, she admitted to having a stubborn streak from a very early age.

"I told Mama I didn't want to go to camp. She told me I had to. Things got really heated right before we left."

Her brow furrowed, Savvy shook her head. "I don't remember anything like that."

"That's because you two were already in the car. I held back, hoping I could get her to change her mind. She wouldn't. And I..." Sabrina tried to swallow and couldn't. The pain was too great.

"What?" Savvy urged.

"I told her I hated her. That it would serve her right if something happened and she never saw me again." Her lips twisted. "She swatted my butt and told me to get in the car or she was going to wash my sassy mouth out with soap."

A fleeting smile appeared on Savvy's face. That had happened to all of them more than once. And to Sabrina, who had been the sassiest, it happened at least once a month.

Sammie squeezed Sabrina's arm. "But what does this have to do with their deaths? I don't see any relationship whatsoever."

"I didn't either for a long time. I'd always felt so guilty that those were the last words I ever said to her. You'll never know how many times I wanted to relive those moments so I could take it all back."

"I can understand the guilt," Sammie said. "I remember how guilty I felt about some of the things I'd said and done that I'm sure embarrassed or hurt them, but that's just being a kid. They knew that."

"Maybe so, but this was so much worse."

"How so?"

"You remember that Aunt Gibby said Mama was upset after we left? That was the reason she and Daddy had a big fight. Everyone assumed it was because she missed us so much. But that's not the real reason. She was upset at me...for what I'd said to her. We didn't talk all the way to the camp. And when I got out of the car, I grabbed my backpack and walked away. Didn't even look back...didn't say goodbye."

"So?"

"So that's why she got so upset that night...why she and Daddy argued. Why she left the club early and came home alone. It was all my fault. None of this would have happened if I—"

Sammie sprang to her feet and whirled around to face Sabrina. "You're blaming yourself for what that scheming, murderous bitch did? That's ridiculous."

"No it's not. Everything that happened that day started with my selfish, immature tantrum. Those assholes may have committed the murders, but I was the catalyst. If I hadn't—"

Savvy grabbed her hand. "How could you even think that, Bri? And my God, how could we not know how you felt?"

"I couldn't tell anyone. I had learned to live with the guilt of what I'd said. It wasn't easy, but I had come to terms with it. I remembered the good times...all the times I'd told Mama I loved her. That's what I clung to.

"But then we found out what really happened. Found out the circumstances behind their deaths... what had started it all and I couldn't deny the truth. Without me causing that, they might still be alive."

Savvy squeezed her hand even tighter. "Bri, first of all, you're not responsible for their deaths. The fault lies solely with her murderers."

"But if I hadn't—"

"No…wait," Sammie said, "I was the one who mentioned going to summer camp in the first place. If we hadn't gone, Mama would never have gone to the club…she would have been home with us. So I guess it's really my fault."

Sabrina frowned at her. "Don't be ridiculous."

"No, no," Savvy said. "Don't you remember? I'm the one who told you about the camp, Sammie. So technically, it's more my fault than yours."

Sabrina shook her head. "Now both of you are being ridiculous."

Savvy arched a brow. "Oh really? More ridiculous than you are?"

Sammie dropped back down beside her, took her hand. "It breaks my heart that this has been eating at you for nineteen years, Bri. Why on earth wouldn't you tell us?"

"I thought you would hate me for what I did."

Tears filled Sammie's eyes but Savvy glared at her. "Sabrina Sage Wilde, how in the world could you even for one second believe we would hate you? Do you not understand how much we love you?"

Sabrina swallowed a sob. For the first time in her life, she understood the depth of her sisters' love for her. She had enough love for them to fill an ocean but had never realized that they loved her just as much.

"I don't know how I got so lucky to have you both as sisters. I love you guys so much. Can you forgive me?"

Two pairs of arms wrapped around her and they shared a three-way hug.

"There's nothing to forgive," Savvy whispered.

"I agree," Sammie said. "But even if there was, there's nothing on earth that would make us stop loving you."

Sabrina closed her eyes as tears streamed down her face. Even though she still felt the guilt for what she'd said to her mother all those years ago, her sisters' love and acceptance had lightened her burden. Maybe the truth could set her free after all.

CHAPTER THIRTY-TWO

Sabrina sipped her lemonade and enjoyed the last few moments of daylight. She was exhausted but in a good way this time. She and her sisters had spent most of the day in Mobile shopping. Well, Sammie and Savvy did most of the shopping. Since Bri wasn't and never would be much of a shopper, she was the designated opinion giver. And she had plenty of those.

They had giggled and reminisced just like the old days. And for the first time in her adult life, she'd felt free to be herself. All guards down, façade completely gone. Her sisters knew the worst about her and still loved her. Imagine that.

Now Savvy was having dinner with Zach and Camille in their private dining room upstairs. Sammie and Quinn were at their house. And she was here on the back patio, sipping lemonade. Alone with her thoughts.

Nothing had changed and yet everything was different. That only made sense to her. She was still free to be Sabrina, but she was also free from the worry of losing her sisters' love. That was indeed freedom.

Most people wouldn't understand the guilt she'd built up over the years. Not unless they'd experienced something similar. Done something equally as stupid and careless. But that was okay, too. She was who she was and quite honestly, she was okay with that.

"Sabrina Sage, I've got a bone to pick with you."

Startled, Sabrina watched Gibby march toward her like a top commander on a mission. If the pursing of her aunt's lips and the challenging glint in her eyes was any indication, this was not going to be a pleasant visit.

"What's wrong?"

"I'll tell you what's wrong, young lady. How in the name of all that's good and holy could you for even one second think you were in any way responsible for Maggie's and Beckett's deaths?"

Her sisters were loyal to a fault but had no doubt felt the need to let the matriarch of the Wilde family in on what Sabrina had told them. She was torn between anger at their interference and love because they cared so much.

She held up the pitcher of lemonade. "Want some?"

Gibby settled herself into a chair and nodded. "Don't mind if I do. And while I drink, you can explain yourself, young lady."

Fighting a smile at her sweet aunt's snippy tone, Sabrina poured another glass of lemonade. "I know you and my sisters think it's silly, but it's hard to get past what I said to Mama. If she hadn't been so upset that night, they might still be alive."

Gibby swallowed half her lemonade in one long gulp and gave a delighted sigh. "You do make mighty fine lemonade." She settled her glass on the table and then glared at Sabrina. "But you don't know beans from apple butter about why your mama was upset that night."

"But I—"

"Listen honey, I don't know all of what went on that night. None of us do. I do know that everyone has a choice. Some are silly—like your daddy flirting with that waitress. Or seemingly insignificant, like your mama deciding to leave the clubhouse and go home without Beckett. And some are downright monumental, like those murderous monsters that killed your parents and then made it all the worse by covering it up with a horrible lie.

"We all have decisions to make. Sometimes we make very bad ones, even if they don't seem bad at the time."

"Like when I told Mama I hated her."

"Maybe so. But what I do know is, it would literally break your mama's heart if she knew that you had been carrying that around with you all these years. Blaming yourself for what other people are responsible for."

"But—"

"I talked to her that day. Right after she got back home from dropping you girls off. She told me a little about your spat. Even laughed about it."

"She did?"

"Said she was torn between spanking your fanny and hugging you because you reminded her so much of Beckett."

A sharp pain clutched at Sabrina's chest. "You mean she wasn't upset with me? Then why was she so emotional that night?"

"Because she was missing you three something fierce. It was the first time y'all had been away from her. She didn't want you girls to go. Said when she realized that, it convinced her even more that you needed to go. And she was sure that once you got there, you'd have a good a time."

Her mother had been right. Despite the terrible guilt for saying something so ugly to her mother, she'd been having a blast. That hadn't lasted long since her grandfather had arrived the next day with the news that their parents were dead.

Though almost dizzy with relief, she had to make sure. Having carried this awful burden for so long, she couldn't believe one small conversation with her aunt could have taken all of that away.

"Are you sure, Gibby? I mean absolutely, positively sure she wasn't upset because of what I said?"

Gibby's eyes glazed with tears. "Oh honey child, I wish so much we'd talked about this before. She was missing you girls something terrible. Then Beckett, Lord rest his soul, flirted with that waitress at the club. I'm sure—one hundred percent sure—it was those two things together that got her so riled."

No matter what Gibby said about how her mother reacted to Sabrina's temper tantrum, she would always regret those words being the last ones she'd said to her beautiful, precious mother. But to know that her mother hadn't been hurt by them…that she had actually laughed? That the reason for the argument with Sabrina's father hadn't been brought on because of the vile words she'd hurled at her mother? That terrible weight of guilt she'd felt for so long was gone.

She felt lighter than air. And free…so very free. It hadn't been her fault…it hadn't…. A sob, unexpected and violent, exploded from her chest.

Gibby held out her arms and Sabrina practically threw herself into them. Enfolding her in a soft, fragrant hug, her aunt's voice quivered with emotion. "Hush now, darlin'. Everything's going to be okay."

And for the first time since she was ten years old, Sabrina felt they actually would.

Sarasota, Florida

Sweat poured down Ian's face. Switching off the engine of the push mower for a moment, he pulled out the hand towel he'd stuffed in his back pocket and wiped down his face and neck.

Cutting grass in the middle of a summer day in Florida was just asking for trouble. Didn't matter. He had a choice of either working his ass off or going crazy. Working was his only option. Besides, pushing the mower was good physical therapy. As long as he didn't die from heat exhaustion, that is.

"Son, I made some iced tea. Come on in out of the heat and cool off."

Ian looked at the progress he'd made on the lawn. With ten kids to raise, his parents had made sure they had a giant yard to play in. He was only halfway done but figured if he didn't cool down he'd die of heat stroke before he could finish.

Following his mother to the patio, he noticed three glasses sitting beside the tea pitcher. Then his dad walked out from the house. He took one look at his parents' faces and knew this was more than an opportunity to cool off. They wanted to know what the hell was going on with him.

He hadn't told them that he and Sabrina broke up. When he'd arrived on their porch a couple of weeks ago, his mother had taken one look at him and had known something was off. And his mom being the wisest woman he knew hadn't asked questions. She had fed him, mothered him, let him know she was there if he needed to talk, and loved him the way she had from the moment he'd met her.

He hadn't planned on staying so long. There was plenty of work he could do at his office. Plenty of cases he could take on. Concentrating on those cases was another matter. So the choice had been easy. He'd stopped at his house long enough to grab more clothes, picked up Jack from the sitter, and then he'd been off again.

For now, being in the place where he'd always known unconditional love felt right.

Ian dropped down into his chair and gave his mother a smile of thanks for the large glass she placed in his hand. He drank three-fourths down in one thirsty gulp and put the glass on the table.

Instead of meeting their concerned gazes, he stared at his almost empty glass and finally gave his parents an explanation. "Sabrina and I are no longer seeing each other."

His mom grabbed his hand and squeezed gently. "Ah, honey, I'm so sorry."

"I'm sorry, too, son. I know you thought she was the one."

He didn't bother to correct his father. Ian didn't think it... he knew it. Sabrina was the one for him. It was just too damn bad she didn't feel the same way.

His mother was always more in tune with her children's deepest feelings. "This last case you worked on took an emotional toll on both of you. You could've died. I'm sure when things settle down...get back to normal, you two will mend your fences."

If he hadn't called it quits, Ian was sure that would have happened. They could have gone back to their same old relationship. It was definitely what Sabrina had wanted.

With every step that had taken him away from her, his heart had been telling him to turn around and accept what she could give him. What they had was better than what most people had. But dammit, they could have so much more.

"I don't think so, Mom. Not this time. Sabrina and I want different things."

"You broke up with Sabrina?"

Alana stood at the patio door. The disappointment in his little sister's face was understandable. She and Sabrina had gotten along great.

"Yeah."

"But why? She's perfect for you."

"Can't deny that. I'm just not perfect for her."

"Then she's stupid."

"Alana."

Molly Mackenzie's admonishment wiped the indignant look from his sister's face. "I'm sorry, Ian. I really liked her. She was the coolest girl you've ever brought home."

"Thanks, sweetie. She's definitely something special."

"She told me next time she came for a visit she would teach me how to take a guy down with one hit."

"Some guy bothering you?"

The eye roll was one only a teenager could do so expressively. "No. But if I know how, I won't have to worry about it if one ever does."

"I can teach you how to do that."

"I know you could, but not without that look on your face."

"What look?"

"The same one Daddy has."

Ian glanced over at his dad, whose fierce, protective expression would scare the breath out of most people.

Doing his best to cool his own expression down, Ian nodded toward the garage. "Go change clothes and I'll show you a few moves that'll have any guy running to get away from you."

She gave a cute little grimace. "That's not exactly what I want."

Ian swallowed a groan. He still wasn't ready to accept that his baby sister was actually dating. "Don't remind me."

"The lesson will have to wait," his mother said. "Colin, Debbie, and the kids are on their way over."

Colin and Debbie's five kids would definitely put a kibosh on more yard work, too. And knowing his brother, he'd called his other brothers and sisters. Wouldn't be long until the entire house was overflowing with Mackenzies—just the way his parents loved it.

Ian no sooner had that thought when the flood began. Colin walked out carrying his three-year old son, Brett, on his shoulder. Debbie followed behind him with their newest addition, Sarah, in her arms. Their oldest, nine-year old Penny, marched out holding a bucket of chicken, and was followed by Mason and Madison, their twins, who each carried a sack of fixings. Then more Mackenzies erupted through the doors. Soon Ian was surrounded by his brothers, sisters, in-laws, nieces and nephews.

Just the way he liked it, too.

As he hugged his family and accepted the gentle ribbing from those who knew and loved him no matter what, Ian tried to tell himself that Sabrina would never have fit in with his big, boisterous family. That it was better they'd ended things. Problem was, he knew it was a lie. She would fit in here. She was confident and strong-willed enough to put up with his brothers' teasing and his sisters' sometimes invasive questions. She could hold her own with any of them. If she had given them a chance, she would have loved them, too.

He just wished to hell she had wanted to be a part of them… of him.

CHAPTER THIRTY-THREE

Two Months later
Tallahassee

This had to be the queen mother of all bad ideas. That was saying a lot because she'd had more than her share of spectacularly bad ones.

Knocking on a door at two o'clock in the morning was a good way to get your head blown off. Since the door belonged to the man who'd basically dumped her, it was also a good way to get her already bruised heart irreparably broken. She honestly didn't know which one would hurt the most.

She hadn't meant to get here so late. She could've waited until tomorrow and arrived at a decent hour. But when she had finally gathered her courage, she literally could not wait one more moment. She just prayed this wasn't a monumental screw-up.

He had told her he didn't want to see her again until she got rid of the baggage she'd been carrying around for years. And while she may have succeeded in ridding herself of her demons, she was far from the emotionally stable, mature woman Ian deserved. Hot-headedness, stubbornness, and impulsiveness were as much a part of her as her hair and eye color. She might be able to diminish and change them from time to time, but for the most part, she was who she was. Would Ian still want her when he realized she hadn't really changed much at all?

The porch lights blazed and her heart thundered against her chest. Was this the beginning of the end? Or could it be a new beginning for them? She would soon find out.

She had a plan…of sorts. Once she had made the decision to come here, she'd had no time to prepare. However, she had practiced a flowery, heart-felt speech all the way here. Hopefully he'd give her a chance to get it out before slamming the door in her face.

The door swung open and Ian stood there. Though his hair was mussed as if he'd run his fingers through it a few times, his eyes were alert as if he hadn't been asleep at all. And they were wary, and so very cool. Not one bit welcoming.

Sabrina's thudding heart took a nosedive. Even though she wanted to sink through the porch flooring, never to be heard from again, she raised her chin slightly and blurted, "We need to talk."

Well crap. That wasn't what she'd practiced. Where were the sweet, loving words she'd planned? What she'd just said sounded more like a demand…arrogant, prideful. A little bitchy.

"About what?"

Not exactly an invitation to come in and chat, but what had she expected after her not so friendly demand to talk? At least he hadn't slammed the door in her face.

She tried again, this time with all the humbleness in her heart. "I wanted to—" She swallowed hard, started again, "I thought if we could…I want…I mean… you…us… I—"

"Sorry, Sabrina. We don't have anything to say to each other."

Of all the responses she had expected, this wasn't one of them. She thought the worst would be a bit of yelling or a simple door slam in the face. Of course her hope had been the exact opposite. She had wished for so much more. But this cold, unemotional reception was even worse. As if he didn't care at all.

Nodding, she backed away, mumbling an apology. Not even really sure what she said. She just needed to get out of here before she cracked completely open. She flew down the steps, her only focus was to get away as quickly as she could.

Halfway to her car, strong arms grabbed her, pulling her off her feet.

"Put me down, dammit."

Instead of answering her, he did the most infuriating thing he could do—so Ian-like. He threw her over his shoulder and headed back into the house.

Sabrina saw red. Not only had he rejected her, he was treating her like a sack of grain. She pounded his back, fighting in earnest, determined to make him pay for not only breaking her heart but treating her so poorly. Okay, maybe she deserved it but that didn't negate the hurt.

"I said put me down, you lowlife, scum sucking—"

He laughed. "Sabrina, darling, you really do need to come up with some new insults. Those are quite dated. I think maybe you— " He broke off on a strangled gasp. "Holy crap, woman, what the hell are you wearing?"

Another cringe-worthy moment. It had been meant to be a symbol, but instead, Ian was taking advantage of her act of humility in a most unromantic and unchivalrous manner.

"Get your hands off my ass."

"You mean your very bare ass, don't you?"

"Still my ass, asshole."

"Now that's something I haven't touched, but who knows. We could experiment if you like."

"Ian Mackenzie, if you don't put me down within the next second I will take my gun and part your hair in a different direction."

"Okay, but just one more second." He took that second to fondle her naked backside again and then dropped her to her feet.

Sabrina looked around, realizing he had brought her into his living room. The television was on a replay of a college football game.

She searched for a friendly face. "Where's Jack?"

"He's asleep. Had a long day playing with the neighbor's kids."

She gestured toward the television. "Sorry to interrupt your guy time. If you'll excuse me, I'll leave you to your game."

"This game sucked, anyway." He clicked off on the remote. Crossing his arms in front of him, he arched a brow. "So you want to tell me why you're here?" Smoldering brown eyes swept over her body. "Dressed like that."

All the fire went out of her as she looked down at her almost non-existent clothing. The barely there, see-through dress had been a spur of the moment purchase with one intent only. Now she felt more exposed than she'd ever felt when she was completely naked in front of him. What had she been thinking?

She shrugged defensively, resisting the urge to cross her arms in front of her. "It seemed like a good idea at the time."

"Good thing you didn't get stopped by a cop on the way here. I'd hate to have to bail you out of jail for indecent exposure."

She turned to the door. "I'll get out of your way."

"Just like that, you're going to run? When did you become such a coward, Sabrina?"

She whirled around so fast she almost lost her balance. "I'm no coward, you jerkwad, pinhead. I just changed my mind."

"Ah…there she is." Relief flooded through Ian and he couldn't contain his delighted grin. He'd hated the defeated, sad look on her face. Her stumbling, rambling words had revealed how insecure she'd felt. Riling her up was the only way he knew to get her back on track.

"There who is?"

"The Sabrina Wilde I know." He didn't add 'and love.' Not yet. Yeah, he adored her, but he'd spilled his guts all over the floor way too many times to take this visit for granted. Who knew… maybe she'd come to grab his heart out of his chest and stomp on it again.

"Now tell me why you're here."

"You're not going to make this easy for me, are you?"

"Easy has never been our forte. Spill it, babe."

Breath shuddered through her as if she was gearing up for battle. Setting her chin at that stubborn angle he knew all too well, Ian braced for the worse.

"You told me a lot of things the last time we saw each other. Some hard truths I didn't want to face. Things I didn't think I could ever face. You told me unless I disposed of all the baggage I'd been carrying around with me, we couldn't see each other again."

Her slender body shook as though she was freezing and her expression went from determined to fearful in a flash. Ian watched with awe, wonder, and not a little astonishment as she wrenched the dress over her head and stood before him gloriously and beautifully nude.

She held her arms at her side, her body vulnerable and exposed. A defenseless, open target for whatever he wanted to dish out to her. "And here I am. Without baggage." Her mouth curved in a wry smile. "Without clothes." She swallowed. "Yours, if you still want me."

He almost went to his knees. Instead he took a step toward her.

She held up her hand to stop him. "Wait. I need to get this said or I won't be able to. You were right. I had a lot of baggage. Things my sisters didn't know and I believed if they knew, they'd never forgive me. Even stop loving me."

"You're not that easy to stop loving."

"Thank God for that. My sisters…well, they kind of forced it out of me. The whole ugly truth. I'll tell you all about that in a minute. The thing is… I should've had more faith in them. They don't hate me…still love me. Said there was nothing to forgive.

"It's taken me a long time to accept that. Longer than I thought it would because I realized that even if there was nothing they felt they needed to forgive, I needed to forgive myself. That took some doing."

"And now?" he asked softly.

"I have…for the most part. I still have moments of sadness, but nothing like before. I wanted to come to you without anything weighing on me. But here's the thing…I'll always be kind of screwed up. I'm not perfect, never will be."

"And thank God for that."

"What?"

"You think I want perfection? Sweetheart, I've never wanted perfect. I wanted the beautiful, spirited, stubborn, intelligent, opinionated, sexy, ridiculously brave and ridiculously foolish Sabrina Wilde. You may not be perfect, but you're perfect for me. I knew that almost from the moment we met."

"So do you think…you could forgive me, too?"

Without a doubt she was the bravest, most enchanting creature in the universe. In three strides, he stood in front of her but refrained from holding her. The instant his fingertips touched silky flesh, all coherent thought would vanish. He had to get this said.

"There's nothing to forgive."

"But I said some pretty horrible things."

"Believe it or not, those horrible things actually gave me a little hope."

"Really? How?"

"I decided to go with the old adage, you only hurt the ones you really love."

"Wow, that's...um, kind of dumb."

Ian laughed. Oh yes, his Sabrina was back in full form.

"True. And remember, I said some shitty things, too."

"Nothing I didn't deserve."

"We'll have to disagree about that. We both said things we regret. Question now is, where do we go from here? What do you want, Sabrina?"

"I want it all, Ian. Marriage, kids, house in the country with some land for lots of Jack juniors to romp around."

Fighting a smile, he said, "Marriage? I don't believe I asked."

She beamed up at him, not one bit put out or deterred. "Only one of us needs to. It is, however, the responsibility of the other one to say yes, though."

"Is that right? Then I'd better do my part." Finally allowing himself to touch her, he wrapped his arms around her and whispered gruffly, "Yes, my darling, Sabrina. Yes."

Gently, oh so very tenderly, he kissed her, tasting, savoring, cherishing. This woman who meant everything to him would be his wife. His partner in life, the mother of his children. His... for always.

"I thought, maybe, if you want to, we could go see your family tomorrow."

Those words confirmed everything. She was all in.

"You ready for a thousand hugs, kisses, and at least a dozen inappropriate jokes?"

"Can't think of anything I'd like better."

"Oh yeah?" he whispered. "How about this?" And then he kissed her again, this time with all the pent up desire and love he'd held back for far too long.

As his hands roamed over creamy skin and satin curves, Sabrina's hands became equally busy divesting him of his shirt and jeans. Seconds later they were skin to skin, heat to heat.

His mouth covering her in kisses in every place he could reach, he warned, "I can't go slow…not this first time. I've missed you too damn much. Want you…" He licked a taut, coral nipple, drew it into his mouth.

"No, don't go slow." She bit his earlobe, her hands roaming everywhere they could reach. "Take me fast…hard and deep. Take me now."

"Put your arms and legs around me and hang on tight."

As she complied, he hooked his arms under her legs, spreading her wider. Taking two steps to the closest hard surface, he pressed her against the wall and pushed in deep. They both groaned at the connection.

This was perfect—all she could have asked for and so much more. Her face buried against his neck, Sabrina tightened her legs around Ian's waist and let him take her harder than he ever had before. It was as if he couldn't go deep enough, get his fill of her. She loved it.

Riding him furiously, she crossed the finish line much quicker than she ever anticipated as climax crashed down upon her and ecstasy erupted.

With a loud groan, Ian followed seconds later,

Breathless and happier than she ever thought was possible, she pressed a kiss to his shoulder, wincing as she noticed the teeth marks in his skin. Kissing the small wound, she inhaled the scents of musky sex and virile man. Life simply could not get better than this.

Biting her earlobe in a tender nibble, Ian growled softly, "Let's go to bed and do this all over again. This time, real slow."

Okay she was wrong. Life could get better.

CHAPTER THIRTY-FOUR

Ian held her close, savoring her sweet softness. How many times had he dreamed this? Of Sabrina showing up, throwing herself in his arms and declaring her love? Dozens. But none of those dreams came close to the reality.

As he listened to her words, her explanation of the pain she had endured for nineteen years, he couldn't help but be humbled by this amazing woman he adored. What courage she had to face her pain and darkness.

"So anyway, after blubbering to my sisters and finally owning up to what I'd kept from them for years, I felt much better."

"And did they help you to understand you weren't responsible?"

"They tried, but I wasn't there yet. Just knowing they didn't hate me helped a lot, though."

"Oh baby, they couldn't hate you. Not in a million years. You did something thousands of kids have done. Most of them either forget about it or have a chance to apologize and make it right. You weren't able to do that so it seemed magnified."

"I guess you're right. I'll spend the rest of my life wishing those hadn't been my last words to my mom, but I remember all the times I told her how much I loved her. I hope that's what she remembered and not my petty juvenile rant."

314 | ELLA GRACE

"I'm sure she did."

"Thanks to Aunt Gibby, I think she did, too."

"Really?"

"She told me that mama told her what I did and she…" Her voice went husky. "That she actually laughed about it. Said I was so much like my dad."

"That's got to make you feel better."

"It does. I was so worried that what I said was the reason she was upset that night. Turns out she was missing us and then my dad did something stupid, pissing her off."

Ian gathered her closer in his arms. It hurt him that she'd carried this around with her all this time. "Why didn't you talk to somebody about it?"

"Like who, Ian? I couldn't tell my sisters. How do you tell the people you love most in the world that you feel responsible for something like this? I was so ashamed."

"And that's why couldn't you tell me?"

"I guess that seems silly. I—"

"No sweetheart, it's not silly. You were hurting. And it hurts me to know that and not have been there for you."

"But you were, Ian. All those nights I woke up crying and you held me. All those times I did stupid things that almost got me killed. You saved my life and my sanity too many times to count."

"And the nightmares? They're better?"

"Mostly. I've had an occasional one…nothing like before, though. My doctor said they should eventually go away for good."

"Doctor?"

"I took your advice and got some help."

He kissed her for her bravery. "I know that was difficult."

"With my history of sharing?" She snorted softly. "It was a piece of cake. I was through with my first session in five minutes flat. My doctor, on the other hand, insisted on the full hour. He let me talk about whatever I wanted to, which I took full advantage of." She snorted again, this time in disgust. "Guy's not even a football fan."

"And you still tolerated him? Imagine that. Did you set him straight?"

"Tried to. He's from Indiana, where basketball rules, so I cut him some slack. I eventually ran out of subjects to procrastinate with and started talking about the deep stuff."

"Do you know how incredible you are?" He kissed her again, softly, thoroughly. And then he knew he could wait no longer. Rolling away from her, he went to his feet. "I have something for you. Be right back."

Sabrina watched a deliciously nude Ian until he disappeared out the door and then snuggled back into her pillow with a happy sigh. She could not think of any time in her life when she'd been this happy or content. And it was all due to Ian. His love and patience had outlasted her sheer stubbornness.

"I kept a carton in the freezer just in case." In his hand was a half-gallon carton of her number one food weakness—fudge ripple ice cream.

"My hero." Laughing, Sabrina sat up and rearranged the pillows for them.

He handed her the carton and a large spoon, then scooted back under the covers with her. She dipped out a large bite and held it out for him. As his lips closed around the spoon and he made a groaning sound, a flush of heat swept over her. Only moments before his mouth had closed over her nipple in just that way and they had both made a similar sound of pleasure.

Risking brain freeze, Sabrina took a giant size bite of ice cream to cool herself down.

"Good?"

Unable to speak, she rolled her eyes in ecstasy.

"I have something else for you."

Swallowing the last of her spoonful, she shook her head. "Nothing could get better than this."

When she noticed the nervousness on his face, she sobered up. Ian never got nervous.

"What it is?"

He took her hand and placed something in her palm. She looked down to see the most exquisite ring she could ever imagine. Only those who knew her best were aware that she adored vintage jewelry. Trust Ian to know exactly the kind of engagement ring to buy.

"Oh Ian, it's absolutely the most perfect, loveliest ring I've ever seen."

"I've had it a while. Wasn't sure I'd ever be able to give it to you, but I knew there would never be anyone else I'd ever want to give a ring to, so I kept it. Just in case."

"I couldn't imagine anything more beautiful. When did you get it?"

His self-conscious laugh brought her head up.

"I'm almost embarrassed to tell you."

"Now I'm really intrigued. So when did you get it?"

"Remember the Sanderson case?"

"Of course I do. That was our first case together."

"Remember we went to Key West to interview that witness?"

"Yes, Sanderson's ex-wife."

"You went back to the hotel to work out. And I took a little detour to see an old friend who deals in rare and antique jewelry."

She was shaking her head before he could finish. "That's not possible, Ian. We had only known each other a few weeks. We hadn't even slept together. Hell, we hadn't even kissed."

"No, but I knew what I wanted."

Tears filled her eyes before she could control them. Any other time she would have worked like hell to rein in her emotions. But as her doctor had told her and she was realizing more and more—showing the depth of her feelings was not a weakness. And she didn't mind that Ian knew how very touched she was by his confession.

"Oh baby, no. Don't cry."

The panic on his face lightened the moment, and she laughed. "These are happy tears." She sniffed indelicately. "I've not shown you too many of those."

"As long as they're happy tears, you can cry all you want. I never want to be responsible for making you cry from sadness."

Needing to be back in his arms, Sabrina placed the ice cream carton on the table beside her and turned back to him. She wrapped her arms around him, held him tight. "I love you, Ian Mackenzie. You're everything I could have ever dreamed of and so much more."

His answer was a corresponding hard squeeze. "You don't know how I've longed to hear you say those three words. I love you more than anyone or anything in the world and if you'll have me, I'll spend the rest of my days making sure you never doubt my love."

Drawing him down with her onto the pillows, Sabrina proceeded to show him with her body what she felt in her heart. Of all the doubts she'd had in her life, Ian's love wasn't one of them. She had always known she had it—even when she knew she hadn't deserved it.

Her mouth whispered soft brief kisses on his face. Ian moved his head and tried to catch her mouth with his. Sabrina laughed softly, avoiding him. She had an agenda.

"Are you going to torture me?"

"Oh yes, my darling Ian. I most certainly am."

Dropping his head back onto the pillow, Ian growled, "Then have your way with me, woman."

"My pleasure." And it was.

The kisses continued, trailing to his neck, down his beautiful chest, to the hard planes of his stomach. When his breath hitched and his body stiffened, she smiled her delight. The man had issued a challenge and he knew better than anyone that Sabrina Wilde never backed down.

She licked a particularly intriguing indention just above his hipbone and was delighted when he caught his breath again.

Her fingers lightly, gently skimmed the hottest, hardest part of him and as his entire body went still and stiff, she looked up at his face. Though his eyes were half closed, she saw the glimmering heat in their depths and despite the rigid control he was forcing himself to maintain, a small smile played around his mouth.

"What are you smiling about?"

"You."

She tilted her head. "Me?"

"I see you."

She glanced down at her very naked self and laughed. "Yep. This is me."

He shook his head. "No, sweetheart. All of you. Your heart, your beauty. That indestructible, courageous spirit. It's all there for me to see. Nothing's hidden. Everything you are...it's mine."

Months ago he had said he wanted all of her...not just the parts she was willing to give. And she realized he was right. She was offering all of herself to him. This man who had offered all of himself to her long ago. Ian had seen the very worst of her and loved her.

"Thank you for loving me, Ian. All of me." She lowered her head, blew softly on the steely length in her hand. "Now, let me love all of you." And she took him in her mouth.

Ian groaned and arched his body. Knowing it would drive him crazy and increase his pleasure, she deliberately swallowed, then relaxed her throat, enabling her to take him even deeper. And when he groaned again, she did, too.

"You win," he gasped. "I'm toast. I'm...done for. I'm—"

She raised her head, releasing him. "Not through."

Straddling his hips, she held him in her hands and brought him to her. They both watched as he disappeared inside her, and the moment he seated himself deep, Sabrina closed her eyes, relishing the connection. This hot, hard male part of him that could give such pleasure. Pleasure she only ever wanted from this man. Her one and only love.

With a half curse, half laugh, he lost control. Grabbing her hips, he pushed her down hard onto him, brought her back up and repeated the motion over and over. Heat washed over Sabrina as her orgasm gathered like a thundering, violent storm in her body. The tingle began in her toes, zipped through every part of her body. Losing herself in Ian...in the way he loved her, was the most exquisite ecstasy in the world. As she gave herself up to the glory of his lovemaking, she gave herself to him, wholly, completely, and forever.

Wrapped tight in her lover's arms, his release surging through his body and into hers, she silently vowed that there would never be a time that he doubted her love for him. Ian had never given up on her even when she had given up on herself. He had loved her during her worst. She would spend the rest of her life giving him her best.

EPILOGUE

One month later
Midnight

The bride was beautiful in a cream silk off the shoulder sheath. The groom was tall, handsome and dashing in a black tuxedo.

The matron of honor wore a soft peach gown that draped lovingly around her slender shoulders and made her skin glow. The maid of honor wore a mint green gown with an overlay of ivory lace. It was the first time in years that Sabrina felt like a girly-girl. And even though she'd had to wear three-inch heels and a little flower in her hair, she had to admit she kind of liked the feeling.

"Ready?"

She glanced over at her escort. No man should look so devastatingly gorgeous or dangerous in a tux. Ian Mackenzie, her fiancé, the love of her life, put every James Bond actor to shame.

She took the arm he offered and squeezed it slightly. "You're sure this isn't the kind of wedding you'd rather have?"

"Absolutely not. Besides, with my family, having a large wedding is pretty much in the cards already."

She smiled at the truth in his statement. Ian's family was ecstatic over their upcoming wedding and even though it would be a simple affair, she spoke with his mother and sisters almost daily about hairstyles, colors, and flowers. Ian's sister Callie was making Sabrina's bouquet.

Their wedding was planned for the week after Sammie and Quinn returned from their honeymoon but would be nothing remotely as elaborate as this one. A large wedding with hundreds of guests, thousands of flowers, and multiple attendants was Sammie's dream but not Sabrina's.

Her idea of the perfect wedding involved comfortable clothes, good food, and most importantly everyone she loved. She never believed that she would ever find the right man to have her perfect wedding though. Until Ian. He had made all of her dreams come true.

Weather permitting, their wedding would take place outdoors, in Midnight's park. Since everyone in town was welcomed to attend, she had a feeling it would be quite large in numbers. She hoped so. She had so much love for this town and its residents. They had come to her rescue, saving her and her family's lives. How could she not invite them to the happiest event in her life?

A nervous, frazzled looking woman with wiry gray hair whispered loudly, "That's your cue, Sabrina. Go!"

Her smile bright, Sabrina held Ian's arm as they headed down the isle. Three weeks from today, they would be reciting the same vows that Sammie and Quinn were today. She couldn't wait. For so long she had been sure that the shadows of her past would forever darken her future. But thanks to Ian and her family, those shadows were gone for good.

And she knew without a doubt that somewhere above them, Maggie and Beckett Wilde looked down on their daughters and were smiling, too.

Thank you for reading *Midnight Shadows, A Wildefire Novel*. I hope you enjoyed it. If you did, please help other readers find this book:

1. This book is lendable. Share it with a friend who enjoys Steamy Southern Suspense.
2. Help other people find this book by writing a review.
3. Sign up for my newsletters at *http://authornewsletters.com/christyreece/* to learn about my new releases.
4. Come like my Facebook pages at *https://www.facebook.com/EllaGraceAuthor?ref=hl* and *https://www.facebook.com/AuthorChristyReece*

Other books by Ella Grace
The Wildefire Series:
Midnight Secrets, A Wildefire Novel
Midnight Lies, A Wildefire Novel

Books by Christy Reece
Last Chance Rescue Series:
Rescue Me, A Last Chance Rescue Novel
Return To Me, A Last Chance Rescue Novel
Run To Me, A Last Chance Rescue Novel
No Chance, A Last Chance Rescue Novel
Second Chance, A Last Chance Rescue Novel
Last Chance, A Last Chance Rescue Novel
Sweet Justice, A Last Chance Rescue Novel
Sweet Revenge, A Last Chance Rescue Novel
Sweet Reward, A Last Chance Rescue Novel
Chances Are, A Last Chance Rescue Novel

Grey Justice Series:
Nothing To Lose, A Grey Justice Novel

LCR Elite Series:
Running On Empty, An LCR Elite Novel

ACKNOWLEDGEMENTS

Special thanks to the following people for helping make this book possible:

My husband for his loving support, numerous moments of comic relief, and always knowing when chocolate is needed.

My wonderful family who loves me through thick and thin.

Anne Woodall for her copyediting and sound advice.

Marie Force's eBook Formatting Fairies, who always answers my endless questions with endless patience.

Tricia Schmitt (Pickyme) for her beautiful cover art.

Reece's Readers, my incredibly supportive and fun loving street team.

My beta readers for reading a rough draft of this book and offering some excellent suggestions.

And a very special thank you to the readers of the Wildefire series, not only for their insistence that Sabrina had to have her story told but also for their incredible patience. I hope you love Sabrina and Ian as much as I do. Thanks so much for waiting!

About the Author

Ella Grace lives in Alabama with her husband and numerous fur-kids. Ella Grace is the pseudonym for NYT Bestselling Author Christy Reece.